Dawn of the Goddess

Dawn of the Goddess

Gordon Strong

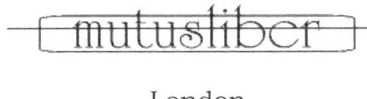

London

First published in 2011 by Mutus Liber

BM Mutus Liber
London WC1N 3XX

A CIP catalogue record for this book is available from the British Library.

ISBN-13: 978-1-908097-03-3

www.mutusliber.com

She is called by many names by many men; but to all she is the Great Goddess, space and earth and water.

Dion Fortune

Author's Note

While writing this tale, I sometimes wondered if it was actually me driving the pen. Perhaps the words upon the page were really those of some long forgotten bard who had lighted upon me as his willing scribe? If so, I consider myself fortunate to have been the one chosen to spin such an extraordinary story.

I was born in Somerset, England and readers may recognise parts of that particular landscape in these pages. Given the mystical heritage of the South West, it might be more than a coincidence that the novel features what are quaintly referred to as 'myths and legends'.

Giving characters or places a name is never straightforward. The particular tone I wanted led me to adapt, perhaps promiscuously, words from the Welsh language. If any citizen of that country is offended by my licence, I apologise unreservedly here and now.

A few words may require a gloss:

Nadoman Feasts: The time of Yule.

Gwalstan: a Maypole.

Hidych: a puzzle.

The story cannot be described as entirely a happy one, but, 'it all comes out right in the end'. Often, that is all we can say of much that happens in our own lives.

Finally, thanks are more than due to Sean Martin for his diligent editing and extremely valuable suggestions.

Gordon Strong

Portishead,
April 2011

Dramatis Personae

Brynan	King of Irlas
Rhaldon	Prince of Irlas
Barud	King of Techlyn
Galar	King of Blauwyg
Gwirel	Queen of Durasglyn
Anfad	Prince of Durasglyn
Tulrech	King of Melynas
Tegwyn	Princess of Melynas
Derwen	A Knight
Paldarch	A Wizard
Hog	An Orphan
Wythen	A Water Faery
Rhi	A Wood Sprite

The Deities

Nen	Chief among the Gods
Loenel	The Great Goddess
Cyngerl	Goddess of Nature
Hudew	God of Magic
Marak	God of War
Fawreth	Goddess of Fortune
Gwemed	God of the Earth
Angaz	God of Death
Cythras	The Dark One

The Seasons

Gwan	Spring
Ufeln	Summer
Hafwan	Autumn
Rhagel	Winter

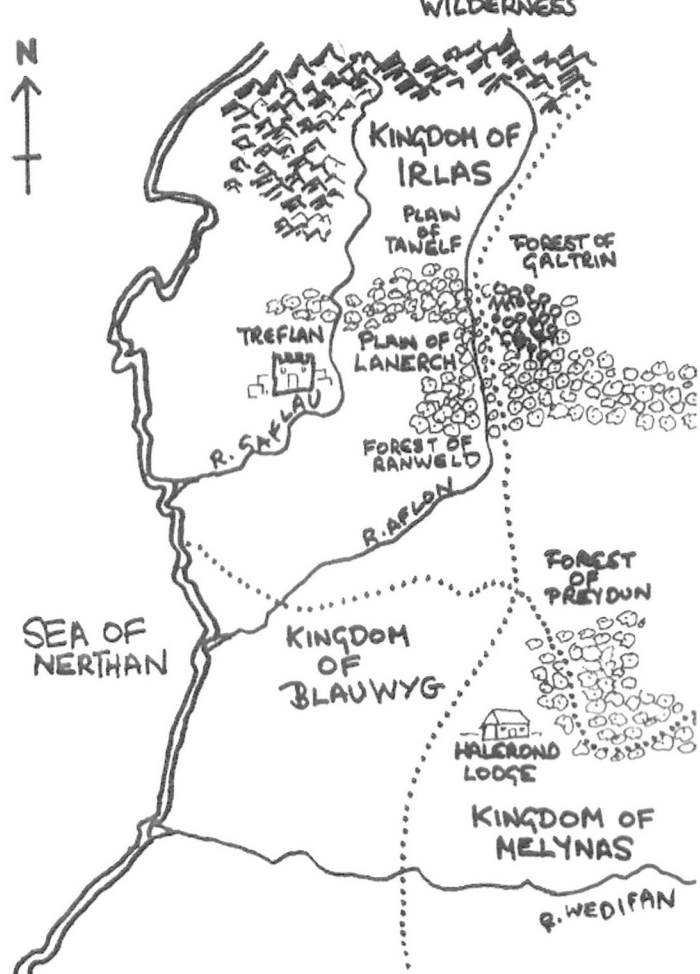

OF THE NORTH

THE LAND OF
THE SIX GREAT
KINGDOMS

NIWEL
MOUNTAINS.

KINGDOM OF
DURASGLYN.

KINGDOM OF
TARTH

ELLION
HILLS.

PLAIN OF
CYFREN

LAKE
FIOLETH

MEFYNON
(SPRING OF
WISDOM)

BRIDGE
OF
ENFLAW

TEMPLE
OF
RHINLAIS
(GOLDEN
PEACE)

THE
WASTED
PLAINS

TOWER
OF
GAFRYD

KINGDOM OF
TECHLYN

WILDERNESS OF THE SOUTH

I

The sky was as black velvet stretched from one horizon to the other and the stars were as diamonds in the heavens. On a rocky ledge, a restless fox watched the dark figure climb slowly but purposefully up the mountain side. His pace never changed as he strode between the great stones that flanked the narrow path. At last he gained the ridge and went toward a great stone there, one shaped like a low table. A black cloak swirled about him as he walked, and his long white hair streamed out in the wind. He settled his heart and mind for a moment then laid his staff upon this altar of stone. Bowing his head in silent prayer, Paldarch the Wizard made ready to perform his magic.

After invoking the gods and goddesses to aid him, the wizard breathed deeply the air of the mountains. As the spirit of the winds entered his inner being, he immediately felt a great change within himself. He acknowledged the ground beneath his feet, and the potent forces deep within the mountains. A whirlwind of energy ascended through his body and beamed out from the crown of light that was now suspended above his head.

Once more, Paldarch stood in the kingdom of magic, one where he had existed even before he came into this world. This was a place not beholden to time or reason – it was as the universe before creation had begun. And why did such a venerable magician feel so comfortable here among the rocky peaks? Because it was he, when chaos ruled – that time before the sun became the sun – who had helped to create the world. And why not? It was the role of the gods to shape the stars and the planets, but it was the magician who might determine how these wonders were to be perceived. Now he would invoke those magical forces once more.

Paldarch felt a further vortex of energy descending upon him. The now very curious fox saw the wizard begin to sway with the power that surged through him. Paldarch could feel his very self becoming more mighty, so that his cloak became as the sail of a ship, his hat reached up to the stars and his staff grew to the size of an oak tree. All the time, the tips of his fingers glowed, and his feet became at one with the rocks beneath him. The wizard raised his staff to the heavens and made to summon every vestige of power that he knew resided in the celestial heights.

"Let the Ancient Gods who from storm set the Sun and every star in the great void, and who caused the mighty seas to flow, hearken now to one whose devotions have helped to make every part of the cosmos ever more the mighty." Silhouetted against the moon, his tall hat making him appear to be the same height as the peaks around him, the words echoed among the rocks and stones.

Then the winds began to roar in the valleys below, the stars grow brighter. On the oceans many leagues away, waves were suddenly pulled high, to crash moments later in a great tumult against the shore.

The gods were answering him! Paldarch pointed his staff towards the heavens once more. "May the Wind that is Justice stir the minds of Men, that their thoughts be noble and fine. Let the Fire of Inspiration shine upon the World. May the Waters of Mercy flow into every heart. Let the earth be blessed and peace, hope and goodness brought to every place upon it."

And those same heavens hearkened to the words of the wizard, so that thunder crashed and boomed over the plains and forests far away. Silver threads of lightning played over the hills, and the night was alive with spirits. In the valley below, poor shepherds sheltering in their coves were greatly alarmed.

"May the blessings of god and goddess, the compassion, mercy and love that is felt for those here below rain upon the Earth. Let light and harmony pervade the shadows, driving forth all fear and doubt and let all be as one."

After the wizard's words had dwindled away there came a profound silence, one in harmony with the stillness of the moon. Great she was when Paldarch had arrived at this sacred place. Now she was so very full that the hem of her silver skirts caressed the earth. The moon is woman in her every guise – at once beautiful, mysterious and alluring. She is maiden, bride and crone in turn, and changing at every turn.

Paldarch was almost prompted to dance a jig in the mantle of her pearly light. But he could sense something else – a presence was approaching, getting nearer every moment. The emptiness in the air had become as it is after snow has fallen, when every atom that makes up the air is tight, like the skin of a drum. There was a tension, a sense of alarm – always the companion of fear. Not that a wizard feels fear. How can he ever be afraid when he is, as the warrior, the constant companion of death? If the end of life holds no perils, then how can that which proceeds it ever succeed in alarming him?

Paldarch knew too that, if he needed to be protected, he had merely to summon the spirits of the trolls that dwelt in these mountains. Such was the power of his magic in this place – one which he had claimed as his temple long ago – that he never considered he would have a need for such allies... and yet... Paldarch sensed the nature of the company he was about to encounter; whoever it was had no love for wizards.

Now, without a footfall, came the wraiths. Shifting in and out of the silver moonlight as if they were at one with it – but they were not. Grey they were, the colour of ash, that of spent fires. Spectral, a different light – one that was fitful and told of eternal unrest. Each had a long cloak draped over its ghostly form and, as they grew closer, their mournful features could be clearly seen.

They were the ghosts of the old kings, those who had ruled in times long gone, and whose earthly power was so great that even death could not take them from this world. Some had fallen in battle, others had perished in riot and rebellion, a few had been the victims of treason and foul plots. The reign of some had been just, of others cruel and despotic. Even those who had been weak and ill-starred were there, but all were still crowned, and all stern and grim of feature.

Paldarch eyed the many score who now slowly marched towards him. They halted, as if knowing they must, and began to gather about him. The wizard knew that the circle of protection he had cast around himself prevented their coming any closer. The mightiest mortal could not gain entry, and those who were not of this world would also be restrained. Still stood those kings, and Paldarch was as a rock also, and his voice was as the strength of the mountain itself. It rang out now, clear as the note when true steel is struck by the hammer of the smith.

"Why do you come here, O ancient kings? You would be better to seek the land beyond the West, where the dead find eternal rest. There is nothing for you here among the mountains," Paldarch said.

The silence grew heavier, the eyes of the pale retinue ever more dull. One of their number was taller than those about him, with locks hanging down to his shoulders like grey-green weed. Now he was a shade of doom. Once he would have owned such command that all who rode with him would have followed their leader even unto the Land of Uffern, from where none return. No more was this so. For this king, the candle of life had been blown out long ago. He spoke:

"We have come to take what is rightfully ours." The voice was thin and querulous, like the sound of dry grass caught by the wind.

"You are wrong!" Paldarch intoned. "Go! There is nothing here that belongs to you."

"The Sword of Pengyron is ours. It must be so."

Deep within him, the soul of Paldarch trembled. How were these ghostly monarchs aware of the most treasured secret in the world? How had they come to know that it was he, Paldarch the Wizard, who was its guardian? Perhaps some fell demon had born witness to its creation and, desiring all noble things to be sullied and then perish, whispered of its power to one, or many, of this withered horde.

The danger was only too apparent. Paldarch knew that if ever the Sword was held by any other hand than for whom it was meant, the whole of Creation would come to an end. That was the power that resided within its tempered blade. It must not be! Long years ago the wizard had sworn a sacred oath that he would give up his own life rather than see the Divine Will perverted by evil men, be they the ghostly dead or living warriors! The image of the Sword filled his consciousness and lit an eternal flame in the eyes of Paldarch the Wizard, its noble keeper. He spoke now as a god – infinite, and above all that he might perceive.

"None may wield the sword that was forged so long ago. Even the Great Warriors, who came before the age of Kings, did not know of it. Those of the blood of the high kings of Goerlwin were not worthy of that honour. The hero has yet to be ordained who may claim this blade. Forget this empty desire, O king, forthwith. You will gain nothing by it, except to add yet more pain to those longings that burden you, and those others of royal blood I see now before me."

The king spoke once more, his words as if addressed to a child who knows little, and can be softened with honeyed phrases. The thin smile that hovered about his lips had no warmth, and his eyes were those of the dead - seeing nothing. "Is it not written in the Great Book of Diras Pechlin that the Kings of the West will rule in an unbroken line for ever? And also is it not written in those hallowed pages that the Sword of the White Prince will be seen again in the kingdom? And when this comes about, the age of Kings will return, that they may rule as ever before and with even greater might."

Paldarch answered him with words that seemed to blaze in the night. "The lines in the Great Book, of which you speak, were written at the behest of a usurper and a tyrant. King Camilir was not worthy to bear the name of monarch and forever he has blackened the name of the Kings of the West. If you be of the blood of Camilir, O King, then your claim to the Sword of Pengyron is as the cry of the wolf in the empty wilderness, and nothing more."

"What does an ignorant fool of sorcerer know of such holy things?" the king hissed. "Your learning is not of the wisdom of my ancestors, it is fools' talk of sprites and imps, of the enchantments of maidens. You are not worthy even to speak of such secrets. They are the heritage of only the blood royal."

Paldarch allowed himself a brief smile.

"This King of the West before me must know little of the bounty of Haelmaw, guarded by the Nine Great Dragons in the caves of Myndifyn. Nothing remains of that hoard, not one silver goblet, except that treasure of which you speak. I, Paldarch the son of Teranstaf, am the guardian of the Sword of Pengyron and the oath that I have taken ensures that this thing is hid from the eyes of all upon this Earth."

The features of the king twisted into a grimace. When that haggard face settled once more, it was dark as the coldest shadow.

"It cannot be hidden from these eyes of mine, wizard. The sword is there upon yon stone. Now give up to me what is truly mine."

With its blade plunged some way into the rock that formed the altar's top, the Sword shimmered in the moonlight. It cast no shadow, as the blade had been sanctified by Loenel, the moon goddess. It had been a gift to her from Hudew, the god of magic. Long before that, by stealth and trickery, that mischievous god had taken it from Cledoth, the swordsmith who served the gods. It is a long tale and will bear the telling once more, but at another time. Now we must observe Paldarch, a devotee of Hudew, as he thinks with all speed.

"I grant you may have the power to look upon the sword, O King. And I also have the power to change the world - so it is no longer there."

And with that, the Sword of Pengyron faded until it was a flickering outline and, like mist upon a lake, it was gone. The frame of the old king shook and a muted scream came from him.

"It *will* be mine!"

He made to move a pace forward. His cohorts all appeared to tremble, as if willing him onward.

"Hold! You cannot enter here," Paldarch thundered.

"You would command a king?" the old king said, icily.

Paldarch did not falter. His words were clear and strong, and on hearing them, many of the phantom host fell back: "Only I have command in this sacred place. I... and the Wind."

Straightway a sound could be heard, low at first but gathering strength, even as a lion gathers pace when it bounds across the plain. Now, the approach of a great tempest could be felt, strong enough to roll rocks the size of a man's head along the ground; clouds of dust and showers of pebbles followed in their wake.

As the full force of this sudden storm became apparent, the previous resolve of the kings began to break, and many of them fell back into the shadows.

Then the sylphs appeared. Spirits that abound in the element of air, they cared little for men or any other creature. Being full of a dark mischief, they were famed for their ability to disturb the minds of mortals. Leaping back and forth, darting gleefully among the company, they caused great havoc. The ranks of the kings were buffeted, and some even tumbled over in their dismay, like pieces upon a chessboard. Only their leader held his ground, but fear had begun to creep upon even those ashen features.

Paldarch locked his gaze upon the king, and at the same time brought the heel of his staff down hard upon the ground. At the place where it struck, cracks began to appear in the rock floor. That same stone split open in a spider's web of furrows that streaked towards the company, widening by the moment. The cracks grew broader until, one by one, the figures began to fall like lifeless puppets into the abyss. Their cries echoed as they plummeted into the depths, and soon were heard no more.

"Return, you shadows of life, thence to the roots of the earth that bore you! Your time is forever gone, O kings of Olden Times!" Paldarch declaimed. "That age has claimed you at last; the years now will have their fill! Let Gwemed, whose kingdom is the Underworld, give you peace in his stone halls beneath the mountains. I command this to happen... *now!*"

This last word was as the sound of a great door being closed. The old king who stood before Paldarch trembled, and his hands began to move fitfully. The eyes of Paldarch were as points of light, more intense than the heart of a blacksmith's forge. The old king followed his shadowy host deep beneath the mountains, from where they would never return. Their fate was in accord with the sacred nature of the Sword of Pengyron, for its guardian must vow never to

8

destroy the evil or the undead, but instead to ferry their souls into the great void.

Paldarch struck the ground with his staff once more and the fissures, plainly to be seen a moment earlier, closed forever. In those mountains all became as it had been before. Paldarch leaned heavily upon his staff and let his breath become still. With a few incanted phrases he calmed the spirits of the wind, and caused the circle of protection to recede into the aether. His magical workings were at an end.

No man of magic could tell how any ceremony would turn out, or what strange events might occur! Why should he have chosen to invoke the sword this very night, so that its presence was visible upon the altar? Paldarch reflected, perhaps wearily, that he had been tested once more, as a wizard always must be. He had been reminded that the Sword of Pengyron was so powerful that it had the power to manifest itself even without any mortal willing it to be so. The power in the sword was greater than the man who held it, that much was certain. Within that blade was the might of the smiths of the Age of Steel, men whose favour even kings would crave. And soon the sword would be taken up again. Of that, he was sure. But by whom? It had attracted the spirits of the old kings, and now they were no more. Marak, the god of War, would soon be hungry for blood and strife. Paldarch knew that only too well, and already he could feel the fire of that deity's angry breath. Where or when this war would be, he knew not yet.

The wizard gathered together the rest of the magical weapons and returned them to the leather pouch. His lantern he held firmly, and in the other hand gripped his staff. As he did this, he was aware more than before of the presence of the moon all around him. The Goddess was not just shinning upon him from above, but from every direction. The moonlight was as the milkiest marble and so bright that the wizard was forced to shield his eyes from

9

the luminous glare. Knowing this light to be more than just the moon, he called out to the heavens.

"I know you to be Loenel, the Queen among the Stars. I pray you do not blind the eyes of this old man. Your power is greater than mine; do not use it to bring pain and fever to my mind."

Paldarch was aware of a sound, like water cascading into a deep pool, then the peal of distant bells, sweet in tone. A dreamlike melody came to him. Paldarch knew that sound of old - it was the voice of the Goddess.

"Cast aside your fear, O wizard, the Queen of the Night means you no harm. Was I not watching over you when the Old Kings came? I would not have let you come to any harm. 'She who is among the stars' does not forget that it was you, Paldarch, the Great Magician, who loved my blessed daughter, Gwirel, and schooled her in the ways of the Otherworld. Do not be afraid! Raise your eyes, O Paldarch, for do you not know that to look upon me is to know the greatest rapture? Come, you may do so as none have ever done before. Such a privilege you will own, O mortal man. Surely you would wish to see the beauty of the Woman of Wonder who, in her purity, has no rival?"

Paldarch stole a glance in the direction of that sweet, yet awesome voice, and looked upon her. There before him was the Goddess. Her smile was as a thousand silver suns and welcoming him to her, to be embraced by an overwhelming love. Yet Paldarch was also aware of a presence so aloof that the air was chill. No matter how enchanting her slender figure, and brilliant her eyes - brimming with glistening jewels – he knew the Goddess had her dark, terrible side. Loenel owned the power to comfort and also to cast out. Her any whim would always determine how she would be with those who felt her power.

In that moment Paldarch wondered why Loenel had revealed herself to him at such a moment. The mind of the wizard was suddenly filled with dread, not just for himself, but for all men upon the earth. His heart felt heavy, his mind troubled and confused.

"You wonder, do you not, what matter it is I wish to impart to you? "

Paldarch, burdened by unease, was drawn to be abrupt. "Yes, my lady. What matter is it?"

"Patience, O Man of Magic. Do you not know that the Goddess lives only in eternity?"

Paldarch bowed his head in silence. The Goddess laughed, a laugh like the sound of pebbles falling into a deep well.

"Nay, do not sulk - as men always do - be they young or old. Look upon me, Paldarch. Look deeply into my eyes. Tell me what you see there."

The wizard hardly dared to do as he was bidden, but by summoning all his courage, he gazed into the face of Loenel, the Great Goddess. Her eyes were now as vast saucers of light. Paldarch could feel himself drawn into that swirling centre where there was a great orb, black and streaked with gold. This opened, as a rose does to worship the sun, and he saw an ocean, calm with not a single wave, stretching to the horizon. The waters were turquoise and, floating upon them, a great white shell. Within the depths of this secret place of beauty, Paldarch knew there resided unimagined visions. The shell opened and the wizard fell back as if struck by an invisible hand.

"What do you see there in the *Mirror of Insight*, Paldarch?"

Paldarch peered into the great glass. He spoke slowly and carefully. "I see people... many women... girls dancing... holding up their hands to the skies and laughing."

"Indeed, you speak truly... they are rejoicing because the time of the Goddess has come. And when a new age comes, then the old must make way. Do you understand this, O Great Paldarch? The Time of The Kings has now

11

passed and the Earth waits for the Great Mother to return. When she does, there will be peace and joy, and all shall be as one. Every soul will be as a star, and like the stars, shine in heaven."

Paldarch continued to study the endless reflections.

"I see yet more! Now, there are many birds in the skies... the animals have left the forest, for it seems there is no longer anything for them to fear... even the fishes in the pools and streams are to be found in great numbers. What does this mean, O Loenel? What has brought such changes?"

"It is because soon there will be an end to strife. No longer will there be the fear and terror that war brings. How will this be? Why, the era of man, as the one who decides the fate of the world, will be over. It is his partner, woman, who now has mastery over what will happen upon this Earth. Is that not a cause for great celebration? You, Paldarch, understand the ways of the sun and the moon. You know the way that power flows from night to day, from heaven to earth. You have the spirit of man and woman in your wise heart, and know how right it is that this shall be. Are you not filled with rejoicing? Will you not celebrate with us, Paldarch?"

Though Paldarch took his eyes from the Mirror, still was he bathed in the light of enchantment. He paused before he spoke, considering his words carefully.

"Men are as they are. I have seen into their hearts many times and know what lies there. They strive and they suffer as women do also. If it is to be that they must fall, as the corn does before the reaper, and new seeds be sown – a different crop to spring from the Earth – then it will be so."

"But this fruit that will soon be gathered may be full of goodness and life, Paldarch. Will you not gather the harvest with us?"

"I shall be honoured to do so when that time comes, and surely it will. Though I fear my own years will not last much longer. Perhaps I shall hear these voices of joy only at a distance... when the cold lord Angaz claims me, as he does every mortal."

The Goddess smiled upon him.

"But you will at least know that you have left a world that is new, and one bathed in warmth and love. A world that will be as it was intended, when the embrace of Nen and Angeln first created the Heavens and the Earth."

"It *will* be a different world, for the world is ever changing. I am of the old ways, the times that went before and so I am able only to watch and wait. In my life I have already seen great turnings of the wheel and felt the wind as it changes direction, these things are not new to me. The will of the great Nen is known only to him."

"It will never need to change again, Paldarch, for who would wish to alter paradise?" Loenel's tone was one of gentle chiding. "The Great Mother that nurtures us all, whose spirit I am will provide all, and provide for all eternity. Her children will want for nothing."

"This may be so. I cannot tell. The gift of prophecy that I was given by Hudew, the god of magic, has begun to fade as I have grown older. I can no longer see over the horizon of the years and into the far future."

"You do not need to strain to see any longer, my Wizard, for all that I now tell you is true."

"It would be unwise, nay foolish, of me to question the word of the Goddess."

Loenel continued to smile.

"You will never lose the gift of using words well, Paldarch, that is certain. And none but such a great wizard would even consider that he might address the Queen of the Night as an equal."

The eyes of Goddess flashed, but for the merest moment, and Paldarch knew he must remain silent. He turned to the mirror again.

"You think you will see more? Tell me if you do."

"There is someone who flies across the sea," Paldarch said. "See, there."

The Goddess started.

"Where? Ah, a youth. Who can this be? Ah, I see he looks out and greets you, Paldarch. You know of him? Answer me! Who is this?"

"I do not know who it may be. If he has the gift of flight he must be one of the chosen of Hudew. Perhaps he is also the spirit of the New Age of which you spoke." Paldarch said, his voice as sound as seasoned timber.

The tone of the Goddess was merely even: "I think you know more of this than you will say, O wily wizard. The truth is hidden deep in your heart. But let it remain there for I will not force you to reveal this thing, even though I have the power to do so."

"I do not doubt you powers, O Great Queen. Yet Loenel has always been renowned, among those who worship her, for that great mercy and even greater understanding that she always shows."

The Goddess blinked once and the Mirror was no more. The light about her also began to recede. Now she spoke to Paldarch as one to whom she had revealed her presence for an instant but now, no longer.

"Farewell, Paldarch. We shall meet again, perhaps when the moon is full once more."

To the wizard, Loenel suddenly seemed to fill the whole of the skies... and then there was only the sight of the Moon. Serene and in majesty among the stars, she was, he mused, and turned away, retrieving his pouch once more, and began his slow descent from the mountain.

Before he did so, he reflected upon the vision he had seen of the slender youth, so free and without a care flying in the heavens. Loenel was right, he did know more than he would tell, for he perceived that if any mortal man could rival her powers it would be the airborne figure. There was also much about this youth that he did not know, but doubtless this would become clear as time passed. Paldarch made his way slowly down the mountain path, pondered on youth and age and their various virtues and weaknesses.

II

Hog was hungry. If the life of a youth of near twenty years is filled with carefree days, sporting or idling in taverns, Hog had never known such things. He had only ever been dimly aware of the gods and, if he had, he might have reasoned that Fawreth, Goddess of Fortune, had not smiled upon him for some little time now. He was as thin as a bean stake, and empty-bellied most of the time. The season of apples was long gone, and lately Hog had been forced to gather berries and nuts to quiet his hunger. Nature's bounty was often hard to find, and the squirrels always seemed to be there before him.

Hog was as an orphan, and in those days, the motherless were left to fend for themselves. So no one, apart from an old woman in the village who occasionally gave him scraps, cared very much about what happened to Hog. Precious little kindness came his way, though this same widow did on occasion let him sit by her fireside, and glad was he to do so in the cold season of Rhagel. As yet, Hog had not turned to thievery or murder, but perhaps Fawreth always keeps such a path open for those who are born to misfortune. In those days the laws were harsh. Whether villainy has ever been diminished by the threat of punishment, is another matter. Wrong will always be with us, that is the way of the world.

Hog knew the Nadoman Feasts would not be long in coming; the short days and endless, freezing nights told him as much. At this moment however, a quartern loaf would have been his idea of a banquet. He imagined sinking his teeth into the thick crust, and stuffing pieces of barley bread into his mouth. It turned out to be a cruel thought, for it only made him the hungrier.

Today his wanderings had taken him to the outskirts of a hamlet in the next valley to his own. Some distance from the way he was travelling, there was a barn. Hog reasoned that, even if he could find nothing to eat this night, at least he would have a place to sleep. He crept warily along one wall of the barn until he reached an open door, then peeked inside. A fire in the middle of the dirt floor had burnt low, but a pile of logs stacked nearby meant that someone, not long before, had been feeding the flames.

Hog hesitated. If he was discovered, there might be a good chance he would be thrown back into the cold night. Worse, he might be regarded as a young vagabond; one who should be hanged from the nearest tree. In those dark days, justice was often of a summary kind. The dusk began to grey the light and there was the threat of snow in the air. Hog did not consider long – survival is always stronger than fear. He crept inside, made swiftly for some steps at the corner of the barn, and climbed up into the hay loft.

He had not long lay down and made himself as comfortable as possible – the hay prickled – when he heard the sound of horses. Next he heard the riders halt and come into the barn. From where he was, above them, Hog could clearly hear their voices. He kept very still for some time, but eventually curiosity made him put an eye to a gap in the floorboards. There were three men - all with swords and looking like they were in the habit of using them. One, who moved quicker than the others, and seemed to be in charge, threw a log onto the embers. Flames crackled into life. *Fire and the Sword!* Hog suddenly recalled the old widow's tales of cruel kings and their grim lords, whose only goal was to drive the common folk from the land.

Hog ceased his spying and made do with listening. The boy had the gift of understanding the words of men as well as any priest or scribe. So he attended to what was being said, and the longer he did so, the more he learned. It was well that he did, for part of our tale turns about this starving orphan, and how he was to have hand in the destiny of the world.

This particular world was the Six Great Kingdoms. Once there had been four – Irlas, Melynas, Durasglyn and Tarth – lying together in harmony. The other two kingdoms, Techlyn and Blauwyg, had been united with them during the Age of Kings. Whether the conflict that was to follow was brought about by this addition to the number, later chroniclers often speculated. Perhaps some evil curse was upon Techlyn and Blauwyg, one cast in the dark mists of time, recalled by none.

Now let us be witness to what was in the hearts of these men, know their thoughts and hear their words, be they good or ill.

*

Not even the strongest light could make the shadows disappear from the faces of the trio about the fire. No joy or compassion was writ on any countenance, only the lines that are etched by a terrible will. These warriors were to be the last of the old dynasty, though they knew it not. Now they remained sullenly mute, each daring the other to speak first, in the way that men of a certain kind do. The silence became more and more leaden until one of the company suddenly got to his feet. He kicked at a branch that stuck out from the fire, causing crimson flames to leap almost in protest high into the gloom. When it was heard, the voice of Prince Anfad of Durasglyn was like the cackle of a rooster, leavened with the hissing of a serpent.

"Now listen to me! We will march into the land of Irlas when Ufeln is over. The people there have grown soft with the bounty of rich merchants, and too many good harvests.

It is time good King Brynan shared his riches with those of his neighbours who are perhaps not so fortunate. The mountains of *my* kingdom do not breed fat cattle. It will be good for *my* people to know land that is easy to work. We have suffered long, while others have become lazy in their comfortable castles. Now that is hardly right, is it?"

Prince Anfad tightened a palm on the pommel of his sword as he spoke, and his eyes narrowed to dark slits. The brightest light could never pierce the darkness of his features, surrounded as they were by a mantle of oily, black hair. The two kings regarded him as they might a starving wolf in winter, a creature come out of the mountains in search of prey - any prey.

King Galar of Blauwyg, bearded and with a weary look about his eyes, did not respond for some time. He was gruff when he finally spoke, as if he was not in the habit of giving away his true thoughts to any man – prince or peasant.

"Brynan will fight, know you that! He will not turn and run away when he sees your men on his borders. He has many sons of noble families he may call upon to defend his kingdom, and his people are not all mutton-faced churls either."

"Noble knights, you mean?" Anfad almost snarled. "Naught but fools dressed in mail! They are so much a-sporting at the joust and parading themselves in the courts of love, they have forgotten how to hold a sword. Their horses are put out to grass and only fit for hauling wagons full of turnips. As for his foot soldiers, they are too heavy with ale and pasties to hold a shield or swing an axe. And they have no young men at arms that are not a-sporting with maids in the woods. You think that rabble will be match for my men of the hills? I know my folk, iron they are, not made soft by the attentions of women."

Anfad spat into the flames and regarded the other two with the surly air of the bully born.

Barud, King of Techlyn, the third man there, began to speak. A gross boar of a man, his jowls told of endless greed, while his eyes were smouldering pits of lechery. His voice was languid, almost soft. "So, you wish us both to pledge our armies in order to fight alongside you as loyal comrades. Is that so, Anfad?"

Anfad could detect the mockery in Barud's voice. It took little to heat his anger.

"I am asking you to join me, Barud, but only if you have true warriors in your land - men who are willing to fight. Are the men of Techlyn such as that?"

"Aye, and plenty. But what pickings are there for them in Irlas? They will want to know that, especially if there is a chance their wives might be widows at the end of the day."

Anfad came back at him quickly.

"I tell you, Irlas is a rich land. There is much treasure in Brynan's castle and the merchants, I have heard, hide gold beneath their beds."

"Gold, you say? Good... and what else? Women?"

Anfad spat contemptuously into the fire once more.

"Plenty, if that is what you want. They say the maidens of Irlas are the fairest in the Western Lands."

Barud's eyes grew brighter still. "I was thinking of one particularly choice little thing. A pretty dove, and of royal birth."

"The Princess Tegwyn?" Galar said. "You would not lay waste to Melynas as well? Besides, they say she is betrothed to Brynan, and he is certain to see no harm comes to her, even though she may not yet be his queen."

Anfad ignored Galar, concentrating on playing this fat fish. His mouth shaped into a leer. "You shall have your dainty morsel, Barud."

Barud's eyes glistened all the more. "And how do you propose that?"

Anfad tightened the line. "King Tulrech's kingdom of Melynas lies next to Techlyn. You, Barud, shall attack them first. Brynan will go bravely to the rescue, and Galar may then march up from the south and lay siege to Brynan's castle - it will scarcely be left defended too heavily. Brynan will then hurry back to rescue his own... with you, Barud, in pursuit. Along the way, my own army will lie in wait, and then cut them to pieces. Perfect, is it not? By this time next year, all Irlas, and Melynas as well, will be ours."

Galar eyed the other two, his expression fixed and grim. "And you plan all that, Anfad, that you might raise better swine on another's lands, and Barud here get his hands on yet another poor wench?"

Barud chuckled quietly. "I shall dream about the moment, Galar."

"And what makes you think she will do your bidding, Barud? She might sooner throw herself from the castle walls than be mauled about by you."

"You obviously do not know the ways of women, Galar," Barud chuckled. "They are like dogs, and soon get used to a new master. And there is always the threat of a beating, if they do not obey."

Galar kept silent. Then he too rose, to stand opposite Anfad. In the firelight he towered above the prince. Galar, now in his middle years, was not the great warrior he once had been, but he still had a commanding air.

Anfad kept his hand upon his sword; the other was put defiantly on his hip.

Barud watched them both carefully. Galar, when he spoke, appeared to choose his words carefully.

"There is one thing that you have forgotten in your pretty plan, Anfad. Or rather, one person."

"And who is that?"

"Paldarch..."

Anfad glared, but Galar went on.

"...have you thought about how you might go about defeating a wizard?"

Anfad laughed out loud, a mirthless sound that echoed from the walls around them. "Paldarch! The trickster! The buffoon! His foolish games are only fit to amuse brats. I have no concern of him." Anfad gripped his sword and this time he drew it, the steel glimmering dully in the fire light. "What can any wizard do against the blade of the Prince of Durasglyn? Answer me that!"

"Others in the past have thought the same, Anfad, and they too were shown to be wrong," Galar said in measured tones. "Beware of the wiles of sorcery, Anfad. Beware."

In his mounting anger, Anfad might have raised his sword, even against Galar, had not Barud roused himself at that moment. His voice was as steel on stone.

"Hold that vile temper of yours, Anfad. Sometimes I think you believe a blade is all that matters in this world. Besides, there will be plenty of time for heat and blood, if battle is what you crave. Let us not break this alliance we have agreed upon before it has yet time to yield some fruit. We have much to gain. As for Paldarch, he can be dealt with all in good time, of that I am sure. The sun will have grown bigger and made its round by the time we meet again..."

Anfad put away his sword, almost reluctantly.

"...calm yourself, Anfad," Barud continued. "Put that fire into making all ready with your army. Remember, all will be ours in a season or two."

Each grasped the others' hand in silent union, as chiefs among men are wont to do. Then they made ready to depart, for the fire had burnt low. Even with a thick cloak about him, each felt the chill air as it bit at their throats. The days were still gripped by the winds of Rhagel and now they could see that snow had fallen in the last hour and lay thick on the ground. They hurried out from the barn, each to return to his kingdom.

Above them in the hay loft, Hog, who had listened intently to every word, marvelled at all he had heard. Significant to our tale, is that he remembered it all.

III

The year had more than turned, and glistening snowdrops covered the banks alongside the river Gaflau. A cart trudged through the mud, its wheels making soft, squelching sounds. Much rain had fallen in recent days, but now the sun was daily growing greater in the sky. Soon the water that had lain long on the land would be gone, leaving only a smooth greyness upon the grass. A man could rise with a gladder heart knowing he might go dryshod to the plough. After the planting, as at every Gwan, folk would offer prayers to Nen - the father of the gods - for a good harvest. This year the ewes were big with lambs, and the cattle, being well foraged during Rhagel, were bright of eye. As for the swine, they always seemed content to be in the forest, snuffling for acorns.

Irlas, the most westerly of the Six Great Kingdoms, had at her heart Treflan - neither town nor village, but a parcel of dwellings clustered about a knoll. Upon this stood a castle of stone and below its walls, the smith, stonemason and carpenter each had their own workplace. None was favoured above the other, but held a higher rank than the other craftsmen housed in smaller huts below them, among them the potter, the workers in leather, the weavers and dyers. Above all, and most favoured, was the swordsmith. He lived within the castle walls, and his calling was regarded as being akin to that of a wizard.

The times when hunters roamed the land had long passed, and folk had taken to remaining in one place. Here they had settled because of the river Gaflau, which rushed through the valley, to end in a lake. The water was easy to fish and the catch plentiful. At some time a mill had been built and after that, granaries and a bakehouse. Of the rest of Treflan, not much was noteworthy, save for the square before the castle. Here folks gathered on market days, or to hear their king address them.

The central street, like the smaller streets that led off it, was unpaved, often becoming muddy after rain. At one end of this was the Temple, at the other the Tavern, and both had their loyal following. The storytellers and the minstrels divided their time equally between both places, so it was often hard to tell whether a ritual or a revel was taking place. Perhaps that is the best way for things to be, for our spiritual life need not always be solemn.

Forest covered much of the land, and deer walked the ways unmolested. The charcoal burners and their families lived in the clearings, safe from the outlaws that infested other kingdoms, such as Durasglyn. Irlas had never been a lawless land, for the kings before Brynan had ruled with an iron hand. Although not displaying cruelty for its own sake, they showed little mercy toward wrong-doers.

Kings are but mortal men, and thus it must follow that some are good, others bad, many indifferent. One ruler may deserve his rank, as if born to it, while another should never be permitted to take up the crown. From ancient times the gods have ordained that a king, in return for loyalty from his people, must serve them and their land. Pity the kingdom that has a weak or wicked ruler for, in no time, it will be naught but waste and ruin. A cursed king means a cursed kingdom. Those who were ruled over by Brynan were indeed fortunate, for he was a just, generous monarch. The full title of His Majesty - *Huan* Brynan – meant 'chosen king' in the old tongue.

As every year at this time, the traders had begun to arrive for the Maiglan Fair. It was a cheery time for all, and much feasting and sport would ensue. The tavern would invite visitors to taste their festive brew; while the merchants in their fur lined linen cloaks would take their ease with wine and sweetmeats in the Great Hall. At the stalls in the square, silver was never as welcome as gold, but this bright metal was much in evidence in the fine jewellry for sale. Many a young maid yearned for a betrothal ring at this season. Pretty they looked too, in their simple lemon and emerald skirts, belted at the waist.

It was much rumoured that Brynan was soon to take a wife. The people felt the time was right for a Rhindas, as they called the exchange of rings, and for their king to have a queen by his side. Rumours were also abroad as to who that might be – but we must not let our tale get ahead of itself. Next, let day become night.

*

It is said that an owl can see further into the darkness than any other creature. Yet, an owl can still be puzzled, as was this particular night bird. It perched on an oak branch in the moonlight and watched curiously as Paldarch the wizard, wrapped tightly in his black cloak, brought his horse to halt. This strange being, thought the owl, had nearly become the darkness itself. Next the owl felt that he had become part of that all-embracing night. He, and the figure he had been watching, were as one.

Paldarch flapped his newly acquired wings, and waited to feel the sensation of claws gripping the bark of the branch beneath him. He had changed his shape many times, but he still felt a strange sensation as he observed his other self upon the horse. Paldarch shook the blanket of feathers about him, and passed deep into the soul of this creature of wisdom. The owl is the night eagle, the all-seeing eye and now the wizard entered the universal mind to discover what he might.

He flew within an immense cavern, one with no roof or floor and everywhere he met stars. The wizard was waiting for a certain one, marked out from the others. He knew that soon this being would reveal itself.

Voices were all around him, some sweet, some discordant - the cooing of a mother over her babe, the cries of hunters – a tapestry of sound. The owl knows instinctively where deception lies and, as he flew, Paldarch listened for a particular tone, one that would alert him to the presence of malice. There! A rasping, sound, not in harmony with the other voices around. Paldarch strained to hear the words but they were somehow snatched away, like the cry of gulls in a storm. Paldarch tried again and again but it was of no use.

After some time, dense clouds obscured his vision, and the wizard knew that the one he was seeking in the Otherworld was under another's protection. The wizard had been seeking the soul of Prince Anfad of Durasglyn, but in vain. At least he was now certain of the prince's guardian – Cythras, the Dark One. Dread was that name, arousing fear in all, even on occasion a mighty wizard.

The coming strife was not to be any ordinary chronicle of misdeeds; it was to be a magical combat. Paldarch returned to this world, still in the guise of an owl, and flew on, to another place and another time.

*

A damp dawn saw three riders meet beneath the black boughs of a huge yew tree, one that dripped steadily from the night's rain. Few ever ventured into the depths of Preydun forest except those, like Anfad, who preferred the company of shadows. Some days before, the prince had sent word to Galar and Barud that he had news to impart, and grudgingly they had agreed to meet him. A pale light could now be seen in the east, but it heralded only a weak orb; one that passed for the sun in this season.

"This news of yours had best be ripe, Anfad, dragging me from my bed at such a time."

Barud managed to be cheery, even though his hair and beard were quite damp. Even the thick hood of his sheepskin cloak was not proof against such weather as this.

"Ripe? Aye, ripe you will think it when you hear what I have to say, Barud," Anfad replied. "You also, Galar."

The latter merely responded with a grunt from beneath his fur cap. These last years, in the cold seasons, the king was aware more and more of the damp creeping into his bones. The sensation did not serve to improve his temper.

"Well?" Galar said.

"I have made it my business to find out a little more about these two lovebirds, Brynan and the Princess Tegwyn. It seems that our lusty young king is in the habit of visiting the castle when her father, Tulrech, is about his rounds of the kingdom. He is even known to stay in her bedchamber until the next morn."

Galar shrugged impatiently. "What of it?"

"Tegwyn's chamber maid has, in return for a few silver coins, informed me that the princess is now with child. Do you not see what this means? When her father, King Tulrech, sees how things are, he will insist their union is announced. The Rhindas will then be quick in coming. The kingdoms of Irlas and Melynas will be so taken up with riot and celebration that our doings will not be noticed. Now we have only to decide when to move against Melynas."

Galar merely shrugged. "Perhaps."

Barud was more inclined to be encouraging of the prince. "So cunning you are, Anfad. You have worked well at your plans. Now tell me, is this maid comely? What else will she do for a little silver, eh?"

Anfad pulled abruptly at the reins of his horse.

28

"Pah! Curse your filthy appetites, Barud! We have other, more important, matters to consider. What think you of the high time of Hafwan?"

Barud raised an eyebrow.

"How can you be so sure that this Rhindas will not take place before then, particularly if our little princess is getting rounder by the minute?" he asked. "Surely, there will be talk among the other ladies of the court? They notice these things, so I am told."

"With the coming of Gwan, Tegwyn intends to confine herself in her Lodge at Halerond. She has told her father that she wishes to spend her time in devotions to the gods."

Barud's rough laugh was heard.

"Devoted to the gods? Only to Cyngerl, the Goddess of Love, I'll warrant, to whom she has been most attentive, it seems."

Anfad ignored him.

"What say you both? Is it to be Hafuan when we march on Melynas? That will be a fine Rhindas gift for the royal couple, will it not?"

Barud nodded grudgingly. Drops of fine rain were now spilling from his beard onto his gloved hands, and he had heard enough of Anfad's shrill voice. It tired him to listen further. He turned to the silent figure of Galar, hunched in the saddle.

"And you, old friend, what do you say? Do you agree?"

The eyes of Galar were dull, even in this sombre light. He barely moved his lips when he spoke.

"Aye, as you say. Send word when you wish my armies to join you. Now, permit me to leave, for I must seek a fire this bitter morning."

As if in mocking answer, the sun rose suddenly over the hills - a yellow disc with little promise of comfort or warmth. Galar glanced at the sky, bid the other two farewell, and turned his horse towards the amber flush now gilding the tops of the trees. They watched him depart and slowly descend the hillside to the way that led to Blauwyg, his kingdom. Barud looked away shook his head.

"If this all comes to pass, it will be the last battle our King Galar fights; I can tell you that, Anfad. There is little fire left in his belly methinks."

Anfad shrugged.

"If he falls on the field, then there will be more spoils for us both to share, Barud."

"All men go to the fight thinking they will have the victory, Anfad. It is impossible for the god, Marak, to serve every warrior in battle that cannot be."

Anfad replied with sly confidence.

"Have no fear, Barud. I have other plans that I know will bring fruit and ensure our victory."

"You are as full of scheming as the dykes are with the winter rains, Anfad. Let us hope your plans bring us good fortune. I bid you farewell."

Barud was about to urge his horse onward when a sudden noise so startled Anfad's horse that it bucked high in the air. Anfad recovered, but froze as if he was tied in the saddle.

"In the name of Nen, what was that?"

"Only an owl, Anfad, there... flying over the kale in yonder field."

The bird flapped lazily through the sky and was gone. Anfad watched its flight. His voice was cold with fear.

"They say it is a bird of ill-omen".

Barud did not respond. He slapped the flank of his horse and moved off. But as he did so, he called over his shoulder,

"It is your enemies you should be afraid of, Anfad. They will make you jump like a frog, not an owl. And jump you will, maybe higher than you did just then."

Barud's mocking laughter gradually died away in the distance, but the scowl upon Anfad's face remained. He continued to stare out over the land until he too left the forest behind.

Apparently oblivious to all this, the owl, that same bird that had so alarmed Prince Anfad, seemed content to perch among the red willow stems. Its head was cocked above its wing, as if listening intently to everything that went on in the world of men.

IV

Ufeln had come and the dust was so thick in the lanes that it was sometimes difficult to make out the way ahead. The blossom lay heavy on the thorn and many trees were in full leaf as if in celebration. Each morn the birds sang loud and long. About the town, the day's doings gathered momentum like the wheel of a cart.

Well after noonday, Paldarch eased his horse along the way that led to Treflan. Behind and before came other travellers, some on horseback, and others on foot. All mingled with the carts, loaded with provender, bound for the Maiglan Fair. Paldarch, emerging from between two rows of elms that marked the end of the way, eased his mount towards the crowded square.

The wizard was soon caught up among the bustle of folk moving around the tents and stalls. One or two faces turned to look at him, and some in the throng would even nudge a neighbour and point in Paldarch's direction. On his white steed, he would have been a commanding figure in any company. Among these simple peasants and farmers, the wizard was the closest thing to a god they would ever see.

Paldarch turned his horse Teryngar towards the castle and slowly crossed the bridge between the henge and the knoll. The palace guard, adorned in crimson and gold, stood erect by the gate house. Paldarch hailed him.

"A fine day."

"It is that, Master Paldarch."

"Is the Chief Steward within?"

"Indeed. He awaits you."

Paldarch raised his hand in friendly salute and, passing beneath the high arch and into the courtyard, saw to his right the Great Hall. There, on Maiglan night, the favoured would gather to carouse beneath the tall rafters. Rich merchants and those who owned lands, would be entertained by tumblers, minstrels and jesters and all would make merry.

Each of the oaken doors of the hall was emblazoned with a winged serpent, a legacy of ancient magical ways, their significance perhaps forgotten. Before this grand entrance stood Cydlon, the Chief Steward, equally as imposing – his tunic cut of sumptuous silk, as befitted the senior member of the royal house. All smiles, he raised his arms to Paldarch in honest welcome.

"Master Paldarch! May Nen be praised that we see you in yet another Ufeln! How was your journey?"

"As comfortable as these old bones will allow, Cydlon! Teryngar, my faithful steed, still holds me well over many miles."

"He will be fed and stabled for as long as you decide to honour us with your company."

"That will not be for long I fear…"

Cydlon's face fell for an instant.

"But you will be staying for the Maiglan Feast tonight, and perhaps the Great Games on the morrow?"

Paldarch smiled.

"Indeed. I have brought my best cloak for the occasion. It is in my pack… so tell the ostler to take it with care."

"It will be done. You will not be alone in the wearing of your best. For many, the Feast is an even greater occasion than Nadoman."

The wizard dismounted and, after he had spoken softly to Teryngar, allowed him to be led away. Then, his satchel on his shoulder and his staff in his hand, Paldarch started in the direction of the private apartments. Such was the power of the wizard over the minds of others that Cydlon found himself mouthing words he was hardly aware of speaking.

"I know the king awaits you, Master Paldarch. I beg you follow me."

Paldarch nodded almost imperceptibly. Once past the great oaken door in the castle tower, he was led into an ante-chamber to wait. The Chief Steward hurried away to inform the king of his visitor. A moment later he returned.

"King Huan Brynan bids you step this way."

Those who had set out the king's apartment long ago were masters of the art of building. Glass was hardly known in those days and yet, by some means, a quantity had been brought into Irlas from afar. Tinted panes had been fitted in the west and south walls of the long chamber. During the hours of daylight, even in the winter months, no hint of gloom was ever there.

Crimson and ochre tiles made up the floor, the black tracery of their design heightening their rich hues. Rugs and animal skins covered much, and the bright hangings upon the walls were so bathed in light as to make them almost animated. There was furniture enough, ornately carved chests covered with linen cloth that doubled as benches, and chairs of elm wood. Presently, the young monarch sat upon an oaken throne.

He rose to his feet as the wizard entered and gave a gesture that showed he regarded Paldarch almost as an equal to himself. They faced each other, the king with sunny locks and youthful beard, and the old wizard, his white mane flowing to his shoulders. Brynan was dressed in a fine purple doublet and wore pointed boots of the softest leather, while the wizard cut a more sombre figure in his grey cloak.

"My Liege," Paldarch said, and bowed as he always did in the king's presence. It was never a gesture of deference. A wizard, like Death, does not consider rank in his dealings with others. Paldarch simply acknowledged that his sovereign was the earthly counterpart of a Divine Principle. From the beginning of the Age of Kings, it had always been understood that the almighty Nen gave his blessing to those who ruled upon this earth. In his journeying through many realms, Paldarch had known not a few kings, and he continued to be surprised at how deep an affection he felt for Brynan. The king grasped the arm of Paldarch firmly, not only in welcome, but perhaps to reassure himself the wizard was actually there with him and not away journeying in some unseen realm, perhaps even in another form.

"You are looking as fine as I have ever seen you, Paldarch. But have the stewards given you refreshment… a cup of wine, some meats?"

Paldarch held up a hand in mild protest.

"Thank you, my liege, but I assure you, water and wafers sustain me well enough. That is the proper fare for one of my calling. A slight hunger keeps one constantly aware."

The king eyed the imposing frame of the wizard.

"As you wish. It must be said your abstemious ways seem to only benefit you! But come, sit you down. You know I have great news to impart."

Paldarch chose one of the finely carved chairs, settled himself down, and nodded gravely.

"My, Liege?"

The king allowed himself a smile of amusement.

"But then of course you will know these things already! Are you not the great wizard Paldarch? The one who reads the minds of men as if they were set out upon a parchment set before you, and seeing into the future as a child gazes into the bottom of a pool? So you know I am to take a wife?"

It was Paldarch's turn to be merry.

"It would be untrue to claim I had seen all this in the scrying bowl, my liege. Why, in every part of your kingdom the talk of the people is only of these matters. They say that soon a queen will be seated beside their king, and they are glad."

"Know you that my father always wished me to wed before Ufeln had come five and twenty times. By Nen's will, he was taken before then, but now I am of that age. King Tulrech of Melynas has a daughter, Tegwyn, his only child. The mother died bearing her, as did my own parent. Nen moves in strange ways." Brynan fell silent for a moment.

"Indeed," Paldarch replied.

"I have known my future bride since we were but children together. So, I am glad that at least my father knew of my betrothed. Though, I fear he and King Tulrech were not on the best of terms."

"I heard this was so."

"It matters not, for it is all in the past and this day is what matters. My emissaries were sent out before the first Rhagel moon to negotiate for the princess' hand. It seems that all parties have agreed."

Paldarch could not help but reflect wryly on the formalities of match making among those of royal status. It was certainly a very different matter for many a youth and maiden who, around the time of the Maiglan, would enjoy an earthy union in the woods. Perhaps the lovemaking of Brynan and the Princess matched the passion of any peasant swain. What he had heard of Brynan's amours, whilst eavesdropping upon the three kings in Preydun Forest, he would keep to himself. Paldarch suddenly realised the king was regarding him anxiously.

"Does your silence mean that you are not pleased, Paldarch? Do you not regard the Princess as a suitable match?"

Paldarch quickly abandoned his reverie.

"Forgive me, my liege; I must be more tired than I thought after my journey. It is true that I had but little sleep last night."

The king was then all concern, and leaned toward him.

"Then you must rest before the festivities tonight. But before you retire, I would ask that, when the festivities are over, you will ride with me to Melynas that you may meet the Princess Tegwyn. It is but two days' journey if we make a good pace."

"I would be honoured to accompany you on any journey."

"Good. Derwen, my most loyal knight, will accompany us the day after the morrow."

"A wise decision to have company of three, for a triune is always powerful..."

Something in the wizard's tone puzzled the king. Paldarch weighed his next words carefully, as a merchant might do precious stones.

"...it is right that we should journey together, but as to our destination, that may be very different."

Brynan leaned anxiously towards Paldarch.

"How so?"

"It is only right that I should impart certain things to you, my liege, before yet another moment passes."

Brynan felt a strange sense of foreboding, almost as if he had known that Paldarch would bring unwelcome tidings. He spoke briskly, perhaps to conceal such fears, even from himself.

"Pray tell me all, I am ready."

Paldarch began in an even tone, as if imparting a lesson to a child.

"This is an auspicious time in the history of the Old Era. It is not just the season that is about to turn. The times are changing also. Most assuredly, we are poised between one age and the next, even as the shore is the meeting twixt land and sea."

"Change is always with us, Paldarch, I know that. But you speak of great changes and have a serious air about you, one not in accord with our time of feasts and rejoicing. Tell me more, I beg of you."

"My liege, you must prepare yourself for the worst. The kingdom will soon be in the greatest danger."

A silence entered the chamber, dulling the light that entered there, as if a cloud had covered the sun.

"What means this, Paldarch? Your words come strangely to me. Why, the kingdom has never enjoyed such peace since the Golden Age of my forefathers. Already more are gathered here for the Maiglan Feast than ever before. Irlas has never known such harvests of recent years. And you talk of alarms? How can this be? Will not the presence of my new queen bring even more joy to the people and the land? Is it not said that the queen brings fruitfulness to the earth?"

Paldarch looked long and hard at the king. His features were the more grave.

"Often the greatest harm befalls us when we least expect it. This Ufeln will herald such things as you cannot now imagine. Nevermore will Irlas be the same, nor any one of all the Six Kingdoms, mark you that."

Brynan was silent, attending.

"By Hafwan all will have changed. In these coming days kings will have a part to play, as well as wizards and warriors. But make no mistake, for a time the sun will not shine as bright as it once did. I cannot give you words of comfort, my liege, would that I could. But it is only right that I, who gave much counsel to your father, should speak thus to you, his son."

Brynan was suddenly pale, whether with anger or fear; none, save a wizard, would have been able to tell. When the young king spoke his tone was almost shrill.

"Have you gone mad in your dotage, Paldarch? How can you speak of such things? Not one word that you have spoken has made the slightest sense to me. In the name of Nen, speak no more in riddles, I beg of you. What is it that is about to happen?"

The eyes of Paldarch were dark as night. He spoke one word.

"War."

It was as if all light in the chamber had become dulled. Brynan turned his head away, as if he did not want to even imagine such a thing might come to pass. A broken whisper gave life to his thoughts.

"How will it come?"

Paldarch shook his head.

"I cannot tell. I have found out much already, but not enough. Only a god may see everything. It is certain that dark forces are gathering, as clouds before a storm..."

The king cried out hotly.

"Then let us prevent this happening! We will gather our armies, seek out these evil-doers and punish them."

"If only it were as simple as that. We must hold ourselves in readiness... and not behave rashly. Nor must we forget the simple faith that reminds us, 'All will be well'".

Brynan was dismissive.

"That is the sentiment of foolish peasants."

"Simple, some folk may appear to be, but they are not always that simple. There is a belief in the rightness of things, my liege."

In the silence that followed, Paldarch reflected that in the coming months there would be much Brynan would be forced to think upon. He would endure many nights of troubled dreams. Kings, as all other men, must learn patience and fortitude in the face of adversity. Brynan was but a young man. While silence ruled in the chamber, beyond the windows, the sound of the crowd could already be faintly heard. The hour of evening approached, and the revelry would soon begin in earnest. The kingdom was oblivious while wizard and king pondered its fate.

"You must advise me, Paldarch."

The words tumbled into the silence of the chamber, like whispers in a dark cave.

"I will do all that I am able, my liege. It is the wizard's vow to always be in the service of the king. Now, what of your brother?"

Brynan was surprised by the question.

"Rhaldon? Why, he tends flocks of sheep on the Plain of Tawelf, beyond the forests. My brother was never one for court life, even when he was a young man. As soon as our father died, he would not tarry here, but set up a home with his livestock around him. I am told he is well regarded by the many that live in the settlement he has made. Why do you ask of Rhaldon?"

"It is as well to know where any allies may be found when times of strife are upon us."

"Perhaps, though my brother is no warrior..."

"It is often not as important as to what we are, but what we become..."

Brynan was silent, but only for a time.

"You spoke of a journey I must take, Paldarch..."

"Indeed. This we must take together, and as soon as the Maiglan feasting is done."

Hearing these words the king was suddenly all alarm.

"By all the gods! The betrothal ceremony! I was to journey to Melynas with a full retinue three days hence! What a rage Tegwyn's father will be in if I do not appear at his court! Paldarch, it is impossible for me to change my plans like this."

Paldarch was firm.

"I fear you must. Not just for the sake of Irlas, but for the future of all of the Six Kingdoms of the West. There is a great darkness gathering beyond your borders, and it will grow the greater. But you, Huan Brynan, must gain certain wisdoms, that you are ready to meet this threat. I cannot say any more."

The king spoke with an air of resignation.

"I will do as you say, and word will be sent to Melynas... but at least tell me where we are going and what we are to do..."

"We must journey to the kingdom of Durasglyn, and then perhaps further."

The king's features darkened.

"Durasglyn? That is said not to be a fair land."

"It has beauty of its own, as all the world. We go to the mountains of Niwel..."

"And you will tell me why we must go?"

"All will become clear upon the way. That is the most I can say now."

Brynan sighed.

"Riddles again, Paldarch. When will you ever cease to be a man of mystery?"

The wizard laughed, and at that sound, light entered the chamber once more.

"But that is what I am."

The king joined in his laughter.

"Indeed you are, old fellow, and I love you for it."

Paldarch paused, then appeared to look most serious.

"Have you ever cut into a leek?"

"A leek?" The king was baffled, but kept his humour. "Is that not what the peasants eat in their huts? It does not grace the royal table, so far as I know. I am not one to be fond of turnips and the like..."

"If you had, my liege, by some mischance perhaps, encountered this humble plant..."

Paldarch was suddenly full of mischief, and the king knew it.

"Now you jest with me, Paldarch! What is all this talk of leeks, pray?"

"It is just that there is an outward part, while inside the rest consists of many rings. These inner parts are as important as the outer. Neither the one nor the other is more valuable. Like the leek, we all appear to be one thing, whereas we are another. That other… hidden part… is the soul, and its journey continues all the while. The soul will never perish, but the body surely will, and many men care too much for that part of themselves, filling it with wine and meat and the like…"

"I know this to be so. At table, the greed of some of my lords is beyond belief; they will stuff themselves until they are sick, then ask for more. I do not often reflect upon those in the court, Paldarch. I let them be… yet there is one who…"

"Yes?"

"Prince Anfad. He troubles me when I am in his presence… there is something about him that I do not favour. He seems to be a creature of shadows and whispers, one who shuns the light of day."

Paldarch's face grew grave.

"I fear it is he who threatens us. After the harvest, a cold wind will blow across these lands. It comes from Durasglyn …"

Brynan gripped the arms of his throne..

"It is he that seeks to wage war? But he has no army to match our own…"

"I believe he has allies."

"So the wolves gather in one pack! This is ill news, Paldarch."

"At least we have warning of our enemies' plans. That alone may save the kingdom."

"*May* save the kingdom? So this is my royal inheritance… the suffering of my people… their lands burning… fathers slain… women and children led away as slaves?"

Brynan got to his feet and began to pace the hall, holding his hands above his head as if to appeal to all the gods.

"Calm yourself, my liege. It has not come to this yet."

"But you said yourself that before a season is out, war will come and we shall be fighting against great odds. And I... about to take a wife... and bring a queen to my people. Before many moons pass, it seems Nen will cease to smile upon us."

Paldarch got slowly to his feet and faced the king. He spoke gently, in way that always brought calm to those who were greatly troubled.

"Nen has ways that we mortals cannot possibly know. When danger threatens, all manner of powers rise up to aid us. Do not distress yourself with idle imaginings, my liege. I will do all that I can to protect the kingdom. I gave that very same pledge to your father in the times when he sat upon that very throne, the same times when my powers were first bestowed upon me."

Brynan looked intently at the old wizard.

"The kingdom has never had a greater ally than you."

It was now early eve and the light in the chamber had begun to fade. Paldarch felt a sudden weariness come upon him.

"I wish that I had words to allay your fears, my liege, but I do not."

"I wish the same too, Paldarch."

The wizard bowed his head a little.

"Now I beg that I may take my leave, my liege, so I that may rest before the festivities tonight."

Brynan's countenance brightened, as if a lamp had suddenly been lit. He had now the face of a child, remembering some day of pleasure from times afar off.

"How I loved Maiglan when I was young! Then I knew it was the time when you would come to visit the castle. Oh, how I waited and waited for that day, alway pestering my father and mother for news of your arrival!"

Paldarch looked upon the king as would a kindly uncle. The years fell back once more, to reveal times long gone.

43

For Brynan, his cares had disappeared, if only for a moment. Paldarch continued to smile upon him.

"You were a young prince then. Now you are Lord of a Kingdom."

To the king, Paldarch was the emissary of gods. It was a marvel that he who now advised him, had also given his father counsel. Did Brynan even dimly remember once seeing the wizard in grave debate with his grandfather?

"Aye, and let us hope I am worthy of the title, as all my fathers before me."

"You *are* worthy, and that most assuredly, my liege. A leader of men and born to be so. You wear your crown with honour, and Nen smiles upon your deeds."

Brynan bowed his head.

"I merely pray that Nen gives me strength and faith, so that when the hour comes that I am tested I will banish all doubt."

"He assuredly will, my liege."

Paldarch stooped to pick up his staff from where it lay upon a carved settle. Brynan put his hand on the wizard's arm.

"Go now, Paldarch. We will talk further on the morrow, and make ready for our coming journey. I will make certain my knight Derwen knows he is to accompany us."

"Excellent. I look forward to meeting again that most excellent of men."

"And I know Cydlon the Steward has made ready your usual quarters, and that all is of the finest."

Paldarch bowed.

"Grateful I am, my liege. Always the hospitality of the Royal House of Irlas was the finest in the Six Kingdoms."

Brynan acknowledged the compliment with a nod of the royal head.

"Rest well, before the feast, my old friend."

And so Paldarch the Wizard departed from the king, and presently a steward led him to his quarters. Being high in the North West tower, the chamber was small, with just enough room for a bed and a narrow bench, but to the wizard it felt welcoming and familiar. Before he made to lie upon the coverlet of his bed, he opened the wooden shutter and looked down at the lively scene below. Couples were dancing and frolicking about the Gwalstan, and at each succeeding air, the minstrels introduced a more insistent lilt to their playing. Paldarch could even catch a waft of the roasted meats that filled the air, and hear the hubbub from the mead stalls.

The wizard observed all with a benevolent eye. His gaze did not always radiate such a kindly emotion, as those who had dared to challenge him over the years had learned to their cost. But now the wizard applauded the careless joy of the revellers. It was for the wellbeing of the common folk that a wizard often best employed his powers, to bring some ease to their lives, and vanquish as much misfortune from them as possible.

They were unaware of the role magic played in their lives and rightly so, for they might become anxious or afeared. It was better that a wizard should pass among them, as a shadow in the night, than they be aware of his presence too often. Paldarch respected these folk who worked the land as, in doing so, they served the Goddess. True abundance was theirs, and that same earth would remain, long after those who walked upon it had been forgotten.

Here, ensconced some way above the world, he could enjoy a moment of peace. Later, after walking among the crowd and acknowledging their joy once more, he would attend the feast in the Great Hall. And after that, he would have been glad to slip quietly away, and be alone once more. Paldarch knew this would not be so, for now a great quest awaited him with the king.

A wizard does not seek out the company of lords and rich merchants; their ways do not suit him. He has no regard for the fripperies of court, and the false faces that too often are to be seen there. The sight irks him. Men were often foolish, and that knowledge did not make Paldarch feel superior; rather it added to his melancholy. Strife and discord were about to come to the world, and that knowledge made his heart heavy. It was made worse because he dearly loved the fair kingdom of Irlas.

Paldarch took off his boots and cloak, loosed his belt and lay down. No sooner did his head touch the coverlet of his bed than he fell into a deep slumber, one thankfully not disturbed by the weight of his troubled thoughts.

V

The sunlight dancing upon the walls of her chamber made
Tegwyn wake early. When she turned her head on the
pillow, her fulsome locks streamed out around her, aflame
with gold. She was herself the sun, more wondrous than
the orb now slowly rising in the heavens! The doves that
gathered about her window every morning sang praises to
her, and she sang with them in her joy. Her thoughts
lingered upon her beloved, King Brynan. Soon, he would
be with her again, and then would be the betrothal
ceremony. How she counted the days until then!

The pair had met when youth was upon them both.
Brynan was naturally shy with a pretty maid – the first he
had ever encountered – and, heavily chaperoned, they
would walk together beyond the battlements. Tegwyn
would play a game, cajoling the young prince into picking
wild flowers for her, to adorn her hair. Then she would
dance for him, whirling around and around in her white
gown, her amber beads flying about her neck. When she
ended the dance, Brynan, carefully avoiding the eye of the
lady-in-waiting, would steal a kiss or two. His attentions
were by means unwelcome to the princess. She was
flattered to be courted, albeit in fantastic style, by a boy
who would one day be king.

As they grew in years together, it seemed inevitable that
one day they would become lovers. Tegwyn thought again
of that precious encounter only a few moons ago. Her
father had been away in the North visiting his brother and
Tegwyn had made her plans. Brynan would enter the
castle secretly through a seldom-used door in the Inner
Gatehouse. Tegwyn had, with great stealth, procured the
key. That night, with a heart so excited she wondered its
beating could not be heard in the furthest courtyard, she
had let Brynan into the castle.

Hand in hand, they had crept silently to her chamber where a fire of logs burned steadily in the grate. She recalled every moment. Brynan had warmed his hands and then settled himself on a rug before the flames. How handsome he had looked in the firelight. It took only moments before their arms were about each other and their lips met. Brynan looked into those eyes full of stars, and in his she saw them also.

"And what would you wish of me, O spirit of the night, O great warrior?"

Brynan had replied, with words that returned to her every night, "I would wish to conquer you, my lady."

"Then let us not delay your victory too long, my lord. I willingly surrender."

Then she had taken the pins from her hair, combed it long, and boldly thrown off her gown. All that remained upon her smooth form were her bracelets of amber. They had lain naked before the warmth of the fire and made love, not once but many times, even until the dawn. It was as if their innocence alone brought such ardour. And soon they would be together for ever! Tegwyn felt as one who would sing and declare her love to all, crying it aloud to the very skies. This was how life was meant to be!

Often it is as well that we are unknowing of what life will bring to us. But at that moment, the gods had chosen not to mar one instant of Tegwyn's happiness.

*

Above the hills lay a hint of cloud, but the sky remained sapphire, and spoke of infinity. It was the day after the Maiglan Feast and Hog was, for once, pleased with life. The cold and bitterness of Rhagel was forgotten. Who could not exalt on such a fine day? Yester eve in the square there had been, laid out upon the oaken tables, food aplenty. Many had been generous to Hog, handing him a pastie here, or a hunk of bread and cheese there.

It is the way of things, that if a dog is seen to be often kicked, it attracts yet more blows. However, at the feast folks had been less inclined to scowl in his direction. Hog knew that the widening smiles might be as much due to ale as a warm heart, but he had fed well, and thus slept well, and for that he was grateful. Nen had smiled upon him, albeit briefly, and though he knew it not, Hog had been chosen this day to receive favours of a kind that he had never received before.

He walked among the mauve thistles, docks and soft cooling grasses. The wind caressed his neck like a mother quieting her child. Hog had never known a loving touch such as that. The Goddess, who knows and sees all, felt a great compassion for him. She knew too, that this slim youth had been chosen for a singular part in destiny's play.

Knowing nothing of all this, Hog stepped across the dry bed of a stream – a torrent in the wet season – and entered the woods. The clack of a woodpecker greeted him. Even here, among the tall oak and ash, he could still feel the warmth of the morning sun. His mood seemed to be reflected in everything he saw. Pools of light brought butterflies to bless the brilliance, and seeing them, Hog felt his spirit freed. He was invisible, a spirit roaming the woods.

Even the sound of a dog barking in the distance did not return him to this world. But how wonderful the world appeared! Ivy-covered elder branches lay where they had fallen, and below the russet and emerald carpet of leaves, lay the secret dwellings of badgers and foxes. Coming to a place where broken, old trees seemed to resemble giants, Hog knew that, if just a little life were breathed into them,

49

they would walk. Here, among the periwinkles, anything could happen...

What was that among the trees? A shadow flitting in and out of the undergrowth! Within his being, Hog was always aware of anything or anyone that might be watching him, perhaps to wish him harm. Someone *was* observing him, and he knew it! But he felt no fear. Was he not invisible, hidden by the trees? He returned to gazing at the yellow flowers and the sight of a thrush leaping eagerly among their spiny leaves. The buzzing of insects was a summons to explore further. The trees grew closer together, hazel and hornbeam among their number, but Hog was not deterred.

He plunged further into the woods, to where there was also beech and holly, the latter growing thick and glistening greenly. Suddenly he came into a clearing. This was not any made by the foresters, it was a space set apart from the world. The silence was intense. The rustle of a leaf or the cracking of a twig was, to his ears, almost deafening. The light too, was fulsome, as if it had no depth. Hog stood completely still, gazing at the far edge of the glade.

There was the shadow again! Between two trees, or was it a tree itself?

It was neither... it was a maid... and she spoke... or rather she whispered... his name...

"Master Hog."

The youth was too in awe to reply.

"Master Hog, of nineteen..."

"Tis true. How did you..."

For answer, the maid stood on tip toe and put a finger to his lips. Her touch was cool and she ran her finger down his cheek, all the time smiling.

"I know all about you! But such a beautiful boy you are, and all alone in the woods."

Hog was inclined to take offence at that.

50

"I am not afraid, if that is what you mean, I come into these woods all the time."

She feigned surprise, her eyes growing wide.

"Not afraid? But Master Hog, the woods are full of enchantment."

Hog's tone was now not so assured.

"What do you mean?"

"Did you not see the giants? Or the burrows of the trolls? The little creatures that are birds one minute, and butterflies the next?"

"I did see something like that..."

The maid laughed, a sound that thrilled Hog, though he did not know why. In those tones was the rustling of the wind... the soft rushing of water...

"Sweet Master Hog, you have much to learn of the ways of the woods. Shall I teach you all that I know?"

Hog was gracious.

"I should like you to teach me."

"Dear, sweet boy, you shall be taught all there is to know of the spirits that are in them, and more besides."

"Shall I?" Hog asked, slightly unsure of what the maid was promising.

"But first, I wish you to tell me why they call you Hog. Is it because you roam the woods like a boar? Or are you a greedy boy who eats too much pottage? One who likes to have more than his share of pleasures?"

Hog was inclined to be angry at such talk, but found that when he looked upon the maid's smiling face, it was impossible to be so. When he tried to look away, his eyes returned to her, as if made to do so by some power which he could not understand. Hog could hardly hear her whisper, but he could clearly hear her words in his mind.

"I shall tease you no more."

Her hands went to his face, cupping his head and slowly drawing him down to her. Her lips were now on his and her arms about his neck. At first, her kisses were like the wings of a butterfly, as they grew more insistent, like the nudging of a cat. Hog's arms went about her waist. How slim were her hips, he thought, and what way was this that she moved up and against him? He was engulfed by feelings he had never known before. She was bathed in the scents of the hedgerows, and that sweetness seemed to make his heart pound, and his breath quicken.

"Do you know that I am a spirit maid of the Goddess Loenel? I am Rhi, daughter of Morgalt and my mother was once a maid like myself. My mother was beautiful, but now I am as beautiful as she. Look!"

Rhi wore only a linen shift, the colour of the earth, and with one quick move, she cast it aside. Hog, who had never seen a woman in her nakedness, was overwhelmed by her beauty. She delighted too in watching his eyes feasting upon her body, taking in every part. His glance alighted first on her breasts, then the curve of her hips and thighs, at last to the tuft of hair that hinted of her secret places.

"Does the sight of a spirit maid please you, Master Hog?"

"Yes, oh yes..." His voice seemed to him faint and distant.

"Then prove it."

Hog moved toward her, his arms outstretched.

"But first," she whispered, and deftly took off his doublet and hose till he stood facing her as naked as she was. His first kiss was soft and, satisfied with this for a moment, Rhi was content to put her lips upon his. But then Hog found her hot tongue inside his mouth, and he was overwhelmed by the insistence of her passion. Suddenly she drew away and paraded a little before him. It was a successful move, for now it was not only Hog's face that showed an unbounded excitement.

"Come, my sweet Hog. Now you shall know how it is to love me."

She took his hand and led him to a place where the sun flickered upon a bed of soft moss and leaves. He thrilled to her, but was awkward at first. Rhi encouraged him with gentle caresses, and showed him how he could please her with the same. Then she lay upon her back, and offered herself all to him. Hog knelt between her smooth thighs, spread wide to receive him. As he made to lay upon her, with supple fingers she guided him into her.

Soon Hog was moving with a rhythm that began as his own, but soon was the pulse of all creation. This was the union that, in ancient times, Pan and Aphrodite enjoyed, now evoked in the woods by man and maiden at the Feast of Maiglan. Rhi began to move beneath him in such a way that he might thrust deeper and deeper into her. Hog panted with the bliss of possessing a woman for the first time. He plunged further into the well of desire. And all the time the sprite kissed his lips, his eyelids and his neck, making little shrieks of pleasure, as the wild creature of the woods that she was.

Both wished such a sensation could go on for ever, but even as the thought came, a new wave of pleasure seized them. Rhi locked her legs about Hog as tightly as she could, all the time gasping with endless longing. At that moment Hog let go his seed and she, yearning aloud for the heat that raced into her womb, screamed with such delight. The sounds they uttered together in their pleasure echoed about the woods.

Afterwards, they lay in each other's arms and Hog buried his face in her mane of brown hair. For the first time in his life, he had known the wonder of woman. For what seemed an eternity, they lay together until a sudden rush of wind among the trees broke their reverie. Rhi rolled from underneath him and now, no longer entwined, they held hands and looked up into the sun-dappled branches. Hog thought he had never seen a sight so beautiful in his life. Rhi broke the silence.

"And now, master Hog, I must leave you. Do not look so sad. You have known the love of a spirit maid of the woods, and that is not given easily. Only to the chosen ones."

"Shall I see you once more?"

Rhi smiled and kissed his cheek. Hog closed his eyes.

"Perhaps. Who can tell? One can never know the ways of the Goddess," Rhi teased. "Strange they are indeed."

Hog slowly opened his eyes. Rhi was no longer there. He jumped up and looked around. The wood sprite had faded back into the forest and was nowhere to be seen! Hog was suddenly aware of his nakedness and retrieved his doublet and hose from where they had been carelessly flung. With all speed he struggled to dress himself, and had just completed this task when he was aware that once more he was being watched.

"Who is it that has been so fortunate to be blessed with love by Cyngerl, my sister goddess..."

Hog turned to see a shimmering vision hovering in the glade before him. His emotions were pulled this way and that, as a leaf floats in the wind. At once he was frozen by fear, and also an unearthly bliss. Very few mortals are granted the honour of being in the presence of the Goddess. Hog was one who had been so chosen. Loenel smiled upon the youth, who was aware something about him greatly amused this deity.

"Master Hog, you are a bold young man. You make love to one of my handmaidens and, so full of delight are you, I think you would seek to love me also..."

The Goddess now laughed, and the effect of such mirth upon him was greater than that of Rhi. It was a sound like the rush of silver water over rocks, becoming fainter, until it was like the whispering of winds. The Goddess smiled upon him and quite shyly Hog returned her smile. The next second he almost shook with fear. Before him was no longer a beautiful, ethereal woman, but a being altogether different. She had grown as tall as the world, so that she looked down upon Hog from somewhere beyond the height of the tallest tree. Her tresses were the skies, her silver gown became the forest, and her limbs were the very earth.

She began to spin slowly and, as soon as she began to move, the trees swayed also. They made a slow dance about her. Loenel still resembled a woman, but was so much of the earth that she was all the world – a goddess of the hills, the dipping curve of the valleys, the distant mountains.

"I am Loenel the Goddess who is among the stars, but I am Magweryd of the Woods and Valleys also. I am the Goddess of all things. Without me, not one petal of any flower could any eye ever see. It is I who give form to all in this world. Not one leaf can begin to unfurl without the sweet essence of creation that comes from my being. I bestow upon all the gift of life, it flows from me as does the stream from the mountain. That power of being is the same that is within every mortal. You will grow like a young sapling, Master Hog. You will become a great oak, and then one day you will fall, and the life that I loaned you will belong to the earth once more."

It is the way of youth to consider age as some distant horizon that will never be gained. Hog did not reflect too long upon those last words of the Goddess. But now she spoke to his inner being, as if she held his very soul in the palm of her hand.

"You are the spirit of the New Age. It has been ordained by my consort Nen, the Universal Spirit, that you are to be our messenger. Much depends upon you, Master Hog, but do not fear, for I will protect and nurture you. All of your fate is with my sister, Fawreth – the goddess of fortune."

Hog was struck with an overwhelming silence. It would have been impossible for him to speak, even had he wished to do so.

"You do not need to hear now what I shall say, nor see what I do, but you will know. This I give you, a treasure wrapped in silk. You will know when the time is right for you to bestow it upon he who must possess it – the true king. What has happened here, you will now forget. It is best this way. I give you my blessing."

As the Goddess was speaking, Hog heard her words but did not understand their meaning. He found he was clutching a small silk parcel, but didn't remember Loenel handing it to him. But inwardly, he knew he possessed a treasure greater than gold. As if a player in mime, Hog concealed the gift the Goddess had given him in the inner folds of his doublet. Then all was over, and the youth, beginning to feel the chill of the eve, started on the way that led from the woods back to the town.

*

Strange things were also happening in another kingdom not far away, that of Durasglyn. There stood the Tower of Gafryd, a peak that dominated the lowlands. Crowned with a ring of stones, each twice a man's height, they whispered of mysterious rites and secret gatherings in the cold dawn. These silent sentinels observed each generation as it came and went. They would still be standing long after the men and women who had once gazed upon them had long been forgotten.

This night, a figure standing in the centre of the circle languidly watched a crescent moon rise above the horizon. Prince Anfad had never once considered the purpose of this monument, let alone the nature of the men who had built it. He was a man of little imagination, and even less sentiment. Others might speculate upon the dedication of those who had devoted a lifetime to hauling these great blocks up the grassy sides of the mound, but Anfad would not have been among their company.

He did not feel at ease in that place and, had not his mother Queen Gwirel summoned him he would never have ventured there. A sorceress may send her spirit across land and sea at any time she wishes; this night and at this place she had chosen to communicate with her son. Anfad paced the circle impatiently. All was silent except for the murmuring of the wind. Now this grew stronger until it became an almost tangible vibration in the air above him. The prince knew that the presence of Gwirel was near.

"Anfad! I will speak with you."

Deep in his inner mind, the prince was aware of his mother's voice. Many times, in this way, he had heard her words, but the sound that filled his head, and the manner in which it came, made him tremble.

"Destiny has decreed that your time draws near, Anfad. Is it still your desire to follow in the line of the old kings?"

"You know I desire to rule the Six Great Kingdoms, and when I do so, I shall be mightier than any who have ever ruled in the West."

Anfad struggled to hear his mother's reply, so soft it was. "You cannot rule without the Sword, my son."

At first Anfad was puzzled, then, as he realised the meaning of the words, he began to sneer.

"What sword? You do not mean the Sword of Pengyron, surely? That is a tale told around the fireside at Nadoman by old men with feeble wits."

Gwirel's reply stung him, such was its vehemence.

"Foolish boy! You know nothing of the old ways... you were never one to listen when I tried to teach you the Wisdom. Oh, all that you could have learned! A mighty king you might have been, and so easily, rather than following the low ways you have chosen, with your scheming and your deceits."

Anfad could feel anger rise within him.

"Rarely do I not get what I desire..."

Then he felt the will of Gwirel within him, stronger than his own could ever be. He was silenced.

"You will listen to me, Anfad! The Sword of Pengyron shall be yours. Whether you wish it or not, that is the way. Then and only then can you succeed in your ambition. Once you have the sword, you will be alone. I shall not be there to counsel you."

Anfad cried out in anxiety, "Where do you go?"

"I must leave you, Anfad. This sending of myself I find the more tiring these days."

"Wait! Before you depart, tell me that which I desire to know! Give me peace, mother!"

"That knowing would not bring the peace that you seek, my son."

"Tell me, I beg of you! My father... who was he? Name him!"

"Do not question the ways of destiny, Anfad! When you have played your part, perhaps then you will be told..."

"Mother!"

But the voice of Gwirel did not remain at the Tower of Gafryd, and no matter how passionately Anfad cried out, his voice was lost in the wind.

VI

On Maiglan Eve, Paldarch duly attended the festivities, and later sat quietly at the king's table. He entered the Great Hall in the crimson cloak that he wore for occasions such as these. Fastened with an ornate brooch of lapis and silver, its splendour was reflected in the candlelight.

Though of good cheer throughout the evening, Paldarch ate sparingly, and refused the offers of wine and ale that his fellow guests attempted to press upon him. Some of the company might have been wise to follow the wizard's example. By the end of the evening many, who had dined too well, snored among the rushes that were strewn about the floor of the Hall.

Brynan played his part as a monarch superbly. Never were his subjects so proud of their king as that night, when he sat at the High Table in the Great Hall. His fair hair shone against the dark blue tunic that he had chosen to wear for the occasion. All felt that, in Brynan's regal presence, they were immensely blessed. The merchants toasted him over and over again, and each time they did so, the king graciously acknowledged their fealty.

Throughout the evening Brynan was often reminded of the time when, as a child, those same merchants, or even their fathers before them, would come to the court, and shower him with gold coins. They hoped, by doing this, to curry favour with his father over some matter. And though he might play with these gifts, Brynan was never allowed to keep them for his own, not even one gold penny. Thus, his father reasoned, he would never regard wealth as being of any personal import. He wished his son to value those greater gifts that life owns. It must be said that the royal tax gatherers did not share his father's view and, on his and Brynan's behalf, they continued to garner much silver and gold for the coffers of Irlas.

Now the royal plate and fine goblets had been returned to their oaken chests for yet another year. The season of Ufeln had been dutifully ushered in, and all had foretold a rich harvest and every other abundance in the coming season. The Great Games followed the Maiglan feast and the day after that, the king, wizard and knight would depart upon their quest. To this end, Cydlon had ordered that Teryngar and the horses of Derwen and the king were to be made ready before dawn. This had been done, and various bags also stood ready, filled with the provisions and other necessary items for the journey.

With the rising of the sun, Paldarch strode into the court, his staff rhythmically striking the worn flagstones. On gaining the stables, he thanked the ostlers, and led Teryngar out into the sunlight. Shortly after that Brynan and Derwen came out from the castle together. They were as two sides of a coin, the king, fair and smiling and his companion, silent and preoccupied. On seeing the wizard, Brynan greeted him warmly.

"Paldarch, know you this is the noble knight Derwen, who has been by my side since ere I can remember, and now rides with us."

"Greetings, Master Derwen."

The knight bowed his head in greeting, all the while looking at Paldarch with an ill-concealed suspicion.

"Good day, Master Wizard."

In his turn, Paldarch regarded intently the dark features and piercing eye of the knight. He saw the shadow that is in all men but in some, more marked. Derwen was a warrior who knew much of battle, and perhaps little else. Though the wizard was no stranger to the trappings of combat, the sight of Derwen's sword hilt gleaming dully from beneath his cloak, made him uneasy. In his mind, Paldarch could clearly hear the clang of sword against shield, mingled with the cries of battle. From now on, he reflected, the days of peace would merely be a prelude to war.

After the Chief Steward had made sure all was well ordered, and that nothing had been overlooked, the three mounted their horses and passed through the castle gates. The citizens of Treflan had gathered along the way to cheer their departure. None knew the purpose of their journey, most believing in their simple fashion that the business of those who ruled them was not theirs.

*

The way out from Treflan led onto the soft downs beyond the town. Soon they came to the edge of the woods where mauve foxgloves, wild roses and glistening elder flower grew. From there, they passed onto the Plain of Lanerch, a seemingly endless flat land of tussocks and thorn. The going was not difficult, and they made a good pace, arriving at the Eastern border of Irlas at noon. There they crossed the dry bed of the river Aflon, and entered the kingdom of Durasglyn.

As the day wore on they felt the warmth of the sun only fitfully, and the grey clouds that massed over the hilltops spoke more insistently of storms. Eventually they approached the edge of the forest of Galtrin. This was all that remained of the old wildwood from the First Age, before the four kingdoms had been born. In those ancient days, trees had covered every part of the land. They rode beneath an arch made of elm boughs and into the forest.

As they entered, the daylight ebbed away, and with it their spirits. Brynan was the first to feel a curious melancholy overtaking him and, as much as he tried, he could not free himself of it. The silence was broken only by the footfall of his horse, like a succession of dull blows in

61

his ears. No other sound was heard, neither the crash and rustle of a surprised pheasant or the busy tapping of a woodpecker – no life was there. Once Brynan thought he saw the flash of a deer leaping through the undergrowth, but that was all.

The silence grew heavier as they rode deeper and deeper into the forest. The trees began to tower above them and the three travellers were now lost in their own thoughts. Of the three, Derwen spoke little at the best of times. A son of war, he rarely reflected on his own situation, only ever attending to his immediate wants. Those were of the simplest – fire, food and shelter. A stalwart of many a campaign, he had learned quickly that in order to survive, a warrior never sleeps. Even in his slumbers he never loosed the grip upon his sword. Fiercely loyal to Brynan, he had no other comrades except those he stood beside in battle. He had no family, not even a mother. His life was lived exclusively among men, and he regarded them only in one way: as either friend or foe.

Soon they began to realise that the way had become so narrow, and the trees so close together, that they were riding beneath a lightless canopy. It was not the dark of night that surrounded them but a strange morass of shadow. Even though they rode in single file, the branches either side of the way brushed against them and more roughly as they continued on their way. With some relief they emerged into a clearing though it gave no respite from the stifling gloom. The face of Paldarch suddenly became one of grim resolve. Derwen could see, as did the wizard, that the trees at the edge of the clearing were advancing towards them.

"What is this, old sorcerer? Some trick of yours to amuse us?"

Paldarch's voice was steady. "In this forest, some of the old enchantment from before the First Age still remains."

Brynan, realizing the sight before him was no idle fancy, was ashen with terror. Derwen drew his sword and waited. Without warning, the lower branches on the nearest trees became as serpents, and began to writhe over the grass towards them. All the while, the rest of the forest continued to move its tangled bulk steadily towards them.

One great tree suddenly stood before them, its branches like a dozen arms reaching cut from a withered trunk. As the rays of some evil sun, with numberless eyes looking out from within the folds of its skin-like bark, the tree seemed to have its own fell energy. Brynan thought that nameless demons, deep beneath the earth, were sustaining this monster with their life-blood. Derwen, however, reacted in the only way he knew, spurring his terrified horse forward, he was intent on attacking them.

"Hold, Master Knight!" Paldarch shouted. "What you see is nothing other than your own thoughts seeking to trap you! You cannot fight them! There is nothing to fight!"

Derwen either did not hear, or chose to ignore what was said. He slashed at one of the tree branches, staring unbelieving as his blade passed through it. He cried out in alarm.

"What evil witchery is this?"

Paldarch urged Teryngar across the clearing so that he was between Derwen and the giant tree.

"You cannot slay that which you see before you, Master Knight. Neither would it be right to do so. I see now that it is the Crafendag, the spirit of the forest. To him, we are unwanted strangers. He sees before him only those who might threaten all living things here."

Derwen put up his sword.

"If we are not to fight, then what are we to do?" he said in desperation.

"Remain still, and put up your sword. I will speak with the Crafendag and assure him that we mean no harm."

Paldarch advanced towards the giant tree. It appeared to sense the presence of the wizard and paused, as if deciding how he would deal with him. Moments passed, and the Crafendag suddenly appeared to lose some of its menacing air. Paldarch's voice rang out in the clearing.

"Let us pass, O mighty spirit! We are friends of the forest, not its enemies. Know you not Paldarch? Perhaps you remember me better as Treiwyd the Wanderer? Many a night have I passed among you and your kin. This day, we are but travellers in your land, anxious only to be on our way."

By moving its branches in a particular way, the tree appeared as if it was listening to what was being said. Time passed, and the air seemed to lose some of its heaviness. The shadows made by the trees and the undergrowth pressing upon the clearing began to fade. Derwen eyed his surroundings warily, as if waiting for another attack, while Brynan continued to look dazed and faint. Paldarch was still as stone, then, as if he sensed that the danger had passed, raised his arms high and saluted the tree. It appeared to return his gesture.

"Great Crafendag, spirit of all the forests of the world, you are a worthy guardian of your sylvan flock. Ancient as you are, you still rule the great forest. We salute you."

The tree then appeared to bow, and some of its branches even swayed as if giving a sign of blessing. Slowly it began to move to one side to let them pass and this they gladly did. The rest of the trees parted also and the three riders were amazed to see that they were still in the same clearing, though at its further reaches. Paldarch waved a last farewell to the Crafendag and they moved on.

A little way out from the forest they came upon a strange sight. There stood a wooden hut with a goat was tethered outside it and a pair of cats perched on the roof. At the sound of their horses, a figure came out from the door of the dwelling. He had a black beard and was dressed in green leggings and a buff jerkin. Brynan halted his horse as the man came up to him.

"Hail, I am Helryn the Forester."

"I would ask that you give us shelter, woodsman, for we are sorely tried."

With that, Brynan slid sideways from his horse, and would have fallen to the ground had not the man run forward and caught him. Derwen, who had been riding close behind the king, dismounted. With Paldarch following, the two carried the prone body of the king into the hut. They laid him atop some sheepskins covering a pile of rushes – the woodsman's bed. Helryn put a hand to the king's forehead, not without a wary glance from Derwen, and appeared content.

"It is only rest he needs. There is nothing that ails him."

Derwen eyed the man once more.

"Are you a healer?"

"Those of us who live among the bounty of Gwemed know well of the healing herbs that he provides. Potions... made from sacred plants... those things which may preserve a life, or even take it."

Derwen shook his head wearily.

"I have seen some of this world and I have known many men. Some respect life, others would destroy it at every turn. It seems it is the same here among in this forest. We would certainly have perished by that Crafendag, as the wizard calls it, if not for his own sorcery."

Rushes covered much of the dirt floor of the cottage and the knight settled himself down on a wide log by the fire. Derwen was not given to speech-making but felt, at this moment, that he must attempt to put his thoughts into words.

"I am not beholden to these ways of sprites and wraiths. A knight cannot be prey to imaginings. The way of the warrior is simple – kill or be killed."

Helryn nodded absently, as he busied himself in a corner of the hut.

"We each have our path, the one that is given us by Fawreth the Goddess of Fortune. Even before we are born our fate is decided."

"That may be so, Master Woodsman, I cannot tell," Derwen answered wearily.

Helryn passed to each a pewter mug.

"It is the last of the Rhagel Ale, perhaps not served in the right season, but it will serve you well after your encounter with the Crafendag."

Gratefully they took this proffered draught. As he drank, Paldarch looked about him. The forester's dwelling consisted of one low-ceilinged room. Indeed, all had been forced to stoop as they crossed the threshold.

The common folk lived in cramped and dark surroundings in those days, the only illumination coming from the doorway. When the door was closed, as it now was here, light came only from a tallow candle set on a chest in the middle of the room. This chest also served as a table, and upon it Helryn laid out wooden platters that held cheese, loaves of barley bread, and green onions – a welcome sight to the travellers, as was a bowl of pottage, made from rabbit, pigeon, turnip, carrot and beans.

Such a delicious smell woke Brynan, who sat up and immediately demanded his share. Into his bowl he dipped a wooden spoon, and eagerly took a mouthful.

"This is most fine, Master Woodsman, you feast like a..."

"A king, were you going to say, *my liege*?"

Brynan almost dropped his spoon in surprise.

"You know who I am? How so? Have any of the company mentioned my name?"

Helryn smiled.

"It was not that difficult..."

"...for a wizard."

As soon as Paldarch had said this he began to laugh and, a moment later, Helryn joined in most heartily.

"None may see further than the great Paldarch! Now I know it is true what they say of you."

Paldarch was like a child in his joy at meeting a fellow magus. The more so, as those of a magical calling are not always well disposed to their fellows.

"Master Helryn, who taught you the art, may I ask?"

"My mother and my mother's mother –"

"And no doubt her mother too..."

Helryn smiled broadly.

"Even she could never have known that I would one day entertain such a master of magic as thee."

Here they were interrupted by Brynan putting his bowl upon the floor with a satisfied clatter.

"Men of Magic, be still for one moment, I beg of you. Though I was quite content to listen while I feasted on this most excellent stew..."

"I fear there is no more of the pottage, my liege, but will you take a saffron cake?"

"I will not refuse, good woodsman, if your toothsome cooking extends to sweetmeats as well. But first may I ask if, after your most welcome hospitality, we are to be put out into the night once more?"

Helryn shook his head.

"Be assured you will not, my liege. You and the rest of your company are most welcome to rest here until the morrow."

Paldarch put out a hand and grasped Helryn's shoulder.

"That would be most welcome. We have a long journey ahead of us."

Brynan began to look about him.

"Derwen! Are you there? You are as quiet as a babe!"

"He sleeps, my liege," the forester said.

Brynan feigned as if he had been chastised, but obediently lowered his voice.

"Most wise of him. I presently may do the same. But where I am sitting must be your own bed, Master Woodsman. Pray tell me where I may lie."

"Nay, my liege, it would be an honour if the king were to take my bed, pray do so."

"Very well. I will not refuse your offer. Already I feel I cannot keep my eyes open much longer."

"Will you take the saffron cake, before you rest, my liege?"

Brynan yawned widely.

"No, I thank thee. Perhaps on the morrow. But I thank thee once more for the hospitality you have shown to three weary travellers."

The king raised himself onto the woodsman's bed. He lay back, his eyes closed, and within moments he was fast asleep. Helryn leaned towards Paldarch.

"It seems both your companions reside in the kingdom of dreams. Will you join them, Master Wizard, or will you take a stroll?"

"I would be glad to venture forth Master Helryn, if you will care to join me. I have a question or two I would ask you."

Helryn opened the door of his dwelling and, clasping a horn lantern, led the way into the clearing. The two wizards walked a little distance together and, as they did so, the waxing moon rose above them. Looking up into the heavens, Paldarch was reminded of his encounter with Loenel on the mountain, a time that seemed an age ago.

"Is it the Bounty of Haelmaw that you wish to know of, Paldarch?"

Paldarch smiled sagely.

"Aye, that is so, but it may wait a little yet. For, Master Helryn, I am curious to know how you gained the art of wizardry, and not just at your mother's knee I will warrant."

"I had a master, that is true. My mother sent me to be schooled with him, as she knew I could see far beyond any wisdom she herself possessed. She was wise enough to know that I would never be satisfied just with forest-lore. Mithran was my teacher's name."

Here, Paldarch nodded.

"You knew of him?" Helryn asked.

"An acquaintance of my father..."

"He was, like you, one who followed the old ways. Stern and even cruel, he could be at times. He sent me naked into the outer darkness more than once. I deserved it too, I'm sure... I was forever getting above myself. I had learned quickly and could summon power most easily, and that is not always good for a young man. I was even tempted once or twice to follow evil ways, but thankfully I drew back from the Pit when I saw what lay there waiting for me. Some I have known have become fascinated by the glitter of wickedness, and became enslaved by its shadows, but thankfully not I. Eventually my master knew that I had been tested enough and pronounced me ready for the calling."

Helryn's eyes lit as he recalled his master.

"Now, to see Mithran work magic was the biggest lesson for me. There was nothing he could not do. I have seen him command the lightning to strike a certain rock and it did so. That is the real power given to but a few. Nothing I could ever hope to do with the art matches such skill."

"We all have our part to play, Master Helryn, great or not so great. And you learned much also from the Goddess, did you not?"

A cloud shimmered across the moon before quickly going upon its way, leaving the moonlight that much brighter.

"I had union with one of her handmaidens. Her name was Peldryn. We were not fated to be together for more

69

than a few seasons, but in that time, as you say, I learned much of the ways of the Goddess."

"Indeed? And there was a child…?"

"Hardly a child now, he would be nearly of twenty summers, though I know not where he might be."

Paldarch pondered for a moment.

"Did he possess the gift?"

"I never knew. Sometimes I thought so, by those things that he would say. But he was always a wanderer, even as a little one. When Peldryn returned to serve the Goddess, the lad left our dwelling soon after. He has never returned."

Paldarch thought the more.

"Did he ever venture to say that he wished one day to fly?"

Helryn started at these words.

"You are a great seer, Paldarch, so I should not be too surprised at anything you say. But yes, that is what he once said to me, that he wished to be as a bird of the air."

"And his name?"

"We called him Hawden."

Paldarch looked up at the moon and there he saw in its silver halls, great visions. Past and future were mingled in one; great battles were being fought upon the Earth while Loenel watched passively from the Heavens above. The figure of Hog darted between the two worlds above and below, never uniting with either one or the other. Paldarch spoke not one word of what he had seen to Helryn, then or ever.

"Master Helryn, let us speak now of Cledoth the Swordsmith, and Awren who owned the three great treasures. The Sword, the Spear and the Ring, am I right?"

"You are."

"And?"

"Only by possessing the ring, would the sword and the spear retain their power."

"Where are they now, these wondrous things?"

The wizard spoke in what appeared to be a careless way, but Helryn had been shown in a dream long ago that Paldarch himself possessed the sword.

"The quest that I set myself when I was young was to find the broken spear that Awren left in the land of Asgell. For two seasons I searched the path that Awren was supposed to have travelled, but I could find no trace of the spear. I returned, back over the Great Sea, a bitter and disappointed man. I would have slipped further into despair had not the moon maiden come to me out of the forest one night. The love of Peldryn warmed my heart once more, and..."

"Yes?"

"...she was the water sprite who found the ring. You know the tale?"

"Only too well," Paldarch sighed. "It is as I thought... and you desired to have the ring for yourself, did you not?"

"I admit that I did, Paldarch, for I falsely reasoned that it would be some recompense for failing to find the spear. I dreamed of the ring, though I had never seen it. After only a season's round, Peldryn could see into my heart, and she then took fright, for she knew that my wanting the ring was greater than my love for her. She thought I would even force her to give up the ring and maybe even harm her."

Paldarch sighed once more.

"The lust for power is a terrible burden. And Peldryn did not even possess the ring..."

"That is true also. She had given it up to the Goddess even before she came upon me. So, I was left with yet more sadness and not a little shame."

"Do not give yourself pain, Master Helryn, even by recalling these things. We cannot all expect to own contentment, and if we do so we are fortunate, and should praise both god and goddess. The wise man knows this."

"Aye, you are right."

71

Helryn was lost in his own thoughts for a time, then he spoke again. This time he was full of curiosity.

"But you own the sword, Paldarch... and yet without the ring –"

"The sword is as the mist upon the lake that fades with the morning sun. The Sword of Pengyron has no true form; that has been its nature since the time of Anwen. Now it waits to serve the one who has the true claim to own it. Before that the ring will be restored to him."

"Do you know how this tale will unfold, Paldarch?"

The wizard looked thoughtful. Helryn noticed he glanced again at the moon.

"It is a Hidych that I have yet to answer."

They returned to Helryn's dwelling. On the way, Paldarch saw trees in the shapes of wolves and dragons, a reminder that the Crafendag still stalked the forest.

VII

The next morning they breakfasted on rye bread, cheese, apples and draughts of well water. The dawn came early, as befitting the season. Bidding farewell to Helryn, they resumed their journey through the forest of Galtrin. The early morning light glistened through the trees, and they soon forgot the terrors of the previous day. Although the Crafendag seemed now content to ignore the three travellers, they could still feel his shadowy presence in the undergrowth. Paldarch was aware that they would need all the hours of daylight to gain the other side of the forest. When its gloom was left behind, they would only find the dusk. The wizard encouraged the others to make as good a pace as they were able.

After several hours of hard riding, Brynan was surprised to hear the sound of rushing water. He had fallen into a reverie and this new music took him into another world, one however, that felt strangely familiar. Paldarch halted the company.

"Let us rest awhile here, the horses may drink and we also take a little refreshment."

Brynan heard the wizard's words as if he were in a dream, the more so did it become even as he looked about him. With growing wonder, he knew that he recognised all that he saw, even though he had never ventured into this kingdom or any part of it before. They had halted atop an ancient bank and, from some way down the side of this, there came a stream which eventually flowed into a pool. The trees were few here, but those that overlooked the waters were of great girth and covered in emerald moss.

The king dismounted and took some peppered pork and rye bread from his pack. Saying nothing to the others, he climbed down to the pool with the intention of eating his meal there. Sitting himself down on a flat stone, he gazed into the water, its silver surface stroked by the breeze. Brynan felt a sublime peace, the intensity of which he had never experienced before. Above him, the sun – now at its height – could be clearly seen above the trees. Its presence crowned the scene with an air of infinite majesty.

Something green at the water's edge caught the king's eye. Cress! He remembered being given some of that to eat when out walking with his old nurse as a child. Brynan fetched a posy of it, cold and dripping. It tasted delicious with his meat. As he ate, he could hear the spring and its soothing melody. Eventually he drifted into a state halfway between trance and slumber.

He found himself wandering down dimly remembered ways until he finally arrived at the entrance to a cave. He went to go inside, but was challenged by a figure with a man's body and the head of a wolf. On his breast was the sign of an eagle, its talons raised. This fearsome guardian enquired of Brynan by what right did he enter this place? Brynan answered that he had been summoned, though he knew not why. His honest words were enough for the guardian to allow him to pass.

Brynan found himself in an underground chamber, where the gloom was almost opaque. His eyes having finally pierced those black depths, he saw before him a figure lying upon a bed of twigs. The features were his own. His crown was upon the cavern floor, as if it had been discarded by the sleeping figure. Was he dead or only sleeping? Brynan could not tell, no matter how hard he stared into that still face. All faded and another vision took its place. This was of a crimson rose that turned first to pink and then to white.

"Tegwyn!"

His future queen came out from the very centre of the flower, silently sliding between the soft petals. She came toward him, smiling. Clad in orange silk, she came ever closer, intent on embracing him. Her lips were half open and inviting, her eyes were alight with desire. Brynan, at first attracted, then found himself curiously repelled by her advances. His own desire turned to water and any longing for Tegwyn's embraces rushed from him. He felt a heaviness come upon him, as if the love he felt for her had suddenly become as a great burden. It was a terrible dread that he felt as she came nearer. Then her image floated over him and was gone. He knew that he should not follow her with his eyes, and his obedience to this warning brought with it a strange relief. Some part of him had been left behind, one he was glad to lose.

His gaze returned to the flower and from it came another female figure, this time unknown to him. Accompanying her was the sound of rushing water – the sound of life itself, moving and changing – a dancing figure that sprang and leapt into the air, like a child at play. Brynan watched, entranced by every whirling, twirling move, seemingly painted upon the air and suspended with the glow of its own rhythm. The dance then slowed and the figure began to take shape once more, so that it became the figure of a naked girl. Brynan was astonished to feel that he had at some time known the smoothness of the slender body that appeared before him. When had he felt those slender limbs? When had those sweet buds pressed against him? Not in his recollection, but perhaps these sensations were to come.

As soon as the features became distinct, they too were strangely familiar. The eyes were the colour of jet, the lips of the palest coral, set against skin like flawless marble. How such beauty moved! Gliding upon a silver sea, as light as the clouds trailing behind her, she was there beside him, holding his gaze and whispering wondrous words to him. He was only half conscious of their meaning, but tiny darts pricked his heart and left a bliss impossible to describe. Then all was gone.

Brynan shivered once, and realised he had returned to this world. The sun had retreated behind a cloud and all his body felt cold. He slowly got to his feet and made to go back to where the horses were tethered. Arriving there, Paldarch eyed him with some amusement, as if he knew something of what the king had experienced.

"You have been resting by the waters, my liege?"

"Indeed, Paldarch, I would tell you of the strange dreams I had, but little of them can I recall."

Paldarch appeared thoughtful.

"Where you have tarried is known as Mefynon – the Spring of Wisdom. The guardians of that place are stern and powerful beings. It is said they are the sons of serpents, though I know not whether that be true."

Hearing this, Brynan was suddenly anxious to share with Paldarch what he could remember of his experiences. The wizard listened intently, knowing that for the king the door into the Otherworld had just opened, and he now stood upon its threshold. The wizard was impressed that such fleeting insights had profoundly affected the young king. After Brynan had finished with his tale, Paldarch waited for a few moments before gently questioning him.

"And what now of your betrothed, my liege, does your heart still sing at the mention of her name?"

The wizard's irony was not entirely lost on the king; though it did not appear to lighten his heart any.

"I am troubled, Paldarch. It is as if this betrothal was never meant to be. Perhaps my feelings for Tegwyn are merely the follies of youth and I have grown out of them, as a child one day tires of its toys." Brynan paused, staring into the distance, and shook his head. He looked back at Paldarch. "Yet I am a man of honour, as was my father. I have given my promise to Tegwyn, and to King Tulrech. I cannot withdraw."

"Things change, my liege, more swiftly than the hawk descends from the skies. It is as well to remember that, when we make plans in our lives."

Brynan could offer no reply, though Paldarch was certain he reflected upon these words. A sudden sound made them both look up. Derwen came out of the woods where he had obviously been relieving himself. He looked at Brynan curiously.

"The wizard and I are so glad to see you again, my liege. We thought you might have wandered off and been eaten by the Crafendag."

Brynan smiled at this, but Paldarch was not so easily amused. He held more respect for the spirits within woods and forests than did Derwen. To the wizard, a forest was a mighty a creature, living and breathing as any other. Its soul moved through the net of leaves that reached towards the sky above, and down among the endless roots in the earth beneath. To experience this was to feel the limbs of Gwemed, the earth god, stretching themselves and encircling the world.

*

Later that day, they found themselves on rough moorland. The ground was soft beneath the hooves of their mounts. From now on the going would be slower. Brynan turned to Paldarch.

"What plans, Paldarch? To ride through the night, or shall we find somewhere to rest?"

"We shall have shelter before too long. The way will not be easy, and we must be careful to keep to the highest ground. Many a horse and its rider have perished in the Telchmaw, the great marsh that lies over to the east."

The wizard held up his staff to indicate the direction they must follow. Above them, the canopy of the night sky was pierced by the gleam from an occasional star.

"There lies our way, towards the mountains. We must stay close together. Even those who are used to this land can still be deceived by the lure of a false path."

So began their journey to the Mountains of Niwel in the kingdom of Durasglyn. Paldarch led the way, and as it became more treacherous, his companions were thankful that the wizard guided them. As they started out, a bright moon lit their passage, but soon it was swallowed by inky clouds and became so dark they could hardly see in front of them. Paldarch stopped and regarded the moon, now dimmed to a pale disc. The love of Loenel, safe in her silver palace, was faint at that moment, almost cold and lifeless. The travellers were soon forced to walk their horses for fear the animals might stumble in some hidden rut and become lame.

As the night wore on, Brynan could feel the chill air begin to seep even beneath his jerkin. Like stone statues come to life, they advanced ponderously to the foot of the hills. There they began the climb, the way made even harder by the horses continually slipping on the scree. More than once, Brynan thought they might tumble down the hillside, to land in a broken heap at the bottom. Paldarch, meanwhile, looked neither to right nor to left, and it was the sight of his stern, unmoving profile, seemingly hewn from the living rock, that sustained them. It was marked also, that Teryngar rarely stumbled, horse and rider moving as if part of the earth. It was not only the heavens that gave the wizard his power; his affinity with the very bones of the Earth sustained him as well.

At last they gained the high ground. The moon, losing a little of her sombre mood, began to bestow a watery light upon the scene. Below, they could see a narrow path that wound down to the valley floor. Brynan's gaze was suddenly taken by the silhouette of a castle. Etched against the moon, this great stone edifice, boasted many towers, each as sharp as a scythe point, thrusting high into a blue-black sky.

"What is that place? It looks as if it has grown up out of the very rocks. What can it be?"

"That is where we are bound – the home of Gwirel, Queen of Durasglyn. You are right. Her domain was hewn from the stone of the mountains. The castle was built by the first of the Kings, so long ago that his very name has been forgotten. He caused it to be made in order to guard this realm from the Agenrhaig, the beasts that once roamed the Wasted Plains in the kingdom of Tarth. These fearsome creatures would cross the mountains in search of prey – mortal men."

The wind howled about Paldarch, snatching at his words. Derwen appeared not to hear, yet Brynan took in all. The wizard spoke as if he had known those times, when gods and men were almost as one. With the jagged peaks of the Niwel mountains all around them, it was possible to believe that time had ceased to be, and nameless monsters still ruled the heights.

Slowly, they made their way down to the bottom of the valley where ran the thin ribbon of a stream. The shadows of the three companions fell upon the glistening water. As they began ascending on the other side, the moon suddenly grew bright again, colouring all silver and black. The towers they had seen earlier now rose dauntingly above them. Soon, thought Brynan, they would be in the presence of Queen Gwirel. Like so much, it was as if she was known to him already, and the thought made him strangely uneasy.

The path led steeply upwards, turning in on itself all the while. When at last they found themselves on level ground, with the castle gates before them, they were almost breathless. The horses had not had an easy time of it and

Brynan, ever concerned for their welfare, wondered if there would be any stabling for them in such a wild place. This, and other thoughts, filled the king's mind as he contemplated the grim walls of the castle. Derwen was out of temper, and not being a man to keep his thoughts to himself, began to complain heartily.

"These are cursed lands that you lead us to, old wizard. The forest was bad enough – now you bring us to the hovel of a witch."

The knight's words harshly cleaved the darkness. Brynan would have remonstrated with him, but before he could do so, Paldarch turned and faced Derwen.

"I will thank you, Master Knight, to have respect before the gates that lead to the home of a queen. Gwirel rules this land and we are strangers here, hoping for shelter within."

"I would wish to remain forever a stranger in such a den of darkness."

Paldarch was quick to counter this remark.

"Without darkness, there can be no light. You would do well to remember that, Sir Knight. In the game of chess, the pieces are either black or white, it makes no difference which to the outcome of the game. So now there is a black queen upon the board... and if you wish us to be welcomed as guests and given hospitality this night... I would ask you to hold your tongue."

Derwen might have said more had not the look in Paldarch's eyes warned him that it would not have been wise. Even the bravest knight cannot look into the eyes of a wizard when they are brimming with celestial fire.

*

The great iron gates of the castle were open wide, and they led the horses into the courtyard. It passed through Brynan's mind that the clatter of the horses' hooves on the flags would have warned anyone within of their arrival. A search revealed some stables which, to the king's great satisfaction, were filled with sweet-smelling hay. That task seen to, they took down their saddle bags and made their way towards the great pine door, the entrance to the living quarters. They passed beneath a crumbling porch through a door that lay open, and made their way inside.

Paldarch called out several times to announce their presence, but no answer came from anywhere within. They passed though what might have once been a guard room, into an unlit vestibule. Here they were obliged to feel their way along one wall, groping towards the pool of light they saw coming from beneath a door at the end of the passage. Gaining this, they found themselves in a large hall. Paldarch hailed any who might hear once more, but his cries were only met with silence.

A great oak table was set against one wall, lighted candles upon it, so they could see into the chamber. Chairs and benches were set about, some in the dimmest corners. Upon one of these fell a shadow, darker than any other. Brynan started when he saw the darkness begin to move and slowly come towards them. Derwen put his hand to the hilt of his sword.

The shadow slowly began to resemble a human form, though not one any of them had ever laid eyes upon before. With a crumpled body and a face to match, Queen Gwirel was a sight to evoke sympathy and loathing in equal measure. Moving like a crab, she scuttled out of the gloom and eyed the company with an oblique curiosity.

"Who is there? Who are you... breaking into my home, like thieves in the night?"

Derwen shouted her down.

"So it is you who caused us to stumble about like old men in the darkness, thou childless crone!"

A sound, like the wind that rises in the east, was heard then. It chilled their bones to the marrow. The voice of Gwirel was even, but with a power that could not be ignored.

"Hatred is terrible gift, Master Knight. It soon turns to a restless fear, which then devours he who gives it succour."

Derwen visibly trembled at her words.

Despite himself, Paldarch sought to defend the knight, partly for fear that Gwirel would freeze the very blood in Derwen's veins.

"Peace! The knight you see before you is noble and honourable, but weary from his journey. I beg you to forgive his foolish words, he means no harm."

For an eternal moment nothing was heard in that dark place, save for the breathing of Gwirel – a plaintive sighing, resembling the wind once again.

"Always the peacemaker, Paldarch, are you not?" Gwirel said. "But the time for such constant forgiving of men is long past. No longer will your kind rule, Master Knight. It is the Goddess who will rule from now on. I, her High Priestess, have waited for the time when all of you will fall to the might of the Waters of the West, and those who try to resist will be swept away. Is that not so, Paldarch? You are still a great seer, I presume, and all this you know already, do you not?"

Paldarch leaned upon his staff, and it seemed to Brynan that the weariness that he had shown in the castle at Irlas was upon him once more. He also seemed pained by Gwirel's words, although the king would not know why this was until some days had passed.

"Gwirel, I beg you to remember that also there flows, from another spring, the water of compassion. I, for one, pray it will never cease to rise and to nurture all. This it did even in the Time of the Old Kings, so let these healing powers be also known in the New Age, or even in any time that is hence."

Brynan recalled that Paldarch had spoken of the coming of the New Age in the Royal Chambers. The king remained silent, but realised that for him, many questions remained unanswered. Now, perhaps they soon would be. He was suddenly aware that Gwirel was regarding him with an amused expression, as if she was aware of all that he was thinking.

"And who is this you bring to this lonely place, Paldarch? A king? He has the look of a king. None born to rule can conceal their blood for long. The Queen of Durasglyn bids you welcome, my liege."

Gwirel dropped an ironic curtsey, which might have had charm had she not cut such a grotesque figure. The king, taken aback by such a display, replied awkwardly.

"I thank you for your hospitality, my lady."

Gwirel eyed Brynan once more; the king quailed slightly beneath her gaze.

"Come, permit a humble priestess to show your majesty those things that he may well have never seen before."

Paldarch made no protest, only giving Brynan a significant look as Gwirel led him from the hall.

The king found himself standing in a small adjoining chamber – bare, and with an arched window in one wall. Gwrirel indicated to Brynan that he should look out at the view of the mountains below. The moon, that some hours before had shone upon the peaks, was no longer a pale, wan disc. It had become a glorious jewel among the stars, and its pearl luminescence picked out every knotted crag as if it were daylight. The king stared unbelieving at the sight.

"Yes, my kingly one, it is I who have made the moon to be that way, for am I not the chosen one of Loenel, a queen as well as a high priestess?" Gwirel said. "She has bestowed many a secret spell upon me, as is befitting one who is the daughter of enchantment."

Brynan took his eyes away from the mountains and turned towards Gwirel. He gasped aloud. Was there ever such a figure as stood before him? In an aquamarine gown with a halo of stars, the pale blue of her eyes iridescent against a pair of ruby lips. Her smile gleamed like the foam at the waters' edge.

"Look upon me, O king. Am I now not beautiful?"

When the king looked again the vision had disappeared. There stood Gwirel as he had beheld her a few moments before. Brynan's head reeled and he could only stare. In an instant he had experienced the awesome power of enchantment. This queen could, in an instant, have any man under her command, and yet she perhaps chose not to do so. That was the true essence of owning power – the decision not to use it.

"Now look upon me once more, O king."

Again Gwirel changed and, this time, her beauty was not enticing, but truly terrible. She was arrayed in scarlet and black and her eyes had within them more darkness than the most fearful hours of night. One glance drove Brynan deep underground, to some lightless cavern from where he believed he would never return. Her hands made passes in the air and he could see her nails – crimson, the colour of blood. Her lips, in this face of fright, were of the same hue, and Brynan drew back in terror. When Gwirel spoke, her tone was harsh, like the sound of rocks when they are crushed by an earthquake.

"Do you not find me so attractive this time, my liege? Perhaps it is because you do not wish to know there is a Dark Goddess – one who toys with men as a cat might a mouse, caring not for their pathetic pleas for mercy. If a man chooses to love the Dark Goddess, his boldness will reward him with a wicked fate, that of becoming as a wraith that howls in the night."

Her eyes became as the darkest thing there could be in the whole of creation, such that not a single trace of light existed within her.

"I will cast you aside and break your heart into so many pieces that you will no longer wish to live. Desolate you will be in the wilderness... never have you felt so alone... life will be so unbearable you would cry out in prayer for it to end. Know you, that the Goddess may draw every ounce of life from any man whenever she so desires, for she has that power. O poor man! Thou art helpless before the Goddess!"

Brynan had been staring in fascination at every pulsating pore in Gwirel's ivory countenance. He was as a rabbit when confronted by a snake – losing any power to resist. Then Gwirel was as before. She stood beside him, her words now reassuring.

"The Goddess neither asks questions nor seeks answers. She is content only to be, as her priestess does also. That is the way we are, simply here in this world until we cease to be. Our coming and going... what is that to the stars?"

Gwirel gestured at the great distance beyond.

"The mountains have stood there since the beginning of time, perhaps even before the beginning of time. Who is to say? They will always remain. That is because they are wise, so much wiser than men. How can a man ever believe that he has dominion over the world, yet he cannot order the smallest pebble to do his bidding? Within that pebble is the power, not within him – few know this. If they did so, they would be as Paldarch, and he is a wizard among many lesser of his ilk."

Gwirel held out her hands to the night, almost in supplication.

"If only man was wiser and heeded the words of the Goddess..."

With an effort, Brynan found within him such words as he wished to speak.

"I am prepared to hear the Goddess. What would she have me do?"

Gwirel looked upon him as a mother might her son.

"Huan Brynan, you have so much to learn of the ways of the world, and the ways of the Goddess also. But it is not too late. You must remain here for seven nights, so that in each night you will feel her presence within you. That way, you will be made complete. If nothing else, when you pass into the next world, the Goddess will take your hand and lead you to Gwynfan. That is 'the Place of Peace' where all dwell in perfect harmony."

"And am I to remain here alone?"

Gwirel laughed, such that crystal choirs rippled through the night air.

"Do you fear what might happen if you were left on your own with the High Priestess?"

The king was abashed, and lowered his eyes. Gwirel touched his arm, not unkindly.

"Be at peace! Paldarch and the knight will also remain here."

"Your Goddess seems to have much patience with those who behave as foolish children."

"Oh, that men would always be as children, content to play in paradise!"

"Perhaps it is so. And after we have tarried here for this time? What then, Gwirel?"

"You must journey much further. Into Tarth, and there seek out the Lake of Fioleth. But take heed, O noble King of Irlas, there you may find wonders more than you could ever imagine. The Kingdom of Tarth has never been ruled by a king. It is sacred to the Goddess. It is there you will find the wisdom that you seek... and more."

Upon saying these words, she looked at Brynan in such a way that he almost cried out in pain. It was as if an unseen hand had gripped his heart. The eyes of Gwirel smiled at this, not cruelly, but rather with the utmost understanding. Did he but know it, she saw upon his heart the destiny that was writ there. He could not himself perceive it, and the heavens in their mercy made certain that he did not.

*

And so the three companions remained in that castle, the home of Gwirel, Queen of Durasglyn. During those days, Paldarch appeared to the others to be quietly content, often spending long hours in the company of Gwirel in distant parts of the castle. Brynan suspected that their intimacy was one born of love, but he could not be sure. He was loath to confide in Derwen upon this matter, as he knew the knight regarded any tenderness of the heart only with scorn. Thus, he did not think of these things but instead applied himself diligently to his meditations, beginning each day from early dawn. A special chamber high in the West Tower had been set aside for his devotions, and there, each night, he also slept.

Much enlightenment he soon began to gain from his solitary prayers, and great guidance also was there in his dreams. The visions he experienced during his slumbers were such as he had never experienced, and when he woke it was to know that he had travelled to hidden realms in the company of the Goddess. It was not what he experienced, nor the words he heard, but the nurturing of his soul that was the great gift he was given.

Predictably, Derwen fretted at what he saw as a threat to his liberty, and spent the days pacing the courtyard like a caged animal. His sullen moods betrayed his frustration, and even though he suspected yet more strange happenings would follow in the coming days, the knight yearned to resume their journey.

At dusk each eve the three would gather in the Hall and share a meal. It was always some simple fare that was provided by Gwirel, but most welcome for all that. The table seemed always to be laid with provender by some invisible hand and, after they had partaken of it, cleared in the same way. Their host was never seen, except by Paldarch, and it was evident that she had no desire to seek out the company of her visitors. On occasion, Derwen was heard to mutter about what he considered to be the Queen's strange ways, but he dared not say too much openly.

On the evening before their departure, however, Gwirel did unexpectedly appear in order to wish them well for the morrow. After this she turned to go, but Brynan held her by asking of a matter that had been troubling him.

"What of your son, Prince Anfad? What of his doings? Where might he be?"

Gwirel halted, turning to face the king. She searched his features for the reason for his enquiry, and apparently satisfied, the queen answered plainly.

"He is engaged upon matters of his own in some part of the kingdom, or perhaps even further away. Anfad is a man, not a child, and must live his own life and make his own decisions. I do not speak with him often. Rest assured, he does not know you are here, and neither will he ever know."

Here she exchanged a glance with Paldarch that was almost imperceptible, though Brynan noticed it. Gwirel then left the chamber. At her departure, Paldarch took Brynan aside, leaving Derwen to his own musings at the table. They spoke together quietly in the small chamber where Gwirel had, some days before, shown wondrous things to the king.

"You have gained wisdom from your days and nights of meditation, my liege?"

"I have indeed learned many things that before I did not even imagine existed."

"And soon you will learn even more. The coming days will make our journey thus far seem as the wanderings of a child."

Brynan looked curious, if not somewhat alarmed.

"How so, Paldarch?"

"Many will be the twists and turns before we reach the end of this road. Let us not weary ourselves with false imaginings, for we shall need all the strength we have to endure what is in store for us. Many things I cannot fully impart at this time, even to you, my liege."

"I accept that, old friend. But one thing I do wish to know."

"And what might that be?"

"I dreamed last night of Gwirel. She held a lantern. I knew this meant she is somehow the guardian of the sacred light, one that must never be extinguished."

Paldarch looked at the king with a certain wonder.

"You have seen true, my liege. That divine light of which you speak was once in my keeping, at a time when Gwirel was too broken and weak to carry it herself. It nurtured us both for a whole season. After, I returned that light to the Goddess. As reward, I was given the gift of creating that light myself. It is the light that guides us when, in this life, we wish to journey into the next world. You have known something of that place and you will know it more."

"It seems that Queen Gwirel has, in due measure, bestowed the bounty of the Goddess upon us both."

Paldarch looked out through the arched window at the mountains, standing mighty and steadfast as always.

"We are all given life, the greatest gift we can imagine, and we should be grateful for that, giving thanks for every second that we experience this. But that is not the way of men. They constantly wish to change what they see around them, for they are never content."

VIII

Before dawn the next day, they set out for the Kingdom of Tarth. Paldarch had insisted they depart before the sun rose. Brynan gladly fell in with his wishes, and Derwen was also only too anxious to be off. In the gloom of the Great Hall, they looked about and discovered that on the oaken table, barley bread, spiced cakes and dried meats had been left for their journey. The linen pack that held these gifts was surrounded by heather flowers. Paldarch offered a silent prayer of thanks to the Goddess, but her priestess was nowhere to be seen.

Without a word they made their way out into the open air, closing the great door behind them. As he mounted his horse in the courtyard, Brynan was certain he could feel the eyes of Gwirel upon him, observing his every move. The king even made a gesture of farewell as they rode across the stone bridge, but from none of the forbidding towers came any response. Silence settled once more upon the stones of the ancient castle, as the sound of their horses died away.

The going was not easy, but when the sun appeared above the hills, their spirits rose with it. Eventually, at the foot of the mountains, they joined the way that took them into the Kingdom of Tarth. In the common tongue the name meant 'empty', and true to tell, bleak and uninviting was all that surrounded them. Travellers occasionally spoke of the Wasted Plains that lay to the east of this kingdom. These lands also owned the grim reputation of being described as, 'from where none return'.

As always, Paldarch led them, silent and purposeful. Nothing appeared to affect his resolve for a single moment. What was in his mind none would ever know, for the true feelings of a wizard are never revealed to ordinary mortals. Brynan, in his turn, wondered at all; while Derwen

90

continued to remain aloof from all, his warrior's heart following its own singular beat.

At last, with their descent into a low valley, the tedium of their surroundings was broken. They passed great rocks that, so wantonly were they scattered, might well have been hurled there by some angry giant. Below, they glimpsed the Wedifan River, still swollen by rains of an earlier season. So loud was the furious tumbling of the numerous streams that fed the river from the hillsides, that they were unaware of a rider approaching along the bank. Derwen, suddenly sensing this, sharply turned his steed and eyed the newcomer in no friendly manner.

"Hold, come no further! What is your business with us?"

"Peace! I mean no harm, fellow knight. I come only to know the way you intend to take."

"Why so?" Derwen asked.

"Do you cross the bridge?" came the stranger's reply.

Brynan, meanwhile, was examining this rider with some curiosity. Knight he may well have been, but a pale and fearful member of any company he would have made. The king guessed that he had once been round-faced and rosy of cheek, but now was as gaunt as a scarecrow. It was a fearful disposition that put sweat on this knight's brow, not the heat of the day. Still, Brynan hailed him.

"Greetings, Sir Knight. I am Huan Bryn, the King of Irlas. I and my companions, before we tell you of our own plans, would wish to know why it is you are abroad in this land."

"My liege, I was not aware..."

With a certain alarm the knight made awkwardly to dismount in order to kneel before the king.

"Stay, I beg of you. Now, your name?"

"I am Sir Bulwas of Durasglyn, Sire... the kingdom you must recently have passed through."

Derwen rebuked the other angrily.

"That is no affair of yours whither we travel. Have you been up to spying upon us?"

Brynan held up his arm.

"Derwen, let us not accuse one whom we have only just met of any crimes."

The king looked kindly upon the strange knight, as if he were one of his own subjects.

"We know little of you, Sir Bulwas. What is your company?"

"Sire, I have none."

At this, Derwen could not restrain himself and cried out once more.

"An outlaw! Banished, I'll swear, from…"

Brynan quieted Derwen once more.

"Let him speak! Now, Sir Bulwas…"

"I know such a thing may appear strange in these times, sire, but I will tell you all. I had visions, sire, such that appeared in my dreams in a way that I wondered if I was mad. I left my company and journeyed to speak with Queen Gwirel, that I might ask her of these fearsome things. Her words quieted me, sire, and I saw the meaning of these strange visitations. I made a vow straightway that I would serve Loenel all my days. The Goddess came to me that night, and told me I was to be the guardian of the bridge, once called Enflaw in times of old. Here I have bided since that day."

The king acknowledged his words with a smile.

"It appears you are the most loyal servant to the Goddess. It is said that all of the gods and goddesses ensure good fortune for those who praise them."

Sir Bulwas acknowledged the words of the king with much nodding of his head.

"That is without doubt the truth, sire. I have learned also that, once long ago, a wise woman of the name Gwaruch had her dwelling here and owned the power to turn away those who approached the kingdom of

Durasglyn with evil intent. She would make the bridge to be no longer there and thus even a great army who might be set upon invading Durasglyn would have been obliged to turn back."

Here Derwen could not help but snort loudly. His features could not conceal the contempt he clearly felt for this newcomer. Sir Bulwas was not unaware of Derwen's feelings.

"Wait, brave knight, hear me out, for there is more I would tell you. Those, like yourselves who came to Tarth from the West, have always come in search of great knowledge. All journey to Lake Fioleth and to these honest pilgrims, the wise woman granted a safe passage. She would cause a rainbow to be always in the sky throughout the day, and a cluster of stars in the heavens by night. In this way they were guided towards that which they sought. Is that what you seek this day, sire, you and your companions, the fair lake of Fioleth?"

In the sunlight reflected from the waters of the river, the knight looked almost ghostly. Brynan did not reply, and at the same time Sir Bulwas appeared to notice Paldarch for the first time.

"Tell me, master, who might you be?"

"I am Paldarch."

The knight nearly fell from his mount, so great was his agitation.

"Paldarch the Sorcerer?"

"If you prefer such a title, yes."

"...who at the Winter Feast in Careg put a spell upon the Captain of the Guard..."

Paldarch's features were like a mask.

"Perhaps."

"...so that he believed himself to be a hound and fell down on all fours and barked most loudly..."

Brynan could not conceal a smile, while Derwen even began to laugh loudly. A rare sight it was to see those dour features alight with merriment.

"I wish I had been there. He is an arrogant oaf, the bane of every man who has ever fought for the king. By Nen, that would have been a sight to see." Sir Bulwas fell silent and did not reminisce further. He thought for a moment. "If you do travel to Fioleth," he said, "then I may be of some service to you."

Paldarch looked questioningly at the pale knight.

"How so?"

Sir Bulwas indicated the road that lay beyond the Enflaw Bridge.

"It is more than half a day's journey to the Lake. If you heed my directions, there will be shelter for you this night, such as you would not expect in this land."

The king turned to Paldarch.

"Is this true, that we would not reach our destination before nightfall?"

"Aye, our good knight speaks the truth. Our crossing of the Plain of Tarth took much longer than I expected."

Extending a ragged glove, Sir Bulwas pointed once more.

"Take the way that you see there, by the edge of the forest. You will find on one side will be the Plain of Cyfren, named so in the Ancient Days. It means 'Brother to the Forest'. Do not stray either to right or left. You will, before the end of this day, come upon a knoll that stands in some marshy ground, proud from it. Upon this, built upon a platform of stone, you will there find the Temple of Rhimlais, which meaneth 'Golden Peace'. It has two chambers, The Outer and The Inner. Both are held fast. You may rest for the night in the Outer if you wish. Wooden beds are there which will give you more comfort than a score of goosefeather pillows, for it is a blessed place."

Paldarch took all this in.

"If the doors are held fast, then how may we enter?"

"By saying aloud the sacred words."

"Indeed?"

"The spell that evokes the will of Loenel is for your ears only, master Paldarch. I know you to be at one with my sacred Mistress and I am certain you will guard her secrets as you do your own life."

The wizard bent his head down to hear the whispered words of Sir Bulwas and, at the same time, received another communication also. This Paldarch held silently in his heart, though there was much that troubled him from that moment on. Brynan addressed Sir Bulwas, smiling upon him.

"We thank you, noble knight, for aid given so generously. Mark you this, Sir Bulwas will henceforth be given royal hospitality if he ventures to our kingdom."

At these kindly words, the knight vainly held back his tears. He still sobbed quietly, but blissfully, as the riders crossed the ancient bridge. And the sprit of the wise woman Gwaruch watched them also. Her eyes were clear and far-seeing, even though she dwelt in eternity. It was because of this, perhaps, that she owned such vision.

*

The way was as the strange knight had told. After they had followed it for some time, they cleared a shallow rise. The forest appeared below them, as did the broad plain of Cyfren, which stretched into the distance, almost it appeared, as far as the mountains of Niwel. They rode for the most part in silence, as the wide plains wore a tiresome aspect, and the shadow of the forest only added to its sombre air. The trees that towered above them seemed almost to scowl and wish ill upon them. They longed to see a sight of their goal, the Temple of Rhimlais, but they would have some time to wait. As day turned greyly to night, Derwen began to carp about their situation.

"I'll warrant this place is a dream of that crazed old fool. The only temple to be found here is in his addled head."

Brynan was inclined to pacify the knight, though Paldarch kept silent. There was no moon, and the darkness of the trees conspired with the night to make the way unsure. Just as it seemed to Brynan that they could go no further, Paldarch called a halt.

"I would ask that my horse is held while I venture a little way into the plain. I shall be as swift as I am able, but I entreat you not to call out to me or make any sound whatsoever until I return."

Derwen still retained his churlish air, and was inclined to make yet more comments until even Brynan was angry with him. He sharply commanded the knight to hold his tongue. The king was becoming, by the hour, more aware of Paldarch's magical ways, and less in sympathy with Derwen's fiery moods.

They waited, and in the cold and inhospitable land of Tarth, time seemed to crawl upon its knees like a weary beggar. At last they heard footsteps. His cloak almost at one with the night, the darkness parted to reveal the wizard.

"Come, we must lead the horses a little to the east, and then, I believe, we shall be not far from that which we seek."

Obediently they followed Paldarch, a task that they found not without difficulty, the horses of Derwen and the king both stumbling many times. As they briefly rested, Paldarch gave them a breathless warning.

"We are at the edge of the marsh Sir Bulwas spoke of... it would be wise to hold on to each other... these wet lands are treacherous... the recent rains have not helped... if we are fortunate... we shall gain solid ground soon."

Already the way was deceiving. One footstep might be sound, while with the next a boot might sink thickly into the mud. The horses suffered too and were whinnying in their distress. It was as much as each of them could do to keep his balance whilst holding the reins of his mount, and the cloak of his companion. It was a slow and tired procession, and once they all nearly pitched into a bog. Only by great good fortune, and their staunch obedience, did they not lose the horses. Suddenly Paldarch called out.

"It is the stone platform! There is a step here, take care. Once you have climbed upon it you may rest."

It was a relief to feel a solid footing once more. Brynan, as always, was anxious for the safety of their mounts.

"Is there anywhere the horses can be tethered?"

Paldarch was, as ever, hopeful.

"I think this place was built for pilgrims who visited on foot, yet I feel allowances would have been made for the less devout."

Brynan looked to right and left, willing his eyes to pierce the darkness. He was dimly aware of the sloped roof of a shelter, and descending from the platform once more, he grasped the reins of all three horses. They were all willing to be led, even Teryngar. Despite being in near darkness, Brynan tied the animals, and found fodder for them. The king climbed back onto the platform. Looking up, he was aware of another flight of steps, this one leading to an immense stone tower. They climbed up to reach the topmost stair where they were confronted by a heavy wooden door studded with ironwork. Derwen slumped against it.

"And now what, Master Wizard? Will you blow upon the lock until the door is kind enough to open for us?"

Paldarch was in no mood for such jests.

"If you will stand aside, and that right quickly, Master Derwen, I shall see what can be done."

Brynan watched in fascination as Paldarch, turning his back, raised his staff to the night sky, muttered words long forgotten to all but the most venerable wizards, and then tapped thrice upon the woodwork. A pause followed, and Brynan strove to keep the thought from his mind that Paldarch might fail. Derwen shifted impatiently from one foot to the other. A noise like the crack of doom thundered into the still of the night. The door slowly began to open. Recovering himself, and eager to quit the darkness, Derwen lurched toward the entrance. The voice of Paldarch held him fast.

"Wait! You do not know where you enter! You will be struck down if you do not show respect to the guardian spirits that are here!"

Derwen fell back and Paldarch immediately took his place between the pillars of the door. His voice echoed into the space beyond. To Brynan, he sounded like an old god calling out to the cosmos he had created.

"Servants of Loenel, we come in peace to Rhimlais," Paldarch intoned. "We humbly request that we may remain in your quarters this night. On the morrow we shall leave you in peace once more."

In answer, from the darkness within, came a sound that made Brynan tremble. It was a like a thousand sighing breaths, becoming eventually a tone like a lute string, stroked by an invisible hand. The sound vibrated in the air and then became like birds singing in intricate harmony. The spaces between the music held words, seemingly without meaning, yet they caused the heart to flutter long after the last trill was heard. Paldarch then motioned to the others to follow him.

"We are bade to enter. Lay down your swords as soon as you are within. Come."

Brynan stepped warily inside.

"How are we able to see?"

As if in answer, a ghostly light appeared, and gradually the shape of the chamber began to be visible around them. Paldarch quieted any fears they might have about the ethereal illumination.

"It is a rare property of such stones as these that, in the dark, they glow with their own strange light."

From his brief view, Brynan had not realised that the tower was circular. A wide wooden shelf ran around the greater part of the interior wall, thus providing a place to sit or lie. No other features were there, apart from a small door that led to an upper storey. It was an austere space, yet with a quiet dignity. It seemed right that they should sit together, and Paldarch joined them, once he had made certain the door was fastened.

"We must offer a prayer to the Goddess before we retire this night," the wizard instructed.

Brynan immediately adopted a pose of devotion, and even Derwen was moved to bow his head.

"Wondrous Loenel," Paldarch began, "we beseech that you accept our thanks for your generosity and compassion. We humbly ask for your blessing and protection this night."

The ethereal light about them glowed with a greater intensity. They settled themselves to sleep as best they might. Such was the peace that the Temple of Rhimlais owned that they were all at their slumbers within moments. It would have been a wonder if in such surroundings, they had not dreamed that night, and indeed, the Goddess visited the sleep of them all.

Paldarch's dreams she spiced with a jig so that he danced and kicked his old legs beneath his cloak. He laughed so hard that in his mirth nearly woke the others. To Derwen, the Goddess showed only compassion, promising him peace in the next world and that right soon. In this way, the warrior slept more soundly than he had for as long as he could recently remember. To the King, she bestowed a vision, one of beauty and longing, that was not of this world. Loenel led his soul to a place beyond the stars, where eternity and bliss were as one. For him, the Goddess conjured every endearment. He woke with a bejewelled kiss upon his lips, and knew that it had been bestowed upon him by the water sprite he had seen in the inner world at Mefynon, the Spring of Wisdom.

So it was that knight, king and wizard had all known a hint of the sublime. In the dawn, the ethereal light of the stones faded, and inside the tower another illumination came. High in the east wall, a tiny opening concentrated the light of the sun, and threw a golden beam onto the centre of the floor. Another sun was there also, created from a mosaic of tiles, and the golden rays flickered around this elaborate design. Paldarch eased himself off the wooden platform, and giving this solar deity a bow of thanks, strode towards the door. Brynan and Derwen recovered their packs and followed the wizard outside. Paldarch sealed the door once more with the spell, and they went to fetch the horses. The makeshift stable had protected them from the rain that had fallen in the night. Teryngar greeted his master most affectionately, his white mane flashing in the morning sun. Astride him, Paldarch watched the mist rising from the valley below.

"Come! A morning's ride will bring us to the Lake we seek!"

IX

The water of the lake lay not far from them, the way leading over grassland, neither too soft nor too hard for their mounts. When they came in sight of the low range of the Eilion Hills, Paldarch knew it would soon be in their sight. Before this however, the way twisted this way and that through the heights until they returned to the flatland. Here all was lush, and the rain that had fallen in the night glistened upon each blade of grass. They rode on through this emerald sea until, without any warning, they came upon the lake. As has been told, it was named Fioleth, which means 'Cup of Silver', and truly did it deserve the name.

Although the sun was at its height, much of the lake was in the shadow of a low cliff. Coloured dark blue and grey, this led down to the diamond glare of the water below. The horses were eager to be left in the shallows where they could drink their fill.

Brynan looked past the clusters of tawny-coloured reeds into the distance. Dwellings there were none, and apart from the geese to be seen in the distance, no other sign of life. It seemed as if wind and water had always ruled here, and humankind had had no part to play in the scene. The waves on the shore gently rolled one pebble against another, and apart from the occasional cry of a water bird, no other sound came. Tall willows stood by the banks, their branches like thin fingers pointing at the sky. But for the slight swaying of their leaves, they were as still as the three riders on the shore. The king was the first to break the reverie.

"I feel a great peace here, Paldarch, such as I knew at the Spring of Mefynon. It is true that water brings a stillness to the heart."

Paldarch did not respond. He was staring out into the middle of the lake where something had caught his eye. The words Sir Bulwas had whispered to him at the Bridge of Enflaw had come to pass, that a handmaiden of the Goddess would appear from beneath the waters and her coming would be profound. When he eventually spoke, the wizard's voice was distant as if his whole being had become part of the dramatic scene before him.

"The spirits of water can be loving and tender, but if driven to anger will bind the heart with a fear that cannot be loosed."

Brynan was alarmed by the wizard's words.

"What mean you, Paldarch?"

In answer, the wizard pointed out to the lake. One patch of water was as smooth as polished stone, while around it all was rippled and ruffled.

"Look... there!"

With great wonder, Brynan watched the water stir and break. A form then began to rise. So feminine was this figure, and with a perfect grace, she glided across the surface of the lake to alight upon the shore. Slight, with wide eyes, this maiden of the deep had hair the hue of a raven's wing that reached to her shoulders. She was clad in a silver-white gown that was a shimmer of raindrops. Neither poet nor minstrel could ever have depicted her beauty with any true justice.

If Brynan was speechless with awe at this vision, the effect upon Derwen could hardly have been more different. He sprang down from his horse, his sword unsheathed, and advanced towards the maiden. The knight held his sword threateningly aloft, but even as he advanced, no fear came to the maiden's eyes. She stood in perfect stillness, a mysterious smile playing over her lips. Brynan quickly found his tongue once more.

"Derwen! Hold your sword!"

The knight ignored the command, crying out in a voice that blended fear and anger in equal measure.

"Yet another filthy witch! I am sick with the stench of their evil. Surely this one deserves to die, that men may at last be free of their foul sorcery."

With impotent horror, Brynan watched Derwen raise his sword to strike. The king could only stare and wait for the blow.

It never came.

"Ahhh! What is this?" Derwen shouted. "I cannot move. Yet more vile enchantment."

The voice of Paldarch was as ice, his tone of iron.

"It is *my* enchantment, Derwen. Held like that forever you will be, if I so wish it."

Derwen was obviously in pain but his anger could not be stilled.

"Release me, wizard! I curse you, too! Would that Nen cast the pair of you into the deepest oceans. Let me go, I say!"

"It is time you learned a few manners and a great deal more wisdom, Master Derwen!" Paldarch's voice boomed like a great bell. "Let this be the first of your lessons, that hasty judgments are often followed by endless regret."

Derwen was silent. After what seemed to be an endless time, Paldarch spoke again.

"I believe you *are* growing wiser, Sir Knight. Now give me your oath that you will never offer harm to the one before you again."

Brynan almost felt sympathy for Derwen as the words were forced from his lips. Whether the damage to his pride was greater than the pain in his numbed limbs, could only be guessed.

"There. I have given my word."

"And I accept it."

The hand of Paldarch moved slowly through the air over the knight's frozen body, releasing him from the spell.

Suddenly able to move, Derwen fell to his knees. His sword, still in his grasp, drove deep into the earth before him. All the time he was breathing heavily. Paldarch continued, most reasonably.

"You must learn that what you see, or indeed what is in your mind, is not always what is truly there. Wythen means no harm to you and has not a speck of evil, as you call it, about her."

Wythen smiled upon all of them, as if all that had just passed had never been.

"I see you remember my name, Paldarch, as I yours," she said.

"How could I forget the name of the daughter of Gwirel? I always knew you would become as fair, if not fairer, than your mother."

Wythen smiled in a way that hinted they shared great secrets between them.

"I see you have not lost your wizard's charm either."

Paldarch smiled in return.

"A wizard without charm is no wizard indeed."

Derwen had now stumbled to his feet. He looked shamefaced and sullen. Paldarch turned upon him, his tone still stern.

"You must now beg forgiveness, Derwen. You might even, with regard to your oath as a knight, be obliged to offer eternal service to this lady for your misdeeds."

Awkwardly, Derwen went to get down on his knees once more, but Wythen made a gesture for him to halt his obeisance. She smiled the more and Brynan noticed that her features possessed a queenly air.

"I forgive you, O dark knight, and furthermore I will not hold you to such a promise."

She looked into his eyes and saw the pain and sadness there. As she did this, Derwen's heart felt cold and heavy within him, and he could only look away. Shyly, from beneath her long lashes, Wythen looked now at Brynan and he returned her gaze. Then the king suddenly found himself as equally timid as the maiden. It was as if he were a child once more, and seeing the world in a new way, one that overwhelmed his whole being. He began to look upon Wythen with a fondness that he could neither explain nor countenance. It was as if his soul was celebrating. Had he known Wythen before, in a distant time, in another lifetime before this? He was sure he had, but it mattered little: now they were united once more.

Wythen looked into the eyes of the king for a long time, and with an intensity that would have troubled many a man. She, too, felt some distant soul-bond with the king. Her eyes were of the deepest emerald, and flecked with an iridescent purple. Brynan held her gaze, and the more he did so, the more all of the world that surrounded him seemed to fall away.

The while, Paldarch had taken all this in and he knew the forces of destiny were about to start their work. In that moment he had the choice to act or to remain still. It was within his power to try and rend asunder this extraordinary attraction – one growing every moment – but he knew also that even a wizard is powerless against destiny. Also, he had seen all this before: the king had not been alone in seeing visions at the Spring of Mefynon.

And then Wythen was no longer there.

One moment Brynan had been leaning down from his horse towards her upturned face and proffered lips. The king had been held in an eternal moment, a mere breath from bestowing a kiss upon her. Then, like a star at dawn, she was gone. Brynan was more astonished than he had ever been in his entire life. He cried out, almost in terror.

"Where is she?"

Brynan leapt from his horse and looked in every direction, then he took to running up and down the shore. Each frenzied sprint took him further from his patient steed. He appeared to act like a madman, and his features showed an almost comical despair.

"Paldarch! Surely I have not been in fever? Has the last hour never been? We must find her! Derwen, stir yourself! In this way, you may serve your king and this lady both. Come the pair of you, there is no time to lose!"

Derwen turned wearily to mount his horse and made to move off. It was apparent, however, that Paldarch had not the slightest intention of following him. This was made plain when, dismounting, he urged the king to do likewise, even as Derwen rode off at a slow trot. Wizard and king now faced each other, rather as actors in a revel.

"Calm yourself, my liege. There is much that you do not know and many things that I would now tell you."

In his anguish, Brynan was in no mood to listen to anyone or anything. His passion inclined him to speak hotly.

"All I know is that the most beautiful maiden I have ever set eyes on in my life has vanished like a rabbit into a burrow. That is all I need to be told."

Paldarch waited patiently, until this outburst was over, then spoke ever more quietly.

"I would warn you, my liege, that Wythen is not at all as you see her. Firstly, she is not even a maid."

"What mean you, Paldarch?"

"Did you ever hear tales of the *Ganfaw*?"

"The Giant of the Mountains? Why, yes. Many a dark dream I had of him when I was a child. But what of it?"

"He is the spirit of the mountain, as the Crafendag that we encountered in the Forest of Galtrin, is the great spirit of the trees. There are spirits in all places. Wythen belongs to the realm of water. She belongs to a time when the sun was young, even before the lands were shaped, before the wolves roamed with none to hinder them – the times before man had any dominion over the earth. In those times, thunder roared and the rains were endless. Then the earth was as a woman racked in childbirth. A power so raw filled the air that the very stars danced in the heavens. Those who bore Wythen came before the dwarves, the elves and perhaps even the dragons. Did you not see her walk upon the lake?"

"I... I thought that I imagined it. She seemed to be swimming and then the next moment, she was upon the shore. But she is still only a woman."

"Only? She was held up by the fishes. Sometimes she is as a fish herself. Men call such as her a mermaid when they espy such things in the oceans. You must know this, my liege, *she is not a mortal*. There is much that you could never perceive about Wythen and even more that you cannot be permitted to see. She is a guardian of the secrets of the Otherworld. She is oft the cause of great fear among men when they encounter her, hence the reason for Derwen to act as he did."

The mask of the magician slipped to reveal a momentary anger.

"By all the gods and goddesses, men are such fools!"

Brynan, knowing the wizard had Derwen in his mind, sought to defend his knight.

"Derwen is a noble servant of the realm, Paldarch, that I know."

"Aye, that he is, and soon the kingdom will need every noble knight that it possesses, but there is more to this world than mere swordplay. Even you, O king, cannot know all. Even I, as a wizard, may only see that which is bestowed upon me by the grace of the heavens. You must not meddle in the affairs of fate, believing that by will alone you may change that which has been ordained."

Paldarch sighed deeply. Brynan had so much to learn, and so little time to be taught. The warrior's blood was in him, as it was with Derwen. Fire burned in both of them. Power! Did they both not realise such a thing was as the dew that vanishes with the coming of the sun? It was in

107

the land, the very earth, that real power was to be found. All would remain, long after the last king had been crowned. It was the kingdom that owned the king, not the other way round. A wise king realised he was only a temporary guardian of his realm, while a foolish monarch believed his memory would be cherished forever. Loenel knew that the power of the Goddess resided in this eternal, invisible sphere. In this she was wiser than kings and thus they had, by not seeing all that was before them, consigned themselves almost to oblivion. These things would happen and men had no means to prevent them.

Those who practised magic knew they had no power they could call their own. The only magic was that which was bestowed upon them, and that only for a short time. In his youth, even Paldarch had once been tempted to use power for his own ends, and he had got his fingers severely burnt for his trouble.

Paldarch ceased with these reflections and regarded the king once more. Brynan also, seemed to be lost in his own thoughts.

"Paldarch, I cannot put into words what I feel."

"You have no need to, my liege. I can see only too clearly, as I can with all men, what is in your soul."

"Then, tell me what will transpire..."

"...if you take Wythen as your queen?"

"Yes, yes, Paldarch. Speak... quickly I beg you... my heart is about to break."

Paldarch looked away for a moment.

"You ask a great deal of me, my liege."

"I know, but cannot you see, my whole life depends upon whether you will grant me eternal happiness or endless tragedy."

"*I* grant you this, my liege? Does not the will of Nen, or the spinning Wheel of Fawreth, determine the affairs of men?"

Brynan's voice rose to higher pitch.

"I know of these things. Do you think I do not? Yet I wish to be told of the future."

Paldarch looked away once more. His eyes went out to the distant waters of the lake.

"I am a magician, not a god."

Brynan became impatient.

"Did you not tell me that you have on occasion looked into Glaindu, the Black Stone, and have seen what will transpire?"

"It is true I have done this."

"Then do it now."

Paldarch remained silent for a moment and then spoke slowly.

"That thing of power is hid, many leagues from here... perhaps for ever... and rightly so."

"Then use what talents you surely have about you."

"What you ask, my liege, is not wise."

"Wise or not, I wish you to do what I ask."

"My liege?"

"I command you."

Another moment passed, one that Brynan would always remember. It seemed to stretch into eternity and beyond.

"Very well."

Paldarch's response seemed of no consequence, yet to those who truly knew him, it was far from so. The wizard did not look at the king, instead fixing his gaze upon some point in the far distance. Brynan too found himself looking in that same direction, and gasped in wonder at what he saw. The sun was about to set in the west, but the rest of the vista had changed. The mountains appeared to split in half and the sky filled with lightning. It all happened in the smallest fraction of a moment, but happen it did.

Thus did Paldarch in that moment show that a wizard never relinquishes an ounce of power, even when commanded by a king. Paldarch continued to stare into the distance, but now his eyes were closed. Brynan cried out in his anguish.

"Speak! Speak! Is she to be my love?"

"She will..."

"All praise to Nen"

"...for a time."

Brynan almost fell to the ground such was the emotion that overtook him. He composed himself once more.

"That is all I can hope for?"

"Indeed."

"But where can she be?"

At that moment the sound of Derwen's horse announced his return. Brynan hailed him.

"Have you seen the maid, Derwen?"

"Nay, my liege, and I have ridden quite thrice round the lake," the knight answered wearily.

Brynan cursed quietly to himself.

"Then we must wait."

The wizard and the knight regarded their king. Both knew it would be pointless to question the will of their monarch when he was in a mood such as this. They made themselves as comfortable as they could among the rocks and twisted tree stumps that lined the shore, and resigned themselves to waiting. The dying sun lit the water with molten gold, dusk fell, and with it came the moon. Slipping from her hiding place behind the hills, she rose to greet them. Full she was and though filled with incandescent beauty, the sight made Brynan the more vexed.

They remained there in silent vigil until the time when the moon had risen so far it was directly above them. Paldarch began to stir, looking first into the skies, and then perceiving the figure they had been awaiting as she approached along the shore. Singing softly, and looking as if she were made of moonlight herself, Wythen came into view. She was adorned in a cloak of midnight blue, with silver sandals upon her feet. As she approached, Brynan sprang up almost crying out in his torment.

"Where have you been?"

Wythen put her finger to her lips and Brynan knew he should speak no further. The others watched the water nymph approach the king and put her slim arms about his neck.

"I have been speaking with the Goddess. She has decreed that you are to be my love."

The waves on the shore made a gentle response, echoing her words. Brynan held Wythen close to him in an embrace that they both wished would never cease. Releasing the maiden, the king turned to the others.

"Behold, the Queen of Irlas!"

He hoisted Wythen aloft and put her upon his horse, which shied not at all. So astonished was Derwen as to this turn of events that he could only stare dumbly. Paldarch, meanwhile, quietly asked a question of Wythen.

"And is your prospective queen willing to be enthroned beside Brynan?"

Wythen opened her eyes wide and regarded the wizard with all innocence.

"I am proud to be so."

Brynan mounted his horse. With Wythen clinging to his waist, the king raised his arm aloft in triumph.

"Let us ride to Irlas as swiftly as we may, that all the kingdom may hear of our joyous news."

*

It was soon apparent that not all of creation was prepared to reflect the king's mood. No sooner had they reached the Plain of Cyfren, than a great storm arose. The rains came and began to fall relentlessly upon them. Though the

111

riders each possessed a hood to their cloak, within minutes their hair was matted and twisted, their clothing damp. Then the thunder began. The voice of Paldarch was heard above the tumult.

"Ride for the trees!"

The heavens roared, the horses shying at the sound. Lightning rent the sky, sending an unearthly light over all. The scene was as if observed by a guttering candle, one moment clear, the next full of shadows. The rain fell so hard they could hardly see. They rode desperately for any gap they might find between the trees. Once there, they plunged into the darkness of the forest as deep as they were able.

By some miracle, they all remained together. Sodden and cold they were, huddling like children in the night, frightened by a noise upon the stair. The storm continued in its fury as if it would never cease, but this it did, almost as suddenly as it had begun. The moon returned, and by her light, they surveyed their sorry state. Brynan spoke for them all.

"What is to be done? We are soaked to our very bones. We must find shelter. Shall we return to the temple of Rhimlais? Paldarch, are you able once more to find where it lies?"

The wizard nodded in assent. Brynan was suddenly aware of Paldarch's features and how strained they appeared to be. The king's heart, though full of his new love, suddenly went out to the old wizard. Brynan also realised just how much they depended upon him. The king then turned to Wythen and whispered words of encouragement to her, promising that they would soon be in dry quarters. But fate had determined that their leaving of the forest would not be without incident. As they turned their horses to leave the forest, as one, they shied and would not go forward.

"What is this? Why will our steeds not obey?"

Brynan heard the voice of Wythen from behind his shoulder.

"It is the Cysgeid! They surround us."

"What fell thing is this? Tell me!"

"The ancient spirits of darkness that were in this world before Nen and the Coming of The Light. It is thought that they are only known in Tarth. They are seen but rarely."

"What are we to do?"

The horses were now in a frenzy and rode wildly this way and that, no matter how hard a rein was put upon them. Even Teryngar shied and would have reared had not Paldarch used all his will to prevent this happening. In the confusion, Brynan did not immediately realise that Wythen had leapt down from his horse. When he espied her, he realised she was making a circle around them. As she did this both her arms were raised and she called out in a strange tongue. Paldarch, quieting Teryngar as best he might, quickly dismounted and went to join her, calling to Brynan to hold his horse. Wythen continued with her imprecations as the wizard went to stand beside her.

"Night wraiths, shades of the darkness, fall back before me. Wythen of the Water commands you to do so."

Paldarch began his own evocation.

"I call upon Gwaruch the wise-woman who protects those who make pilgrimage in the land of Tarth. Begone ye dark powers! The Light has come once more!"

Then wizard and water sprite clasped hands and both began to make such sounds as had never been heard before in that forest. Lowing tones that spoke of thunder and the hollowness of caves, piercing calls that resembled creatures of the distant mountains and accompanying these, an insistent drone, the very rhythm of the Earth itself – all these sounds they both made.

The horses having ceased their fevered antics, grew newly alarmed at these strange noises, but soon quieted and were still. Slowly, the ancient spirits of darkness drew back. The night air returned, calm, and without the oppressive weight that had come to be part of it. All returned to how it had been before the Cysgeid had appeared. Paldarch, however, realised they should not tarry in that place any longer.

"Ride out! There is no time to lose!"

With surprising agility, the wizard leapt into the saddle with Wythen climbing up behind him. They sped out onto the plain, the moonlight guiding their way.

X

It seemed as if Teryngar had grown mighty wings, for it was all Brynan could do to keep up with the wizard, as he sped across the plain. The king could see the ethereal form of Wythen as she sat, clinging tightly to Paldarch. How eternal did wizard and sprite look together! Paldarch slackened his pace and, almost immediately, the Temple of Rhimlais loomed out of the darkness. To Brynan, the building appeared far more imposing than on the previous occasion, as if every stone in the tower was charged with some extraordinary power. The horses were duly stabled as before, and they clambered onto the platform. Derwen, who had been some way behind, could be heard approaching them, guided it seemed, by some invisible force.

Wythen was delighted to be with the king once more and they embraced fervently. While Derwen saw to his horse, Paldarch uttered the spell to open the door, but it declined to open. The wizard repeated the words with greater insistence, but the door still firmly closed. In the moonlight, the iron nails seemed to gleam at them in mockery. Paldarch stroked his beard. The moon rose high over the domed roof of the tower. Silver beams played upon Wythen's face as she turned towards the wizard.

"I will try, Paldarch."

She gently loosed herself from the king's arms and stood before the door. Then the others heard Wythen utter cries that sounded to their ears first like the cooing of birds, then, as the murmurings of wind. Slowly, the heavy timbers swung back upon their hinges. From inside the chamber, the light shone brighter than it had before, as if in welcome. The smile on the features of Paldarch grew wide.

"You are truly a daughter of the Goddess, Wythen. Come, lead us into her presence."

They entered with heads bowed, as if Loenel herself was waiting within. Once inside, they stood for some time, content to be bathed in the divine light. It seemed to Brynan as if the chamber was many times the size it had been on their last visit. He could feel his heart beating faster, and he was relieved to feel Wythen's hand clasp his own. She smiled upon the king, then turned to Paldarch.

"I would show Huan Brynan the Shrine of The Goddess in the Upper Chamber."

Paldarch appeared almost to have been expecting these words.

"Master Derwen and I will remain here and rest. May the Goddess bless you both."

Wythen's eyes were suddenly the brightest illumination in that chamber.

"I know that Loenel has many blessings for you also, Paldarch the Wizard."

Paldarch bowed his head. His eyes followed the pair as they ascended the steep wooden stair. The wizard knew that none, except a high priestess, had ever seen inside that chamber. Wythen, as a handmaiden of the Goddess, had the same rank as any who performed the sacred rites there.

Wythen and the king paused before the entrance to the Inner Temple. There, upon the door, were carved two entwined snakes. Brynan immediately recalled the same image upon the doors of the Great Hall, and he knew instinctively that same image would play a part in what was to come. Would he ever see anything in quite the same way again, now that he had Wythen by his side? The king watched, entranced, as first breathing gently upon the lock, Wythen slowly turned the drop handle, and the latch on the other side of the door lifted. Slowly and majestically the door swung away from them to reveal the interior.

They entered hand in hand. At first Brynan was amazed, believing the chamber had no roof. He realised that a dark blue heaven, with a multitude of stars, had been painted upon the ceiling. The great crescent moon, in the centre of this splendorous galaxy, was merely one of the many cunning designs all around.

Each wall was coloured in a different hue. A gorgeous turquoise in the East complemented a tapestry, upon which had been weaved a great hawk, its eyes gleaming with white fire. Opposite, in the West, a curious depiction of two fishes emerging from a silver chalice had been drawn. In the North was a swan made from some light wood, her two great wings spreading from a deep amber background. While in the South, the head of a great stag, its horns glistening with pride, was set against a deep crimson.

The whole was illuminated in the same manner as the lower chamber, by means of the ghostly stones. The floor was a pattern of coloured tiles that led into another design in its centre. Here, lines broad enough to walk upon entwined with each other in a purposeful manner. Wythen took the king's hand.

"Come, let us walk the labyrinth."

Brynan knew not the meaning of Wythen's words but followed her along the tiled way that wound, first forwards and backwards, then about itself. The effect was disconcerting at first, but as the path unfolded, a curious languor came over Brynan, and he walked as if in a trance. At Wythen's every step, it appeared as if the soles of her naked feet never touched the stones.

Brynan could feel his whole body become lighter by the moment, until he thought he might float up to the roof of painted stars above him. When they reached the centre of the labyrinth he felt his whole body tremble. The next moment, he knew that he had been touched by a force that was infinite, one that existed before existence itself. He sensed Wythen's eyes searching his soul, piercing deep into his heart. Her lips were not moving but her voice was clear within him.

"I know you have felt this same power before. Where was that?"

"In Durasglyn, in the castle of Gwirel."

Wythen smiled to herself and her eyes became as clouds drifting across the skies. Brynan shook his hair as if he had been bathing in some deep pool. He waited until he thought he had regained his senses, but more wonderment was to follow. He stared before him. Had he seen this altar before, or had it suddenly appeared from nowhere? The sumptuous silk, ruby red that was draped over it, contrasted oddly with the ethereal scheme of the rest of the Temple.

To his astonished eyes it was suddenly transformed into the purest white cloth, with an emerald border. In the centre was a rose of the same hue, and Brynan saw the holy flower nestled between a sword and a ring. He stared at these two treasures for what seemed an age, and almost as if he had no power to resist, his hand reached out towards the altar.

Wythen screamed, the sound paining the king's ears. In the silence of that sacred place, it was all the more terrible.

"Do not touch them!"

"I am the king and have the right to do so. They belong to me."

Wythen suddenly turned her eyes upon him. They shone like diamonds in the darkness.

"Here in this Temple, no one has rights, save what is decreed by the Goddess."

Brynan almost fell back, such was the cold power of her voice.

"If you touch the altar of the Goddess but once, you will live no more."

118

The king heard only the hiss of a serpent in his ears, deadly and all-powerful. He could feel a sweat forming upon his brow and believed he might swoon, but with a tremendous will he recovered. His own voice sounded faint to his ears.

"Wythen, forgive me, I meant no harm. Tell me, what are these things that I see?"

Her voice was soft and reassuring.

"They are the signs of your destiny. Both the sword and the ring will one day be yours – bestowed upon you when the hour is decreed. What you have seen before you is a vision, one that soon will fade. These things have only been revealed to you, that you may recognise them when the time is tight, that is all. Now you must look no more."

Brynan tried to turn his head away, and was amazed how much strength he needed to pull his gaze from the altar. At last he succeeded, but almost collapsed upon the floor. He felt Wythen's arms, loving and warm, about him.

"My dear heart, you can come to no harm while I am here," she said softly. "Be strong and of great courage."

The king embraced Wythen who pressed herself to his breast. Never had Brynan felt so at one with all creation, there before the altar of the Goddess in the Temple of Rhimlais. At last he opened his eyes, and as if unwillingly, stole a glance over Wythen's shoulder. The altar and its treasures had disappeared. He groaned aloud, as if in pain. Wythen knew what he had seen there.

"It is for the best, my darling one. These things are not for you yet. You must travel further upon your path before you will see the sword and the ring once more."

Gently bringing his head to her breast, Wythen stroked the brow of the king and many times kissed his cheek tenderly. To Brynan her touch was as the coolness of the night.

"Come, it is time to return."

For Brynan, returning through the labyrinth seemed endless. He felt as if great weights were tied to his feet. When at last they came to the end, he almost collapsed again upon the tiled floor. Wythen held him up and led him to bench, ornately carved, where he might rest. They sat there together, Wythen with her head upon the king's shoulder. Then it was her turn to be weary, and she lay down and was soon asleep. Brynan, suddenly feeling strangely restless, left his companion and took the stair to the chamber below.

There, the king found Derwen asleep upon the wooden platform, his cloak beneath his head as a pillow. The knight lay on his back, like some ancient prince laid to rest upon a funeral pyre, in the way the king had heard described in ancient legends. Brynan could not look upon the sight for too long and sought the night air outside. Under the eaves of the porch that sheltered the temple entrance, raindrops were gathered like a parade of moonstones. They were a reminder of the storms from the night before. Brynan looked to the east and saw, behind the distant hills, a faint dawn beginning to spread its light upon the world.

"A new day, my liege."

Brynan turned in surprise, certain he had not noticed Paldarch's presence before.

"I did not see you there. You must have been invisible."

Paldarch's expression was unmoving. Then he smiled.

"Have you forgotten I am a wizard, my liege?"

Brynan returned the smile. In the early morning light the two stood together. Both of them felt this was a moment they would never know again. It was the beginning of the longest day of Ufel and Cyngerl, the goddess of this season, was abroad in all her beauty. They could hear her song, from over the hills from where the dawn was breaking, and sweet music filling the air. The creatures of the forest stirred, and the birds of the air sang in harmony with her.

All this made Paldarch rejoice. At this time, his powers were at their height, and he had only to touch the earth with his staff for life to spring up from its depths. Magic was at its most glorious then, and Paldarch was creation's child – the voice of the heavens, the eye of the sun. Truly, at that moment Paldarch walked with god and goddess alike.

As he stood next to him, Brynan could feel much of his power. He felt his own power too – the divine strength that is given to kings – and at that moment it filled him with a sense of his own destiny. He, Huar Brynan, had been ordained for a purpose that only he could fulfill. In his heart also, was a feeling that he had at last found, in Wythen, all that he had been seeking. It was as if a precious dream had been made real. He had only to reach out and touch this jewel and it would shine the more brightly. Brynan could not find the words to tell of the many things that were in his heart. He turned to Paldarch who, having the gift of knowing the thoughts of any mortal, smiled upon the king.

"You love Wythen, my liege?"

"More than anything in the world that I have ever known."

"Be careful of that love, my liege. Cherish it as the most precious thing in all the world. But know what it is, this love of yours. You are attracted to Wythen, so you have in turn bestowed beauty upon her. This is the nature of enchantment. All those who serve the Goddess have the power to appear as the most profound love in any man's heart."

Brynan was disturbed by the wizard's words, and remembered the power of Gwirel that had been manifested to him in her castle.

"Does Wythen wish only to possess me, to have my soul in her power? Surely not."

Paldarch gently chided the king.

"Beware of pride, my liege. Wythen cares not whether you be a king or his jester. Her only concern is that you are true to her. Mark that simple wisdom."

"I will try to."

"Wythen slumbers now?"

"Indeed, she is most tired."

"She sleeps in the arms of the Goddess. But you must not leave her for too long, my liege, or when she wakes she will look about her and wonder."

"Of what will she wonder?" Brynan asked.

"Wythen has chosen you, my liege, but she wishes to know if you have chosen her."

While an arc of golden fire grew brighter in the east, Brynan pondered these words.

"Does she doubt my love, or my wish to make her my queen?"

"She hears the words you say, but men may be as full of words as they sometimes are of wine. Women are constant, it is their nature to be so, but the desires of men are as elusive as the fishes of the sea. You may want Wythen now, but will you always? If you are to be wed, that union will be an earthly tryst, but if you are truly to entwine your souls, that must then be a mystical marriage. Such things should never be entered upon lightly. If you abuse such a sacred union, the Goddess will never forgive you. Your fate will be decided from that moment on, and neither tide nor time will alter it."

The king protested.

"I will honour Wythen always... all the days that I live. How could I do otherwise?"

"Fine words and noble intentions..." Paldarch said, stroking his beard.

"You mock me, Paldarch," Brynan protested.

"You must allow an old man to sometimes be amused by the ways of the young, my liege. But mark this, Wythen is not as you, she is of the world of the sprite and the sorceress. They are never to be trifled with, for they are as full of spite as they are of love. Your life with her will be as walking upon the edge of a sword. If she believes for one moment that she has mastery of you, she will despise you. You are a king, and mighty among men, and it is the strength in man that a woman is drawn to, not his weakness. But if you attempt to break her spirit, she will break you as a twig is snapped in a storm. The anger of the Goddess is terrible to behold. All creation trembles, for the Goddess is creation in all its moods, and she may do with the world what she wishes. Men must beware of Creation, my liege, all men – even kings."

The sun began to appear in a golden splendour, trailing plumes of red and rose. Brynan found it impossible to reconcile the warning words of Paldarch with such a wondrous and sublime beauty. The king went back inside the Temple, passing Derwen, who greeted him.

Outside in the growing light, the knight yawned and stretched his arms. He noticed Paldarch, staring at the skies and apparently totally enraptured by the dawn.

"You are abroad at an early hour, Master Wizard. Have you been awake all night? I must confess I sleep well here. Even a barrel of ale could not make me sleep better."

"I am glad you have found a measure of peace in the House of the Goddess, Derwen. Are you better disposed toward her and her followers now?"

"I do not deny I have changed my mind about many things on our travels, Master Paldarch. I have seen wonders that I could never have imagined, though I do not pretend to understand them one whit. To me it is all sorcery, these things which concern the likes of you. They are not the business of a knight. It appears also, that our king is also bewitched. What think you of that?"

Paldarch was spared making any reply to the question, for at that moment, Brynan and Wythen appeared, laughing at some private jest, as lovers are wont to do. Paldarch smiled upon them once more before announcing his plans.

"Come, we must not tarry a moment longer, for we have a long ride ahead. To reach the borders of Tarth as soon as we may, then ride hard through Durasglyn, is what we must do. If we halt it will be only to rest our horses."

From the urgency in the wizard's voice, Brynan knew there was a great purpose in their hurrying. What would they find on returning to the kingdom? Derwen had already fetched their mounts. As they made ready to leave, Paldarch leaned toward Wythen, astride the king's horse.

"I am sure you have sealed the doors of the Temple..."

"Tut, Paldarch! Did you think I might forget?"

"I think the Goddess has your ear constantly."

The sun gilded the roof of the building with glory as they rode away.

*

The rains of the night had made the going soft, and the horses more than once lost their footing, but as the sun rose it dried the grateful earth. In the woods about Tarth, the storms had torn many branches from the trees and these littered the way. The party crossed the bridge of Enflaw into Durasglyn, and by midnight had passed through the Forest of Galtrin. When they reached the Plain of Lanerch, they rested. Irlas was near at hand.

Yet another sumptuous dawn greeted them as they approached Treflan. In these outlying parts of the kingdom, the peasants' huts lay among the crops they grew for their sustenance. The corn was ripening with all

124

speed, and an ocean of yellow sheaves stretched into the distance. The rains had brought a richness to the green expanse of the hills, echoed in the leaves upon the clumps of birch and elm. Cyngerl smiled to see her work and all was blessed by her bounty. All living things rejoiced! Never had Brynan seen the kingdom look so fair. He knew in his heart that it was the presence of Wythen, whose arms were clasped about him, that made it so.

Unlike their going, few saw them enter the town. Derwen bade the company a curt farewell and returned to his quarters. He lay down, intending only to rest for an instant, and immediately fell asleep fully clothed. Woken abruptly by a noisy and thoughtless squire, Derwen threw a stool at the lad's head in a fit of rage, whereupon the boy fled for his life. Cursing all of youth, women and wizards – none were spared – Derwen fumed until slumber took him once more.

*

The king and Wythen bade a belated goodnight to Paldarch, who yet again gave them his blessing. Taking her hand, Brynan led Wythen to his private chambers. They stood and faced each other, awkward, and shy even though they were at last alone together. Their first kiss was as gentle as a dove's wing, and the king held Wythen in a gentle embrace. He looked long upon her.

"Wythen, I would know you."

"You shall... every part of me, my love, it is my wish that you shall delight in all of me."

They lay together, hardly touching, and then as if the Goddess had willed it so, sleep came to them. In the full light of day, Brynan woke and began tenderly to stroke Wythen's cheek so that she too woke, and smiled upon

125

him. With gentle fingers he touched her lips, and she would not release his hand until she had kissed it many times. Now roused, Brynan began to endlessly and deeply caress this woman he had suddenly come to love, and she in her turn encouraged his every want.

As she had promised, there was no part of her that she did not willingly share with her lover. When Brynan took her, it was if they had always been united. Such was their union, in earth and heaven, and thus was the nature of their lovemaking. Spent, they remained in a long embrace, one not determined by time or space. They had known love and beauty, and they were as one. Brynan believed Wythen to be his eternal star, one that he had met in moonlight and one that he would love forever.

But as the moon waxes and wanes with the tides, it was impossible for Wythen to be constant. When such a Spirit of Water changes, the past is left behind and the last wave means little; it is the rising of the next that matters. Brynan perceived the beauty of Wythen but he did not appreciate the wonder of her soul. Such blindness would cast a deep shadow over their time together one that would eventually rob it of all light and joy. Wythen was not guilty of any dishonesty; if anything the opposite, for she lived her true self constantly. It was Brynan who was, perhaps cruelly, to be condemned for not being able to see the nature of Wythen and how she was attached irrevocably to the Otherworld.

As she lay with Brynan, basking in the light of love, she cared only for the moment. That her lover was a king meant nothing to Wythen, a water-sprite. Neither did the doings of knights, courts and battles engage her. She was as unknowing and unconcerned with these earthly things as Brynan was of the mystical provinces. It was perhaps inevitable that the two would eventually cease to be as one, and in their parting was yet another sign of the end of the Age of Kings.

XI

In another kingdom, a princess had not slept well for many days. Her troubles had begun many days before, when the message from Brynan had been brought to her. Unopened, how innocent it had seemed and how delighted she had been! Now, in the lonely morning light, she held the cursed piece of parchment with trembling hands, and read once more those terrible words. Many times had she done this, and on each occasion she did not fail to weep. Even now, the hot tears came to her eyes.

Brynan would not be coming to Melynas. Such an apparently harmless missive, yet it caused such pain. So cruel was its stark meaning – never again would she hold in her arms the man she loved. With a heavy heart she knew she would never see him again. If Nen himself had told her this, she would have thought he lied. Even the words of a deity are no match for a woman's intuition. Only to the sad image in her bronze and silver mirror did she confide the secrets of her heart.

"The ways of men are certain strange. I sometimes think they enjoy tormenting those over whom they have power."

Days passed, and Tegwyn was suddenly aware that the whispers from her body were now growing more insistent. She knew, as all women do at this time, that another life was growing within her. Tegwyn stood between two fountains of emotion – of joy and despair. She felt such gratitude to the Goddess for letting her bring a child into the world, but equally strongly, she felt wronged and cruelly abandoned. What was there to do?

It was inevitable that in due time King Tulrech, her father, would get to hear of the matter. He too was filled with equally strange emotions. He loved his daughter well but injured pride gained the victory over his tenderness. His anger rose so that he was more concerned with this supposed insult to the royal house of Melynas than his daughter's heart. Such a stain upon the honour of his ancestors should not be tolerated – it must be avenged! Tulrech began to spend his days pacing the castle courtyard uttering dark imprecations in the direction of the kingdom of Irlas.

Tegwyn had little sympathy with her father's petulant displays. Like most women, she was of a practical turn and simply wished, if not for the return of her beloved, then the unhindered birth of her child. In her heart she knew Brynan would never return, and so she sat alone at her spinning wheel and whiled away the days of her fruition.

At last the appointed time came and a girl was born. She named the child Siricyn, which meant 'Bright Light' in the old tongue.

Then came the days of weaning and wailing. Despite having a maid to help her, Tegwyn succumbed to a feeling of loneliness such that she would never have imagined. Did the princess then become angry and resentful, as her father had done? It is not told whether, in some dark hour when she was in travail and pain, she put a curse upon any other tryst that the king might have. Loenel most certainly guarded over her in the blackest hours of the night, and it was her will that Tegwyn be merciful. This came to pass, and the princess was destined to discover fulfillment, her reward for showing compassion towards an impetuous prince.

*

Though the days appeared the same, the goddess Cyngerl, in her subtle way, revealed to the world the approach of Hafwan. She heralded its coming by deftly painting the leaves with traces of gold, and filling the valleys with eddies of mist. The trees would appear ghostly in the dawn haze when the sun would be as a silver coin, thrown into the air by a Titan's hand. The harvest had long been gathered, and the birds could feast only upon the crimson berries left upon the thorn.

This day ended with that same sun resting upon the hills like a flawless gem. A known company of men, meeting once more at the edge of the Preydun Forest, idly gazed at the sight. Prince Anfad addressed his compatriots with a surly glee.

"It seems the goddess Fawreth smiles upon us. Fortune most definitely, is in our favour."

Languidly, King Barud quizzed him.

"How so, Anfad? What gossip have you lately gleaned in the market place?"

The prince feigned surprise.

"Have you not heard? Our wicked young king has deceived his loved one. He has abandoned poor, pretty Tegwyn and now she cries herself to sleep every night in her father's castle."

Galar grunted.

"News travels slowly to Blauwyg. It rarely reaches my ears even if it gets there at all. But what of all this? How do the king's dallyings bear upon our plans?"

Anfad looked smug and conspiratorial. Like a rat crawling about a dung heap, thought Galar.

"Her father, King Tulrech, is not best pleased. He feels that Brynan's casting aside of his fair daughter is a gross insult to the Kingdom of Melynas. He was also hoping to share a little of the abundance of Irlas, when his daughter Tegwyn became queen. I suspect this added to his ire and why he felt aggrieved enough to send word that he wished to talk with me – an invitation I readily accepted, of course. His anger was something to behold! He now seeks the very blood of King Brynan, so I did all I could to fan the flames. I even offered my army to join with his, so we would

129

together march on Irlas straightaway, and avenge this unforgivable crime."

Barud looked at Anfad with growing interest.

"I vouch you were playing him like a fish, Anfad. Did he bite?"

"Like a hungry pike! He sends his messengers to me almost daily to ask when we may strike at Irlas."

Barud pensively stroked his jowls with a thin, leather glove.

"I think I see where this is all leading..."

Anfad was almost mad with glee.

"Do you not see? I could take an army right to his castle gates and that fool Tulrech would willingly let us in. It is more than we could ever have hoped for. Now we have no need of any siege."

Galar thought it worth his while to mutter an objection.

"But what of King Tulrech's army?"

"They are not worthy of the name, peasants with reaping hooks and a few woodsman with an axe between three of them. Besides, I do not plan to take my army there at all."

Galar looked puzzled.

"You do not? What then?"

"Barud will march his army there. I will tell Tulrech he has two armies to add to his own when we march against Irlas. Of course, we shall do no such thing. Certainly an army will shortly arrive at his gates – yours, Barud. Once there, Barud, you will be invited into the castle. It should not be difficult for some of your men to seize Princess Tegwyn. Then you will tell her father that you will cut her pretty little throat unless his rabble put down their arms. He is a cowardly oaf, and is bound to do exactly as you say. You will have no trouble from him."

Barud leered.

"I like the sound of this more and more. The thought of getting a taste of that sweet little morsel gladdens me this cool evening."

Galar grunted.

"You never give up do you, Barud? Still you think she will give herself up to you, just like that."

Barud sneered at Galar.

"She has been ridden once; she will want to be ridden again."

Galar looked at him with ill-concealed contempt.

"No woman, unless she was mad, would want that..."

Barud ignored him and turned to Anfad.

"And then what would you have happen next, little prince?"

"Once he and his army have surrendered, then Melynas is ours. You may give those of his army the choice of joining your ranks or being put to the sword. Then, as we planned, Galar can move up from the south and lay siege to Brynan's castle. When Barud's army and my own come to join you, Galar, victory cannot be far away. Irlas cannot prevail against our three armies as well as a few of Tulrech's churls who we may throw first at the enemy."

Galar shrugged his shoulders.

"Always with you, everything seems so easy, Anfad. Cannot you see that every battle does not lead to a victory? You are like a child playing with a wooden sword."

Anfad rounded on him.

"But what you do not know is this, Galar – Brynan has taken up with some water-elf from the bogs of Tarth, and dallies every hour with her in his bedchamber. But I have heard in Irlas, the people are not pleased with the thought of having this witch-wife as their queen. Brynan may even find it difficult to rally his own knights, let alone an army. So let that be the proof, if any is needed, that all is in our favour. We cannot fail."

At this, Galar was content to remain silent. Anfad saw that he had won over both kings and he rejoiced yet more within himself. Soon only he would be the supreme ruler of all the Lands of the West. Galar would not last out the campaign, and he could rid himself of Barud by some means or other. His hour – the hour of Anfad – was at hand.

"In thirteen nights the moon will rise again. Let us make that the time for our armies to be ready. I will bring word to you, Barud, when his majesty, King Tulrech, will be expecting you. Also, I will send messengers to you, Galar, when the time is right for you to advance upon Irlas."

Barud and Galar eyed each other, but in Anfad's mind there was little doubt that both would pledge their support. The voice of the Prince now rang out, the voice of a new leader.

"Are we now in accord?"

The two kings answered in agreement.

*

Huan Brynan woke to find himself alone. He wondered for how long Wythen had not been beside him. He suspected it had been for much of the night. She had seemed troubled when they retired, and reaching for her then had brought no response. It seemed that in such a short time, no longer was it for the king's embrace that Wythen yearned. He feared to lose her and even thinking this might actually happen made him tremble with anxiety.

Like many a man before him and since, Brynan was ignorant of the ways of love and of women. In many ways he was an innocent in the world and his knowledge of things beyond it was confined to his vision at the Spring of Wisdom and what Wythen had shown him at Rhimlais. He was not aware that a warrior must be aware of all he *cannot* see rather than the friend of foe before him.

Brynan reflected then on how sweet it would have been to caress his love – if she still was – that morning, but that was not to be. He quit his bed resolved to go in search of Wythen. He would make one more attempt to resolve their quarrels, though even now he suspected his efforts would be in vain. He was too stubborn to admit that he might be at fault and his pride prevented him confiding in Wythen his doubts about their pairing.

The moon was now in wane, and if troubles are to fall upon mortals, they will do so when the Goddess reveals her darker aspect. Two moons had passed since they had returned to Irlas. At the coming of the third, the melancholy king had sent his emissaries to summon Paldarch. Their mission had proved difficult to fulfill, for despite searching his usual haunts, the wizard had proved to be extremely elusive and could not be found.

At last the sound of hooves was heard in the courtyard. Brynan leapt from his seat and rushed up the narrow flight of stone steps that led to the top of the tower. Seeing the swirling cloak of Paldarch as he dismounted from Teryngar did much to calm the agitated king. Brynan descended into the royal chambers just as a steward announced the arrival of his old friend.

"There you are! I thought they would never find you... that you were lost for ever!"

"I came as quickly as I was able, my liege. I had affairs to settle in lands some distance from here."

The king could not fail to notice that Paldarch had, once more, a great weariness upon him.

"You have not been in the wilds of Tarth?"

"Nay, where I have ventured, my liege, the Plain of Tarth would seem as a pleasant land."

"Is that so?"

The laconic manner of Brynan's response told Paldarch all.

"How is Wythen?"

"She... she walks... in the woods I think."

There was silence, and then Paldarch spoke with a voice as clear as wind and water.

"I can tell you are much troubled, my liege."

The king almost stumbled as he returned to sit upon his throne.

"It is true. That is why I asked you to come here, Paldarch. Pray be seated."

Paldarch did as he was bidden, then spoke once more.

"Things are not well between you?"

Brynan tried to force a smile but nothing would have brought joy to those harried features.

"I suppose one cannot expect each day to be as fair as the last."

"Indeed not. We must accept what Nen sends us, and be content with that."

The king's face darkened.

"And what if that which he sends is continual tempest?"

"Then we must wait for the storm to pass."

The king suddenly quit his seat. Paldarch watched him as he paced the chamber.

"I thought I knew the most bliss it was possible for a man to have. That was not so, as I found out. Now I live in torment. It is impossible for Wythen to become my queen, neither can we be wed. I have failed in every way, Paldarch. My brain is fevered by all this."

"You have spoken with Wythen of all that troubles you?"

"I have tried, but I fear that she does not hear a word I say."

"She cannot wish for you ever to suffer, that is certain."

"I would not think that of her, yet I wonder if she is determined that nothing I do can possibly please her. She says that although I am young, I am like an old man, heavy and witless and with no joy in me. That is not true; I had the greatest joy when I met her, as if all the gods and goddesses rejoiced with me. Now I am cast down."

"And in the deeps of your heart, what feelings do you have for Wythen?"

The king threw his hands in the air in a hopeless gesture.

"I do not know! Perhaps I made a great mistake and thought I loved her when I did not. I cannot despise her, even if she feels hate for me. But that is not all that has brought troubles for me…"

Paldarch waited silently.

"The people refuse to take Wythen into their hearts… when first we rode out into the kingdom… as soon as the peasants saw her… they shied away. It is even worse here in the castle, even though the courtiers and servants try to hide how they feel… those in my court do not want Wythen here either. It is as though they are fearful of her, though she has done not the slightest harm to any of them."

The wizard waited with drawn brows.

"And is there more?"

Brynan took a breath.

"I have also heard that Tegwyn's father, King Tulrech, is most displeased. I am told he wishes to put my head on a spike on his castle wall because of the way I have treated his daughter. By all the gods, what am I to do? It is if the world were coming to an end around me."

The wizard made a wry face.

"There may be more truth in what you say than you could realise, my liege, but perhaps this is not the time for jest. I rather feared all this might happen, but destiny must run its course, and to us mortals, the ways of Nen are mysterious indeed. Of King Tulrech I can say little, except that he is an old man with more than his fair share of pride. He has no queen, and he dotes upon Tegwyn as if she were some precious jewel, one that must be kept constantly locked in a casket. If she were some peasant girl who had lost her sweetheart, none would care two farthings."

Brynan went to speak, but Paldarch held up a restraining hand.

"Because she is a princess, the father must go to war on her behalf. I do not suppose Tegwyn regards him as anything but a fool for doing so. Most of his people regard Tulrech as being like a cart with one wheel, that is – almost useless. And yet they would follow him and take his side against you. Many here in Irlas are kin of those in Melynas, and blood runs thick, it is said. That is one reason why they will not accept Wythen as your queen. "

Brynan shrugged nervously.

"All that you say may be true. I know not the ways of peasants. Why do they despise her so much? It is seeing their hatred which has turned Wythen against me, I am certain of it."

Paldarch considered.

"You forget that Wythen is not a mortal. She is one of another world, and we are living in times when these things are feared. Those who lived long ago were not alarmed when they heard the stones talk or saw clouds dance. Now they are more concerned with their cattle and their corn. They do not want the old ways any more. That is the way of folk, they believe they always know better than those who went before. In some ways they do, but not in all."

"I have told Wythen this, but she says she cannot change. She insists that either the people accept her for what she is, or she must be with her own kind once more."

Paldarch's air was almost one of resignation.

"That is understandable. She cannot be at ease in a country where she feels there is no love for her. Neither does she feel certain of your affections either, my liege... and it is with some sorrow that I speak that truth. I voiced

136

these things to you at the Temple of Rhimlais. A king is loyal to his kingdom or he is no king at all. Wythen knows how you feel towards your subjects... as well as how you feel towards her. It is as if, while swimming, she has been caught by too many currents. She is pulled this way and that, and as a consequence, you are tossed and turned by them also."

Brynan sighed.

"That is true. As I go about, I do not know how to be with those I meet. I have taken to going abroad little, and sitting here in my misery."

"And that is not how a king should be. The people need you, and you need them. Mark you... more than ever at this time."

Brynan smote his fist upon his palm.

"All this talk of duty, Paldarch! No more of it, I beg you. It sickens me! My father, and his father, and all those before him, knew so little joy in their lives. Only war and bloodshed was their lot. It seems as if I am to be denied any love or peace either, and any day now, I also must take up the sword of battle as they did."

Paldarch was stern of look.

"Aye, that is true, and I will say this: there are now six Kingdoms of the West, once there were only four. Even in those far off days, Irlas was always the most fair. Many true and noble men laid down their lives for Irlas, and the king stood beside them always and perhaps fought most bravely and untiringly of all upon the field. If peace and joy follow after us when we are gone, then we have done great service to men and to this kingdom."

Brynan was inclined to protest, but Paldarch, perhaps ill-judgedly, would not let him speak.

"Wait! Hear me out!" the wizard said. "You talk of duty as if it is something to be scorned. No! It is our duty to make the world a safer place for those children who are as yet unborn. In the coming years, other tyrants and warmongers may rise, and those who follow us will have to do battle against new evils. Let them be left with a spirit of courage and sacrifice... one that they may follow, so they may be given even greater heart to embark upon their own struggles, whatever they might be."

Brynan was in no mood for such as this.

"Fine words, Paldarch," Brynan said bitterly. "But what does an old wizard know of how it is to be a king?"

For an instant, Paldarch was taken aback, but he quickly responded in the same coin.

"A wizard knows all, my liege, because he is beyond time. He has been all things."

Brynan drew himself up and spoke with a dangerous heat.

"It is said that the sun shines upon those who are born to be kings. None may look upon the sun, Paldarch."

"Unless he is the sun himself."

Paldarch looked upon the king, and the eyes of the wizard were of the brightest fire, burning with an intensity such that Brynan had to turn away, as if blinded. Then he heard such words that, although spoken by Paldarch, he knew to be the very voice of Nen. There could be no mistaking that.

"I am the sun behind the sun, and I am every sun that has ever been, and ever will be. I am the universe and everything within it. All creation is known to me, for I am creation itself."

The sound echoed in the chamber, so loudly that those below in the courtyard hearing it, looked up in wonder. Others swore that they saw a flash of white light come from the windows of the king's chamber. Inside, the king was now blinking a little, and somewhat chastened, settling himself down upon his throne once more.

"I think Derwen is not the only one who has had to learn a lesson from you, Paldarch."

The wizard smiled, as always, generously.

"We all need to be reminded of the power of the heavens from time to time, my liege, even myself."

"And destiny as well, it appears," Brynan sighed. "Is our fate even decided when we are in the womb?"

"Our path may turn to the left or the right, and sometimes we think we have lost sight of it completely, but it always returns eventually to its true course. The brave man always has a choice concerning his fate, the coward not so, for it is said that fortune favours the bold."

It was now the turn of Brynan to look weary.

"And yet, cannot sorcery be used to aid our cause? Cannot the spells of Paldarch turn the tide of war in our favour?"

The wizard slowly shook his head.

"I fear not, my liege. Magic only obeys the divine will. If heaven is not in his favour then there is little the magician may do. He may perform a score of ceremonies to achieve some particular end, but it will all be in vain if it has been decreed it is not to be."

Brynan put his hand to his brow.

"My brain is fevered with all this talk. Come! Let us go and try to find Wythen. She will at least be pleased to see you, Paldarch. Perhaps you may even be able to persuade her that the last thing I wish is for her to do anything against her will."

Paldarch's response was as dry as dust.

"To change the will of a water spirit would be like trying to hold back the oceans, my liege. I suggest you go and look for Wythen yourself, though I very much doubt you will find her. She will return when she wishes, if she does indeed return..."

Paldarch held up his hand as the king began to protest.

"It is no use, my liege. Magic is not to be tamed and neither is the Goddess, to whom Wythen is as close as any in this world. I will tarry here in Treflan another night and the morrow, then I must depart, for there is much that concerns me at this time. The days seep away, like water into the very earth, and there is much that I must do or it will all be too late. I would ask to be left in peace until the morrow noon. It is time that this old wizard reflected on the best course to take in these coming days. I plan to have communion with some of my departed masters. That little exercise takes many hours and much will. I ask that none disturbs me. "

The king readily agreed to his wishes and Paldarch departed from the royal chamber. His heart was heavy: he felt sure the king had lost Wythen, yet he could not alter their circumstances one whit. That he loved the king, and knew he had a mighty battle to fight, did not lighten the burden he felt. And yet, a wizard must confine himself to wizardry if he is to see a true picture of the world, one where he plays a commanding role. Paldarch knew he would not be among the ranks in any conflict, nor could he alter the outcome of the fighting. Greater powers than his decided these things, and he was also aware that Loenel had a greater part to play in the affairs of the world than ever before. The Age of Kings was surely coming to an end.

*

Paldarch had predicted correctly. Look where he might, Brynan could find no sign of the elusive Wythen. It was not until the sun had set that she returned to the castle. With an awkward deference, the gatekeeper had allowed her entry, and in an equally stilted manner the Chief Steward had accompanied her to the king's apartments. All the time, she held her head high, and treated these vassals as if their very existence was questionable. She would have

140

ignored the king also, if, as soon as she gained the threshold, he had not spoken to her.

"Is there nothing that I can do to regain your love, Wythen?"

Her answer was as cold as the stones that made up the castle.

"You do not love me, so how can you bring back something that was never there?"

"Wythen, believe me..."

"I do not. No more... anything that you might say to me."

"But I speak the truth when I tell you that I love you."

The anger of Wythen was of ice.

"Were you speaking the truth when you told Tegwyn that you loved her also?"

About to reply, Brynan hesitated, then realised he could find no words that had meaning.

"You wronged her, and you have wronged me," Wythen said. "It is only now I see how badly you treat us women. You do not deserve so much as for your very life to be acknowledged by the Goddess. All of us are her handmaidens. If you play false with any one of us, you risk knowing the anger of Loenel."

Brynan could only bow his head in growing despair.

"And now you feel sorry for yourself!" Wythen continued. "You did not feel the same compassion when it suited you to cast Tegwyn aside! And then it was my turn! Such a fool you were to think that I could not see into your heart. I am of the sacred waters, the waters of tenderness and mercy and... love. All these things flow within me, they are my very being.

Wythen grew wroth as she continued to berate the king.

"How could you suppose I did not know, or that you could conceal, your feelings from me! I am the keeper of all secrets, all there are in the world, even those that are beyond the world! Every word that has ever been spoken and will be spoken – I have only to ask of the Goddess, and she will share it with me!"

"Wythen, listen to me. I was grieved when I heard that my people did not love you as I did. That pained me greatly."

Wythen sighed deeply.

"I know, and rather than my devotion, you would prefer to have the fawning of your addled peasants, and these clods in their fancy feathers that I see about your castle. Where was your devotion to me when I needed it most? That devotion that you once swore to me on your knees? Did you not have the courage to renounce all the world in the name of love? You swore you would never forsake me. What now of that promise?"

Brynan hung his head even further upon his breast, knowing that there were more words to scourge him.

"I would have given all of myself unto eternity to you; I yearned for you to take my heart when I offered it to you. But you hesitated, and then refused to give even the slightest part of yourself to me. Not a moment of your day would you give up for me. Not one grain of comfort or affection would you willingly bestow upon me. Why? Because, O King of Irlas, you have no love in your heart to give anyone. The lowest ploughman or men of the woods in your kingdom has more love about him than you. I would be more content living in a sty with a swineherd who truly loved me, than in the finest palace with the mightiest king."

Brynan slowly raised himself.

"Wythen, I tell you, I love you…"

The scornful silence that met his words told him all was in vain. Now the king knew for certain he could no longer bear the pain he felt when he was in Wythen's presence. He was to be spared that, for he would never see her again in this world.

142

After she had departed from the chamber and the castle, her face betraying nothing of her true feelings, Brynan called the Chief Steward, Cydlon. He now vowed to sleep in the Great Hall, for in his bedchamber Wythen's presence still remained.

For her part, Wythen had a task to perform. Of the Princess Tegwyn she knew nothing, except her name and the way in which she had been wronged. Yet she knew she must communicate with her, for the sprite had seen visions that could in no way be ignored.

It was Wythen's duty, as an emissary of the Goddess, to use the power she had been given to enter Tegwyn's dreams. This she must do at the darkest hour of the night, and she made ready to prepare herself for a magical ceremony.

Duly, at that hour, the Princess Tegwyn heard, within her dreams, a voice she did not recognise.

"Sister, hearken to me. You must not trust a king and his army that will come soon to the kingdom of Melynas; you will be in the gravest danger. These men wish you ill, and would seek to enslave you."

Tegwyn saw the hot, red face of King Barud staring at her and woke with a start. She knew now of the threat there was to herself and Tulrech her father, and that she must be vigilant in the coming days. Before she sought sleep once more, she thanked both Loenel and Nen, and asked for their protection.

XII

Warm days, one following another, had made those in the town of Treflan believe that Ufeln had returned once more. That forenoon, a hot and thirsty Hog approached the castle. His mission was to be granted a simple request. At least to Hog it was simple, but it seemed that Trafus, the second steward at the castle, did not share his view. He stared at Hog, as if he could not believe what he had just heard.

"You wish to speak with the king? Has it not occurred to you that perhaps the king has no desire to speak with you? Are you a prince of some royal house, or a merchant of some standing? No, I think not. By the look of you, I would guess you are of peasant stock, or even more lowly... with little or no learning in your head... even less rank, and with not even a single silver coin about you."

Trafus was not tall, but most definitely broad. He resembled a barrel, one that by some mischance, had fallen into a stream and was left to bob up and down until it sank. Trafus moved in the same manner as the bobbing barrel – up and down, up and down. When he did so, the red plume that graced his hat of office moved up and down with him. It was often speculated that one day, with the aid of these plumes, he might actually fly. Beneath his hat was a perfectly bald crown and, below that, enormous eyebrows, trying desperately to compensate for the absence of hair upon his head. These extraordinary tufts also had a habit of ascending and descending when the steward spoke. As Trafus talked a great deal, his head was constantly in motion.

Hog repeated his request, plainly, humbly and without rancor – to be rewarded with an even more hostile response.

"Be off with you, you young ragamuffin, and do not trouble those who have important business to attend to. Be off, I say!"

It was of no use. Even if Hog had threatened or cajoled the man, the outcome would have been just the same. Trafus was one of those who, when even the slightest amount of power is bestowed upon them, wield it unceasingly and always ineptly. It was Hog's misfortune, at that moment, to encounter such a one as Trafus and he felt, with some justification, sorely tried. In resigned silence, Hog turned and walked away.

Despite the scalding heat of the day, he was thinking. In his own life, the lessons of books, and indeed, all scholars' learning, had passed him by, but cunning he owned aplenty. If he could not enter the castle the way others did, then he would find another way for himself. More sober heads than his might have reflected that a castle is designed to keep others out, and gaining entry might prove to be more difficult than he anticipated. In his favour, Hog possessed the eternal optimism of youth and he was also empowered by the Goddess – but of this, he was unaware.

Paldarch had been walking in the woods prior to his departure from Treflan, and was returning to the castle. In the habit of using a side entrance, which led to the south tower, Paldarch had not quite disappeared from view when Hog hailed him.

"Sire, I beg if I may ask a favour from you."

Paldarch stopped, and turned in the direction of the voice.

"You may certainly ask, young fellow, though the granting of it might be a different matter."

Hog was somehow encouraged by the expression of partial amusement he noticed on the wizard's face, not knowing perhaps, this was Paldarch's customary look.

"I wish to see the king."

"I see… yes… and on some important matter?"

Hog could not quite tell if this person was jesting with him or not.

"Very important, yes."

"And your name?"

"Hog, sire."

Paldarch turned his inner gaze upon the figure before him and, in that instant, saw again the vision he had seen in the eyes of Loenel. The youth the wizard had seen flying effortlessly across the skies was the same as the one now standing before him. Paldarch decided instantly what must be done.

"I think you had best come with me, Master Hog."

Being in the company of a wizard is always to one's advantage if you are a stranger in a strange place. Few dare to gaze at a man of magic, or indeed those who may be in his company. The magician always decides how he may appear to others; he decides what they shall see. If he wishes to be a daunting figure then that is how he will be seen. Thus, none dared to question why Hog should be found in the castle: he was the companion of a wizard, that was all there was to it.

Hog was himself quite daunted by it all, for the youth had never been inside such a whirling maze of corridors and stairs. At last they reached the small vestibule outside the king's chamber. It was here that Hog came face to face with his recent acquaintance. Spying the youth, Trafus spluttered and squeaked with indignation.

"What is *that* doing here?"

Paldarch did not hesitate to quiet the man.

"Peace, steward. I will vouch for him. Now, will you kindly inform the king that *we* desire an audience."

Trafus pouted a pair of scarlet lips, and proceeded to suck in so much breath that Paldarch thought he might explode. He was all offended dignity. The wizard kept a straight face during this performance but it was not easy and he was rather enjoying the steward's discomfort. The latter turned on his heel and, with as much aplomb as he could muster, knocked upon the door to the king's chamber and entered. Trafus could be heard, in markedly clipped tones, announcing the presence of Paldarch and Hog to the king. The steward then quit the room and returned to stand before them. Stiffly, he led the visitors into the royal chamber. Brynan, whose spirits had been cast low by his ordeal with Wythen, brightened immediately at the sight of the wizard. He almost leapt from his seat.

"Paldarch! I heard that you were abroad on this fine morning."

He then caught sight of Hog.

"And who might this be?"

Hog stared at the king. So intent was his look that Brynan was almost afeared. Trafus, who had been loitering by the door observing this scene, could not resist exerting his authority. To Trafus, there could only be one reason for Hog's dumbness – insolence. He glared at him, and as Hog made no further move to speak, Trafus went so far as to address him in the harshest tones he could muster.

"On your knees before your king, you miserable young dog!"

He might have even struck the boy if Brynan had not raised a royal hand in protest.

"Hold! Leave us, steward. I will deal with this myself."

Trafus regarded the figure of Hog with scorn.

"I hardly like to leave your majesty in the presence of such an uncouth stripling. Sneaking into the castle behind my back! If I had known he had so little respect for his betters, I would have had him thrown into the dungeons, or even made certain that he be..."

He thrust his face so close to Hog the renowned eyebrows almost brushed the youth's cheeks.

"...hanged from the castle walls."

147

With a meaningful glance at Paldarch, Trafus turned upon his heel and left the chamber. The wizard waited until the sound of his angry footsteps had died away. Then he stood by Hog and spoke quietly but firmly.

"Now, Master Hog, you have something to say to your king?"

After some moments, Hog began to speak as if in a trance.

"I was told to give you this..."

Hog reached inside the folds of his doublet and brought out the small parcel wrapped in silk, which he offered to the king. Brynan accepted the packet and, with a good deal of curiosity, began to open it. As he did so, his wonder was manifest. He held up a jewel; and a great light came from it, filling the chamber. It was the ring he had seen upon the altar in the Temple of Rhimlais.

Without a moment's hesitation, the king placed it on his finger. Immediately, he felt the tremor of a great power, one that echoed from the deeps of time. In that moment Brynan smelled a tang of the oceans, and felt the sharp air of the mountains. Hog and Paldarch must have felt something of that which the king experienced, for all three of them now stared in astonished silence at the ring. It looked too as if it had always adorned that royal hand. Paldarch was the first to recover.

"The Ring of Awren! By all the gods and goddesses! How came you by this, young fellow?"

The words of Hog still came slow and haltingly.

"I do not know... in the woods... I saw her... the Goddess... she spoke to me..."

"The Goddess?"

"...it was her... she who gave me ring... and in my mind I saw the likeness of the one I must take it to... then I could not remember... until ..."

Paldarch nodded, understanding.

"That is the way of Loenel, the blessing of forgetfulness, so the mortal mind is not troubled."

Brynan, meanwhile, hardly heard these words, so entranced was he by the jewel upon his finger. When he turned his hand, the ring created an infinity of colours – a kaleidoscope of rainbows. He gazed in awe at its beauty, such that he had never seen before. At last, the king turned to the one who had brought such a wonder to him.

"It seems there is much more to you, Master Hog, than ever we could have known. But first I must know more of this ring. Paldarch, perhaps you may know of the tale that accompanies such a prize?"

The king took to his throne and Paldarch settled himself down also. Brynan motioned Hog to a bench near them. Paldarch began to speak.

"It is an ancient tale, so much so it is almost forgotten even by the tellers of fables. Before the Age of Kings, there was the Time of the Heroes. The greatest of these was Anwen, who owned three great treasures. These had been made for him by Cledoth, the Swordsmith, in the Caverns of Degbryd. Cledoth was of the Bychan, the spirit people, much older even than the most ancient of men. The three great treasures were the Sword, the Spear and the Ring. Only by possessing the ring could the sword and the spear retain their enchantment.

"Taking these with him, Awren vowed to cross the Great Sea of Elgion to Asgell, the land where the winged snakes ruled, and to conquer them. This he did, but the Spear was broken and lost while he fought the snakes, though the Sword remained. On his return across the Great Sea, the Ring slipped from his finger and was lost beneath the waves. Without the Ring to protect him, a storm came. His ship was wrecked and Awren the Hero was drowned. Some say that a water sprite found the Ring at the bottom of the sea and took it for herself. It is also said that later she loved a mortal who coveted the Ring. The Goddess knew of this and caused the sprite to return with the Ring to the sea where she became a great silver salmon. So the Ring again was free."

Paldarch then fixed Hog with his eyes.

"Now it seems that the Goddess, after reclaiming her own, has made to bestow this treasure upon her trusted servant, and trusted him to fulfill an important task, which he has now done."

Hog blushed at this, and both Brynan and Paldarch smiled broadly. Brynan was all for immediate business, and he spoke plainly to Hog.

"Now, what shall be done with you, Master Hog? We cannot have you wandering about the kingdom with your pockets full of treasures as this, and in the company of the Goddess, it seems! We must make use of you. I hear tell that since Derwen returned from our journeys, he has frightened off his squire, so there is a place for you there. That knight will take no nonsense, but that he will make a man of you, there is no doubt. What think you, Paldarch? Is it the soldier's life for our Hog?"

"Certainly, he will come to no harm in that calling. And he will at least be fed twice a day, if he does not bring Derwen's anger down upon his head. Though I would venture to add something else about our master Hog's education, my liege."

"And what is that?"

"There is a scholar somewhere within that shaggy head. Our Hog would benefit from being in the Houses of Learning for some little time, I feel."

"And you will undertake to be his teacher?"

"Certainly I will, and in giving lessons I may also learn much myself. The student is often more informed of certain things than his master."

The king turned to Hog, waiting with some trepidation on the bench.

"So, this appears to be your fate, Master Hog – to be fattened on books and bread. What think you to that?"

"I will do as I am bidden, my liege."

Brynan smiled.

"Good. You are now part of the royal household and you will dress as one of them. I do not suppose you will be aggrieved to lose your present attire. Only one piece of advice I can give you, Master Hog, do not fall foul of the stewards, especially Trafus."

Paldarch now stood up.

"My liege, the days grows short, as we know. I would wish to speak with Master Hog for a time in my chamber."

Brynan waved a hand in assent.

"Do so, do so. I shall perhaps talk with you myself at some time, Master Hog."

The youth made an awkward bow, so deep that he very nearly fell over. Under the amused eye of the king, he and Paldarch departed from the royal chamber.

*

It was now the middle of the forenoon and in the topmost chamber of the highest tower at the castle of Treflan, an old wizard and a ragged youth regarded each other. Amber beams from the window lit the cloth hangings upon the yellowed plaster of the walls. Paldarch was musing upon how he might go about instructing Hog in the ways of magic, when the youth suddenly blurted out some of his fears.

"Master Paldarch, I have seen the king and done what I was supposed to do by the Goddess, bless her. Now I am to become a squire and learn my letters and much knowledge of which I am ignorant, I am certain... but I am sore confused, such that I feel my head may fall from shoulders

151

at any moment. Tell me what I am to do, for although I am but an orphan – some would say a vagabond – I wish only to do what is right."

The wizard looked upon Hog kindly, as if he were a part of himself – one Paldarch had left behind many ages ago, the wandering youth of brook and dale.

"Your first lesson, Master Hog, will aid you in any of your dealings with this world. Things are never as they appear to be. Not all who profess to be noble are so, and many who are branded as evil, deserve it not. Love is a blessing and a curse... loyalty may be like the mist. As for gain or loss, Angaz, the God of Death, is in the end the only one who wins."

Hog had listened closely to all this, but he was none the wiser.

"So how am I to know which path I must follow?"

"As to being afeared of making the wrong choice, there is only the choice that is made for us by the gods and goddesses we follow. That is all. I will guide you until such times as I know you need me no longer, then you will become a guide to others."

Hog could only stare in amazement at Paldarch's words.

"I will tell you a little of yourself also," the wizard continued. "Your name is not Hog at all. Hawdren is your true name, that given to you by your father. He, Helryn, was once a wizard. Your mother was the very sprite that once owned the Ring of Awren."

No sooner had poor Hog taken all this in than he began to weep. Paldarch put an arm about him, and he cried the more. The wizard spoke softly.

"I pondered for some time whether I should speak to you of all this, but it is better always to know the truth."

Hog looked up.

"Is my father Helryn in good health?"

"Most certainly. Not many moons have passed since I was abiding in the forest of Galtrin, and there talked with him."

Hog smiled through his tears.

"I am glad."

"Helryn would be glad to know that you are to be schooled in the arts, for he knew, as I do, that you are suited to the calling. I would prefer it if we had more time to devote to your instruction, but many events are unfolding in the world at this time. At least you have performed the arts before..."

"Have I?"

"Indeed – in your many lives before this one. You have forgotten the way to perform magic, that is all. During these lessons I shall address you as Hawdren, because it is your true magical name. Now you must hearken to me very carefully, for we have but a few hours... but first..."

Paldarch then drew away from the youth and sat once more opposite him. He closed his eyes and, after a short while, was in a trance. Hog, not used to such behaviour, was somewhat alarmed. He was grateful, when, after some minutes, the wizard opened his eyes once more and spoke.

"You must forgive me. I have been communing with a multitude of spirits of late, so it has almost become a habit. Last night I had converse with beings from future times. My, what strange things lie in wait for the generations to come! But, just now, I was hearing what various others who know say of you. It seems your soul is pure and you are destined for great things."

Hog's eyes widened.

"I am?"

"Indeed. And now you shall travel to the inner world yourself and speak of what you find there. It will be excellent practice for you. Come, think only of a sky filled with stars..."

153

Obediently, Hog closed his eyes and followed the wizard's instructions.

With words that first quieted, then guided him, Paldarch gently led his pupil into the endless kingdom of magic.

"What do you see now, Hawdren?"

As soon as he began to speak, his voice changed, as if the words were coming from a long way off.

"I see those three... the two kings and the prince... they make ready for war... I can hear what they are saying..."

Paldarch listened intently to Hog's words. Every detail of Prince Anfad's plans was revealed, and the wizard's brow grew more lined as the tale unfolded. When the youth opened his eyes, he saw Paldarch by the door of the chamber, looking intently at him.

"Come! We must see the king straightway... there is no time to lose."

They almost flew down the stone stairs, Paldarch's voice echoing from the walls around them as they descended.

"My regrets, Master Hog, but your formal instruction must temporarily be halted. We shall resume it as soon as we are able."

Paldarch sought an immediate audience with the king. Trafus was still about his duties, and in his usual officious manner, attempted to create difficulties where there were none. Paldarch was in no mood for petty prevarications, and curtly told him so. In this way, they quickly found themselves once more before the king. With discreet prompting by Paldarch, Hog repeated his tale. As he listened, Brynan grew ever more concerned. As soon as Hog had finished, the king burst out excitedly.

"We have all grown witless in this heat of Ufeln! Now, what is to be done? If we are to engage on the battlefield with the armies of three other kingdoms, then we must ourselves have more men."

"What of Rhaldon, your brother, my liege?"

"The royal shepherd! You think he will come to our aid?"

"I do believe so, my liege."

Brynan breathed in sharply.

"Nen only knows what he will say if I ask him to go to war with me."

"Nen moves in strange ways, my liege, there is only one way to find out."

Within moments, Brynan had made his decision.

"It will be done. I shall rise with the sun and ride to seek out Rhaldon. Now, what will you do, Paldarch, in my absence?"

"I still must still attend to affairs in other lands, my liege. My new pupil will come with me... I may be able to continue his instruction at the same time and with perhaps with a more practical bent. Unless he has any objection?"

Hog, used only to such behaviour when his father had adopted one of his rare magical moods, was somewhat alarmed.

"I would go to the end of the world with you, my master."

Paldarch placed an arm upon his shoulder.

"A good answer – for that is where I intend that we shall go."

*

As he rode along the next morning, Brynan felt as if he were literally being drawn into the sun. A great amber archway rose into the skies above him as he sped onward, into a world flushed with vermillion. As he crossed the Plain of Lanerch, the king felt a new courage start to flow though him. His troubles seemed to fall from him with every league that he covered. He urged the pace and beneath him his horse seemed only the more eager to gallop.

In this way he soon came to the Plain of Tawelf. The king knew that the settlement where his brother Rhaldon had made his home was nearby. The bare outlook changed, and trees began to line the way. Among the rough grass peeped small bushes bursting with colour.

Every prince is entitled to a palace, however modest. Built of elm wood and oak, Rhaldon's dwelling stood in the centre of a group of wattle huts. All blended into one, and gave the impression that Rhaldon's standing with his people was just as harmonious. Brynan slowed his horse and rode between two huts into the centre of the circle.

Faces of men and women peered out of doorways, then just as quickly disappeared. The children were more bold, and some stopped their play and ran up to the king's horse, before scampering away. The sound of hooves had brought Rhaldon out onto his step also. King and Prince regarded each other for a moment, the latter surprised by the arrival of his visitor, but altogether friendly enough. Brynan hailed him.

"Hail, Rhaldon! You look well. The simple life must suit you."

Brynan's brother shared the same fair looks as the king, but he had grown to be as ruddy and tousled as any of the peasant folk that lived around him. The body beneath his rough jerkin spoke of taut muscles and labour never shirked. Brynan dismounted, and the brothers embraced with great warmth. When he spoke, Rhaldon's words retained the royal drawl, but he had none of the air of a courtier about him.

"The days are the same, it is true. We feed our animals and make sure that they come to no harm... then we feed ourselves."

Brynan laughed at this and felt a great gladness in seeing Rhaldon so content. The king wondered, for more than a moment, if in these surroundings, he too might find true peace. He also knew in his heart that could never be so, and he dismissed the thought as quickly as it had come. Brynan was suddenly aware that his brother was addressing him.

"But come, you will need refreshment after your journey. Let us see what we have to offer... a king!"

Rhaldon led the way into a hall that could comfortably accommodate many. There were other doors leading off from this central chamber, to sleeping quarters, kitchens and storerooms. Although the touch of a feminine hand was absent, the plain timber everywhere gave a warmth to the surroundings. Rhaldon led his brother to one end of the chamber. Here the shutters had been drawn back, and the morning light fell squarely upon a long elm table. On this was laid out a rabbit pie and a platter with smoked trout upon it. There was bread that was still warm, a bowl of honey, and cakes of ginger and cinnamon.

"You certainly eat like a king, my brother!"

"There is cider, too, if you wish it, brewed by our men..."

"Rhaldon, I thank you, but even after half a flagon, I would most certainly fall asleep..."

They sat at benches pulled up to the table and ate their fill. After meat, talk flowed in the easy way that it always does among those who are close with one another.

"Now, tell me all your doings and those of the kingdom. We hear little of what may be happening in Treflan. Travellers who pass tell me that the King of Irlas is about to take a queen... but I let the matter rest. If this were true I am certain Brynan would not forget to invite his own brother to the Rhindas."

Brynan's face darkened a little.

"That I fear is a sorry tale, one that I would not burden you with..."

Rhaldon was puzzled but, aware of his brother's anguished look, did not delve any further.

"If the telling of it pains you, my brother, then it is best forgotten. But come Brynan, you would not ride all this way just to watch me feed acorns to swine."

Brynan told of the plot against Irlas. Rhaldon's countenance became more grim as the tale unfolded.

"If it is as you say, then evil times are ahead for us all. If this had come about in our father's time, what would he have done?"

"Doubtless he would have been as troubled as his children are now, though it is fortunate that both my father and I were blessed with Paldarch as an adviser."

Rhaldon had a gleeful look.

"The wizard! I had forgotten all about him, though I am sure I have seen him once or twice in the forest, though one can never be certain with one such as he. But tell me, brother, what is Paldarch's counsel?"

Brynan fixed his brother with a stern gaze.

"It is on his advice that I am here. Now tell me, Rhaldon, can you raise an army?"

The prince was all astonishment.

"An army! One of shepherds and berry pickers perhaps! There are no soldiers in these parts, Brynan."

"Woodsmen? Hunters? An outlaw band or two living on the forest?"

Rhaldon shook his head, but the king was not to be put off so easily.

"Brother, I know my request must seem most strange, yet I believe at least some men may be gathered together. Come, I beg of you, for the sake of the kingdom and our father's memory."

Brynan went on to tell of Barud's plan to capture the castle at Melynas. His brother deliberated silently for some time, and finally he spoke.

"Very well, I will do what I can. Doubtless, there are arms to be had somewhere... When will Barud make his move upon Melynas?"

"At the next fulling of the moon."

"That is not long."

Brynan rose from the table.

"Aye, and I have much to do myself. Rousing the kingdom and telling our people that we shall soon be at war. It is not a task I relish."

Rhaldon grasped his brother by the arm.

"At least you and the kingdom will know that I shall do all in my power. Barud will not have an easy day of it, if I have my way. I shall make sure of that, and so will my followers."

Rhaldon's look was one of quiet determination. He is also our father's son, thought Brynan. The ancestors are truly with us! The two brothers left the palace. A few of the more curious peasants had gathered outside. They were deferential towards Brynan, while with Rhaldon they talked and joked as if they were equals. To the king's eyes, they looked like loyal men who, when called to go with Rhaldon, would do so without a qualm. His hopes began to rise, and it was with a glad heart that he bade his brother farewell, and rode from the encampment.

As he followed the way back to Irlas, Brynan watched a skein of geese as they flew overhead. The king voiced his thoughts aloud.

"They fly south because they sense change. As I do."

XIII

When Brynan returned to the castle and entered his own chamber, he felt time dragging him down with chains of iron. He had briefly met with Paldarch and told of his meeting with Rhaldon, and now the wizard and Hog had left without revealing their destination. Brynan sensed that Wythen was still about in the castle, yet he also knew that in all but body she too had departed. Time meant nothing in the spirit world, yet its denizens always had a sense of occasion. It was not long before that particular drama was to be acted out.

The king sat on his throne and suddenly Wythen was standing before him. It was not he who possessed power at that moment; she had all the might of the Goddess with her and he was in its thrall. Wythen was dressed in the same simple clothes that she had worn on the night when they had arrived together at Treflan. She had refused to take with her any of the fine clothes and jewellery that the king had bestowed upon her. Like worthless trinkets, they lay abandoned upon the couch in the bedchamber, where they had once enacted their passion.

Once more, Brynan found that words would not come to him. Wythen's presence had the effect of making anything he said worse than meaningless. Yet one thing he must know, even though he knew he addressed a spirit. Perhaps it was always easier to gain the truth from the Otherworld.

"At the Lake when Derwen might have taken your life, you showed no fear. I have oft wondered how you were so certain no harm would befall you."

Wythen turned impassive features to the king.

"I fear no mortal man..."

"But..."

"...and I knew that I was protected."

"By Paldarch?"

Wythen smiled as she had that day by the Lake.

"Indeed. Do you not think a father would not protect his own daughter?"

"You mean..."

"Yes, Paldarch is my father, the sorceress Gwirel my mother."

Brynan closed his eyes.

"I... I did not know."

Wythen regarded him impassively.

"There is no reason why you should."

The king struggled to find further words.

"Wythen... I never wished for you to fear me, I believed that you loved me."

Wythen looked at him in a way that held some pity.

"And I thought that you loved me. But you did not, except perhaps for a fleeting moment. In me, you thought you had embraced the Goddess, perhaps you thought you could even possess her. You cannot know love until you truly know the Goddess in every way, and no man is capable of that... not even a king."

And with these words Wythen disappeared from the chamber of Huan Brynan, the place where she had once embraced the ruler of the Kingdom of Irlas. After she had gone, Brynan began to weep silently. When Cydlon entered the chamber, the king averted his head so that the man would not notice his tears.

*

The bard oft sings of the beauty of Hafwan, the time when the goddess Cyngerl chooses to wear a gown of russet and maroon. Birds are black specks against a smoke-grey blanket of sky, and the stillness of the season is akin to

161

that of prayer. In the courtyard of the Castle, where Tegwyn and her father dwelt, oaks had grown as long as anyone could remember, and now a pool of leaves lay about each one. In the old tongue, the spirit of this time was named Gwylaw, 'he who made the earth dark and soft', the branches of the trees heavy with rain.

In the castle at Melynas, the sound of many horses woke Tegwyn as the dawn was breaking. In some alarm, she leapt from her bed and went to the window of the chamber. In disbelief she watched as men, obviously soldiers, began to pour into the courtyard below, while others were gathering beyond the castle walls. Tegwyn suddenly remembered the dream and the warning words she had heard then. What she was now seeing was the same in every detail... and in the midst of the soldiers was that malicious, ugly face. She had woken in such fear when he had appeared... and now... the Princess almost screamed out loud.

Her first thought was for her child. She rushed to the cot where Siricyn lay asleep and gathered the infant in her arms. Then, with the utmost care, she placed Siricyn in her bed so that a casual eye would not detect that anything was concealed there.

Without waiting to summon her handmaiden, she dressed with all speed and raced down the stone steps of the tower. She found her father in the Great Hall, apparently unperturbed, and seemingly dressed to meet some person of import. He was sporting his finest doublet and had a cloak trimmed with marten skins about him. She rushed up to him, clasping his arm in her distress.

"Father, why are these men inside the castle walls? What in the name of Nen has befallen us?"

King Tulrech patted her cheek.

"Hush, my little one, do not fear. These are our allies. King Barud and the Prince Anfad have pledged their loyalty to the kingdom of Melynas."

Tegwyn drew away and stared at her father in disbelief.

"Allies? Why should we need allies? The kingdom of Irlas is our only ally."

At the name of Irlas, her father curled an angry lip.

"Irlas is our enemy! Our armies shall march upon them, and teach that king of theirs a lesson."

Tegwyn could not believe what she was hearing.

"But what has made you turn against our loyal and ancient neighbour? Such strange words you utter. Why should this be?" "

"Why, Brynan has sorely used you, has he not? Surely, that is enough reason."

Tegwyn could feel herself blushing hotly but by great strength of will calmed herself. She breathed deeply before she spoke.

"Father, you must understand my child was conceived with the greatest love, thus I bear no ill-will towards Brynan..."

She faltered for a moment.

"...perhaps once I did, but Loenel spoke to me in a vision... saying that it is not with hatred that we must act in this world. It is time men listened to the words of their womenfolk. We have been silent long enough."

Tulrech spluttered in his rage.

"The kingdom of Melynas has been insulted by the breaking of your betrothal! We must be avenged!"

"My betrothal! To be avenged! And you did not think to ask how I might feel in this matter? Certainly I knew sadness and even anger, but many moons have passed since then. Now I truly believe that it was the will of Nen this should have happened, and we should accept his wisdom."

Tulrech waved an extravagantly gloved hand in dismissal.

"My child, you are too forgiving, and perhaps tired... it is an early hour, after all. Now I must away to greet King Barud..."

"That fat pig on his horse, do you mean?"

"Hush, Tegwyn, you must not speak of the King of Techlyn in that manner. We must always be respectful to others who, as well as ourselves, hold a royal rank."

"He has no more right to wear a crown than a cuckoo..."

"Tegwyn, please."

"I loathe his oily face and I do not trust him. He does not mean well..."

"You are wrong, Tegwyn, my daughter..."

Tegwyn stamped her foot angrily.

"Father, you must listen to me. I dreamed..."

The king smiled indulgently.

"Dreams? Oh, so like your dear mother..."

"Father, hear me out, I beg of you..."

"Do not distress yourself, my Tegwyn. If you do not sleep well, then the wise woman will find healing herbs for you..."

Tegwyn suddenly felt a great rage roaring through her veins, and she almost screamed at her father.

"This Barud, or Prince Anfad I suspect, has tricked you! Everything they have said to you is the foulest lies!"

Shocked and confused, King Tulrech made to move towards the door of the Hall.

"Tegwyn, you must not utter these words... if King Barud heard you... now, I must see him... I cannot delay..."

"Father! You did not see... in my dream... how that beast looked at me..."

Tulrech suddenly halted in his step, a haunted look upon his face.

"What did you say? Looked at you? What do you mean?"

Tegwyn put herself between her father and the door.

164

"I think you must hear the rest of my dream, father, before it is too late, and you find you have given away the kingdom."

Reluctantly, King Tulrech agreed to do so.

*

Paldarch and Hog returned to Irlas with a luxuriant moon rolling along beside them. Bright enough it was to be reflected in the grey green grass of the Plain of Lanerch.

Hog, perched on the back of Teryngar, reflected a little on his first experiences as the pupil of a wizard. He had seen much of the ways of magic and had felt both wonder and fear in equal measure. As he had promised, Paldarch had indeed taken his pupil on a journey to the end of the world. And there, lay to the entrance to the Otherworld, that place that is the dominion of spirits and invisible powers that few mortals could ever imagine exist, even in their wildest dreams. Paldarch had schooled Hog in the ways of entering the Otherworld so that he might venture there at will, and of relating what he saw there. A true wizard learns to know instinctively what is real and what is not. Even in the mystical realms, tricksters and wraiths reside and the apprentice must question them in such a way as to discover their purpose and their usefulness to him.

Hog had learned much. His master had praised him for his triumphs and encouraged him on the occasions when he had courted failure. The province of magic is not for all, and this is as it should be. Paldarch, however, knew that Hog's destiny was already determined, and the path that he must take could not be altered. He was of the blood of a magician and a spirit, and this alone would have marked him as one chosen to be as the gods.

165

With Hog clinging to the wizard's cloak, they rode into the courtyard of the castle in the early eve. Paldarch dispatched Teryngar to the care of a steward, with particular instructions for his welfare. He then bade the youth a good night before Hog went to join Derwen in his quarters for he would begin his duties as squire to that irascible knight the next morn. The wizard had offered Hog what advice he could in his new calling, and wished him well. The candles burned low in the royal chamber when a steward ushered him into the presence of the king. Paldarch took in the situation immediately.

"Wythen has departed?"

Brynan's voice was strained in reply.

"Some days ago, though she returned as a spirit a few nights ago. I have at last realised that one who I thought would be beside me all my life is no longer there. It seems that the Goddess does not smile upon me."

"You have enjoyed the love of two women, my liege, many men cannot say that. And I do believe the Goddess has smiled upon you both. We cannot always know the will of those who dwell in the Heavens. It is right that their ways are a mystery to us, believe me."

"I fear I served neither woman well..."

"None of us knows what is dear to us until we lose that very thing. You have come closer to the Goddess than any mortal man I have ever known. To love a woman is the closest we can ever be to that divine presence."

Brynan stirred upon his throne.

"Perhaps you are right. Is it not said, that 'it is better to have loved and lost'..."

"I believe so, and remember this, without the Goddess nothing may exist, for she is the Great Mother from whom all creation comes. She is, too, greater than man, for without her there is no fuel for his flame to consume. I have known of this since I first practised my art, when I was but a beardless youth. My own mother was a spirit such as Wythen."

The king's eyes were fixed upon Paldarch him. His words when they came were full of wonder.

"And you are Wythen's father. That is how you knew her nature so well. But why did you not tell me this?"

Paldarch looked thoughtful.

"I saw no reason to do so. If I had done so it would have made not the slightest difference to the destiny of either of you. You were supposed to enjoy a union, however brief in this world. I say nothing of the next, and also mark this, both of you have yet a part to play in this world."

Brynan turned away as if seeing Wythen before him.

"I could not bear to look upon her again, not for even the slightest moment. That would be too much for me to bear."

"But you must look upon *me*, now."

Such was the command in Paldarch's voice that the king could not disobey.

"Consider. According to every traveller's tale, beyond the Six Kingdoms, there are only wastes more barren even than the Plains of Tarth. Beyond that again is only the Chaos of the Uncreated where even Nen has no power. It is the fate of our world that is at hand, and what is about to unfold before us means more than just the destiny of a few. Even young Hog and Sir Bulwas have a part to play, though none know exactly what that might be."

At the mention of that oddest of knights, the king allowed himself a momentary smile. Paldarch's features however, were still set.

"We stand at the meeting of ways, and we must follow the one that leads to a greater future, even if we ourselves perish upon that path. It is, too, the way of Nen, and for us there can be no other. We have no choice but to do battle with those who would prevent us from fulfilling that destiny. If Nen has decided that we are to perish in our

167

struggle, then so be it. Even all the will of magic cannot alter that end. Time and Death are ever the victors. I sometimes doubt if Time ever does exist, but Death most certainly does. Knowing our end is inevitable, we should go out to meet Death with a cheery countenance. Those who fear death live with that fear forever."

Paldarch struck his staff upon the floor, hard enough to give power to his words.

"And what matter any of it? The deeds of men mean nothing. To the universe, no word or deed is any more than the whispering of the wind. Life is either triumph or loss, whether great or small. Be it the widow's relief when the hearth fire is alight, or the victory of one kingdom over another, it is all the same. But we must fight, whatever the cost to ourselves. My liege, speak truth to me... is there fear in your heart?"

For some moments Brynan could not look upon the wizard.

"I do not know. Even though I have seen much, and doubtless I will see more before my time is over, sometimes, when I wake and the night still rules and the rising of the sun is far away, I feel as helpless as a child."

Paldarch nodded.

"Then let it be so! A man must acknowledge his fear, only then can he hope to conquer it. Only a fool or a liar boasts that he is never afraid. Even a wizard may sometimes feel fear, you know."

He suddenly assumed a most serious expression, and Brynan looked at Paldarch with some alarm.

"Is that so?"

"Yes, but I make most certain no one may see it!"

Paldarch's laugh boomed out, and every candle in the chamber seemed to burn the brighter. Paldarch's mirth always had the effect of raising Brynan's spirits. His features still bore a trace of sadness, but now there was the dawning of a new courage. The wizard spoke strong words of encouragement.

"The task of any king is bound to be harder than that of other men. He must be the mightiest of warriors, his blade the keenest, his sword thrust always telling. Kings are not ordinary men. Call upon the ancestors, Huan Brynan! Their spirits reside within you, their blood runs in your veins... their spirit is always in your heart. Ask for their wisdom and courage, they are only too willing to aid you. They honour you and you stand as one with them."

Brynan could feel himself smiling once more.

"I think of my grandfather often, and when I am puzzling over some document, he comes to me. He was a great scholar, the match for any of our wisest priests. When I was a boy, I neglected my letters and should have been schooling in the Temple, instead of hawking and fishing with the sons of the stewards. How my mother, the Queen, did despair of me, thinking I would become as a man of the woods and spurn my royal destiny. Yet grandfather never once scolded me for my truancy, and I loved him the more."

With the powers of the seer, Paldarch could clearly see the benign countenance of this noble and loving man as he stood behind the throne of the king, gently but firmly guiding him.

"It is as you say. Deep affection lies between you."

Brynan's voice now suddenly rang out in the chamber.

"I will lead my people to victory! I vow, also, to stand and fight until I feel the icy breath of Angaz upon me, and then I may fight no more."

Paldarch looked upon him proudly, as a father might a son.

"Spoken as a king, and truly a king! Nen smiles upon you, that I know. That which you need will be rendered unto you. However, you are no longer a king. The Age of Kings is over."

169

Brynan eyes were full of wonder.

"Is that so?"

Paldarch now looked upon the king, and the will of heaven was in his gaze.

"Because you have known the waters of the Goddess and the fire of the gods, you are now a god yourself."

Brynan looked into the eyes of Paldarch and he saw that the wizard spoke only of what he knew. A wizard does not lie. Lies are of no use to one who lives only in a world that is created from eternal truth.

"You possess the Ring, soon you will have the Sword, for you, Huan Brynan, are destined to own it. When you were given the Ring, I knew so then, for the one is of no use without the other. It is also the sign that I must depart from you."

Brynan could only stare, his mouth open wide.

"You are leaving? Now? When the fate of the world is hanging in the balance?"

Paldarch took up his staff and studied it, as if seeing for the first time the signs and sigals engraved upon it.

"That is exactly why I must leave, for this war will not be fought only upon the field of battle. It is to be fought also in a kingdom beyond this world. My presence is sorely needed there, and thus I must depart. But know you this... I shall be with you in spirit and guiding your hand from this moment onwards."

Brynan was suddenly overcome with anxiety, and would have clung to the wizard's cloak if he thought that would have somehow persuaded him to change his mind.

"You are going just at the moment when I need your words the most, Paldarch."

Paldarch smiled gently upon him.

"I think you are in need of no one to advise you now. Your hour has come, Huan Brynan. It is you who rules the kingdom and who will lead your people, and they will follow you, mark my words."

"I will do as you say, Paldarch. Truly, I am now aware of my destiny, though before perhaps I did not."

The wizard looked upon him and his eyes were as clear as the air upon a mountain peak.

"I am leaving Teryngar here. It is upon his back you will ride out to do battle... and what better steed to ride to victory..."

"Teryngar! Your own horse? But it is the mount of a wizard..."

Paldarch laughed.

"Fear not, Teryngar will not ride away with you to the stars. I have spoken with him and he is quite agreeable to the arrangement."

"Then I accept your offer, Paldarch! It is such an honour, and I do not know what to say..."

"You need say nothing; I know that Teryngar will have the best master that I could wish for."

Brynan stood then and looked upon the wizard, desiring to keep a memory of this moment.

"And now, like a fox, you slink away into the shadows..."

"It is from the shadows that I came, and now I must return."

The two regarded each other, and then embraced. It is not often that a king acts this way with one of his subjects, but a wizard is not as ordinary men.

"Farewell, Paldarch, may Nen go with you."

"Farewell, my liege, and do not forget to call upon Loenel in your prayers, also."

"I do, constantly."

"It is as well, for now She has the fate of us all in her hands."

And thus Paldarch left the Great Hall and Brynan's heart was heavy once more. He looked upon his throne and the rest of the trappings of kingship and wondered if they meant aught at all. As the wizard withdrew from the king's presence, the king again wept, for he knew that the two of them would never meet again, at least, not in this world.

The shadows became longer in the chamber, and the king reflected most deeply. Eventually he returned from those dark places, and with a greater sense of purpose. Regrets had he none, his thoughts being only for the kingdom. He summoned the Chief Steward.

"I wish every knight be present in the Great Hall tomorrow eve. Gather them all! I wish to address them, every one."

Cydlon was inclined to protest.

"My liege, many of the knights are abroad and..."

The king interrupted him sharply.

"...and after you have done that..."

The Chief Steward almost jumped.

"Yes, my liege?"

"Send word that all the people, from every corner of the kingdom, are to be in the square before the castle. I would speak with them at the noon hour a day's hence. Is that understood?"

"Yes, my liege. At once, my liege. It shall be done."

"Then see to it."

The Chief Steward hurried off.

The jackals of war were about to be unleashed. All must be summoned to defend the kingdom and Irlas was to be roused; the king had commanded that it be so.

*

Barud sat upon his horse in the courtyard of the castle in Melynas. He was visibly preening, and congratulating himself before he debated his next move. He thought it might be good sport to hunt the wench Tegwyn out from her warm nest, but his reverie was interrupted by a cry from one of his captains.

"An army approaches, O king! There! It is nearly upon us... from the west."

Barud was taken aback. Surely, this could not be Brynan? None in Irlas could have had word already that he was here. As fast as he could, Barud mounted the steps that led to the top of the West Wall. From there he looked out, and gaped at body of men, twenty score or more, approaching at a good pace over the grasslands. They were mostly on foot, with a few riders, one of whom was carrying a standard, upon it a device unknown to Barud. Neither was their leader familiar to him. Whoever they were, he would go out to meet them first before embarking on any hasty course. To this end, he shouted to the captain from the battlements.

"Call Aruth and Slondar! We ride out, the three of us."

For a man of some girth, Barud descended to the courtyard with impressive speed. Once there, he encountered King Tulrech, swaggering a little in his fine outfit. Barud would have spoken with him, and assured him in his oily fashion that all was well, if it were not for these new happenings. The king of Melynas had also seen the approaching army, and in his turn was inclined to be curt with Barud.

"Who are those others beyond the walls... more of your army?"

Barud, in the act of mounting his horse, was equally abrupt in his reply.

"None of my men, that is certain."

Barud swept out between the gates, his two cohorts behind him. Rhaldon halted his army and waited for these riders to approach. His men stood, resolute and still, not so much warriors, but all stalwart fellows, the strength of the forest and the honesty of their simple calling about them. Barud rode up to within a yard or two of their ranks and faced Rhaldon who sat easily in the saddle. The prince was impassive, even as Barud, in his lugubrious way, smiled at him.

"What means this, that you threaten the kingdom of Melynas?"

"Rather, I think it is you, King Barud, who threaten the peace of the Six Kingdoms."

So addressed, Barud was inclined to let loose a peal of laughter, though there was little mirth in it.

"Who speaks thus to King Barud of Techlyn?"

"I am Rhaldon, Prince of Irlas, and know you that my father did swear an oath of allegiance with the kings of Melynas. It was made in the olden days, when the Six Kingdoms were even as Four."

Despite himself, Barud recognised that this was no upstart churl he faced. Nevertheless Rhaldon's assured manner did not lessen his empty bluster to any degree.

"Indeed, and are you aware that my army came here only at the request of Melynas and its king?"

Rhaldon eyed him for but a mere instant.

"I am aware that you and Prince Anfad have sought to deceive King Tulrech. You are a false friend and must be treated as such."

Barud was not pleased to be addressed so. He snarled a reply.

"You doubt my honour?"

"I have never been aware that you possessed any such virtue. I hear tell that your intentions towards the Princess Tegwyn are far from honourable."

At this, Barud's eyes blazed as he struggled to control himself.

"Such talk is only to be expected from a lowly prince as you."

Rhaldon delivered his riposte with care.

"Better to be a lowly prince than a king who is no more than a common villain."

174

Barud flinched at this and would have shown more anger but chose instead to eye Rhaldon's company with as much contempt as he could muster.

"Begone from here, before I lose all patience with you and your ragged following."

Rhaldon eyed the other steadily.

"Rest assured, we shall be gone, King Barud, but only when you and your men are far beyond the borders of Melynas."

The fire in the king's eyes kindled once more, and seizing the bridle of his horse he turned for the castle. Unmoved, Rhaldon watched his departure.

"Now you shall feel my wrath!" Barud called out over his shoulder.

Rhaldon wasted no time in addressing his men.

"Horsemen, remember your orders, men-at-arms, yours also. Now, fall in, as I have trained you, in four ranks. My stoutest warriors at the front. "

Immediately they fell to.

"Make ready to do battle, my brave fellows. They outnumber us, but we have one great advantage. Barud is angry, and angry men are likely to make mistakes."

*

Try as she might, Tegwyn did not succeed in convincing her father of Barud's evil intentions. Realising this, and alarmed by the arrival of the second army, she fled to her chamber in the East Tower and barricaded the door as best she might. Tegwyn gathered her child to her breast, offered prayers to Nen, all the while attempting to calm her thundering heart as best she could. Suddenly a great clamour, impossible to ignore, came from below.

She looked down into the courtyard and saw that there, all was confusion. Men were shouting, running this way and that, and all with one end, that of making their way out of the castle gate as quickly as they could. Orders were being shouted and, equally orders were ignored, all to the accompaniment of the high-pitched whinnying of the horses. Angry voices and recriminations filled the air, and chaos ruled. In no doubt however, was that Barud and his army were quitting the castle. It seemed that the king's plans had gone awry.

Tegwyn's concern now was for the safety of her father, who she could plainly see caught up in the frenzy. The king appeared to be pleading with Barud, while the other, his sword raised, tried to ignore him.

"But what of the alliance, Barud, that which Anfad and I swore together?"

"Alliance? Quiet your nonsense! Now, out of my way, before I ride you down!"

Taking their king's lead, Barud's men showed Tulrech even less respect. He was jostled and abused by many of them. One coarse oaf took hold of the king by his velvet doublet and bellowed into his face.

"We only came here to rumple your daughter, you old fool."

At these words the king raised his fist to strike him, but the man threw Tulrech to the ground. The others laughed cruelly, as his head struck the stone paving and he lay helpless, in a tangled heap. Seeing this, and forgetting her own plight, Tegwyn freed the door of her chamber and rushed to the aid of her father.

*

So began the first battle in the War of the Six Kingdoms, as it would later be called by the chroniclers. Not since the time of the Old Kings had blood been shed in the West. Melynas had since that time been known as the 'Kingdom of Peace', and so history had indeed changed. Now, King Barud of Techlyn led out his army to do battle with Prince Rhaldon of Irlas. Ranged on a slight rise beyond the castle, Rhaldon's troop waited for the onslaught. It was not to be long in coming. Barud, in his rage, was almost falling from his horse, as he shouted imprecations a plenty at his foe.

"Show them no mercy, men of Techlyn! They are only filthy peasants! A crock of gold to any man who brings down that fool of a prince!"

Waving their swords, flailing axes and hurling spears, the screaming mob of an army, made more frenzied by Barud's wild cries, threw themselves upon Rhaldon's troops. Resolutely did the men of Rhaldon withstand this onslaught. Their courage could not have been greater, but it was the will of Rhaldon that united them. Not one among them would have broken ranks and the charge by Barud's men was so disorderly that it was soon beaten back. Rhaldon's soldiers showed that, not only could they fight as stoutly as any troop, but that they possessed an innate discipline – invaluable in battle.

The few horsemen he had at his command, Rhaldon kept back until the last moment. He then ordered them to charge at Barud's foot soldiers on both flanks. Caught between this onslaught from two directions and unable to move forward, they were forced so tightly together it was impossible for them to engage with Rhaldon's men. So frustrated and maddened did they become, that they were soon fighting among themselves.

Rhaldon, seeing their confusion, shouted his orders above the melee. With an apparently practised precision, as one the front ranks of Rhaldon's men moved sideways. Suddenly freed from their constriction, Barud's men

177

rushed into this space, but were incapable of rallying when the back ranks of Rhaldon's army ran upon them fiercely and at great pace. The slaughter was immense. Barud's men fell like corn to the reaper. With growing horror, their king realised what was happening.

"Fall back! Fall back!"

This they did, abandoning the dead and the wounded that had fallen, and made a stumbling retreat. Harried and fearful, they clustered about Barud's knights. None had expected such stern resistance to their attack. Only a score of Rhaldon's men had fallen, while half of Barud's army lay dead and dying upon the field. The king surveyed the carnage with fevered eyes. His captain, suffering from a gaping wound in his shoulder, so that he could hardly ride, came up to him.

"My liege, what are we to do?"

"If we lose any more men, we shall be a pretty sight indeed when we come to stand with Anfad at Irlas."

About to faint and fall from his horse at any moment, the captain stared dumbly at his king as he issued his final order.

"Leave the dead and wounded. March out! We must be in Irlas by nightfall."

The captain, as if in a fevered dream, acknowledged this with a nod of his head. Somehow, Barud's men gathered themselves together into a troop shambled off, watched by Rhaldon and his men. Barud allowed himself a glance at the castle with its gates now firmly locked against them. He shook his fist, cursing both Tulrech and his daughter. Not daring to look back at the battlefield, his bitterness and humiliation was great.

Upon the rise, Rhaldon praised his men and they, in turn, cheered their leader. The first battle in the War of the Six Kingdoms had ended in a victory for Irlas. But, in his heart, Rhaldon knew this was only the beginning, and not the beginning of the end.

XIV

At the going down of the sun, the castle servants lit a great number of candles in the Great Hall. The oaken doors were then opened so that the knights might take their places within. Each man knew intimately where this was for there was a strict order of rank among the king's chosen fighting men. Those who had served the king for the longest time sat closest to their monarch, and their sons sat with them. Those who had chosen to follow the knightly calling, the unblooded knights, arranged themselves as best they could at the back of the hall, often with robust jostling. Such behaviour always amused the more venerable of the knights, who were reminded of their own youthful days.

As they arrived, all surrendered their arms to the stewards at the door. A formidable pile of weaponry soon began to amass by the entrance way. This custom had been established long ago, when fiery tempers among fighting men were less restrained. In even more far off days, it was not unusual for the king himself to subdue with mailed fists those who violated the peace of any warriors' gathering.

The squires of the knights did not attend these gatherings – at least, not usually. On this occasion, Hog had accompanied Derwen. The irascible knight had twisted an ankle, falling over some piece of armour in his quarters. Since dismissing his previous squire, Derwen had been living in some disarray, and it had been Hog's first task to restore order to the knight's chambers.

For this Derwen was gruffly grateful, so their association started off in the best possible way it could have done. Tonight, Hog had also to actually support Derwen as he hobbled into the Hall. Some of the knight's companions made to chaff him about his injury, but only the boldest were inclined to do so. Derwen did not take kindly to being the butt of jests, and it would have been unwise for any of them to have taken any such ribaldry too far.

All rose when the king entered the Great Hall. As they had been called together so quickly, the knights had little opportunity to discuss among themselves the reasons for the summons. None really knew, but when they saw the king, not in full armour, but unmistakably displaying the royal trappings of war, they realised what was to come. Brynan's opening words were all they needed to know. They must stiffen their sinews and speedily.

"I have brought you all here that you may listen to my words... and words of the greatest import. Deep treachery has come like a poisoned wound to the Six Kingdoms. Anfad of Durasglyn, Barud of Techlyn and Galar of Blauwyg have, as one, risen against us. They plan to steal the grain from the farmer, the land from the peasant and the gold from the merchant. Then to make slaves of the folk of Irlas."

At this, a murmur of astonishment from the assembled company began, turning quickly to a muted roar of anger.

"I Brynan, your king, tell you that they cannot succeed. Any enemy of ours will lie in his own blood before ever he may conquer Irlas."

A great cheer went up at that, and every knight raised his fist in allegiance to king and kingdom.

"The time has come, knights of this realm, to show that Irlas has the courage of the stag, along with the tenacity of the bear. We will strike too... and as the hawk. We may be mightily challenged... sorely tried even... but always shall we put our enemies to flight. For Irlas will ever be, not only the fairest of the Six Kingdoms of the West, but the proudest."

Brynan looked about him, and a profound silence fell upon the Hall and those within, such as had not been since the days of the Old Kings. It was as if those stern patriarchs were there watching, and their might was once again gathered to help in the coming fray. In those ancient days was the iron of Irlas forged; now it would be tested. Brynan could feel a tide surging about him, holding him up, pushing him onward. His voice rang out, as the voices of the old battle leaders of yore must so many times have done.

"Ride with me, my knights! We shall vanquish our enemies! If we must fight to the last man, then so be it! For we shall ever gain the victory!"

The knights roared their support, as if they would shake the rafters from the roof. The sound was deafening, and Brynan could only just make himself heard above the uproar.

"I vow to lead you my knights... into battle... that we may drive out this evil invader who dares to stand with such impudence at the gates of our kingdom... with every noble knight gathered here... we shall vanquish the foe... this will be the finest hour of the Kingdom of Irlas!"

Brynan ended his speech at a crescendo, and none could have better raised the spirit of Marak, the god of war, as the king had done. Brynan had sown the seeds of valour and courage in the heart of each and every one of them. The stewards were hard pressed to restrain the knights as they reclaimed their arms. They rushed out from the hall with a great clamour, the younger knights waving their swords in the air and singing lustily the songs of the ancient heroes and their great deeds.

In the streets, the citizenry gazed at the sight and, when the knights told them all, a tremor of pride went abroad in the town. By the next day this spirit had spread throughout the entire kingdom. In the huts on every hamlet, all were aware that the king had made a proclamation of war against the scoundrels that would wrong Irlas. The king had sworn to defend his people! No emotion goes so deep into the heart of a nation than that their king will lay down his life for them. The spirit of Irlas was alight and those flames grew higher and higher and were heard to roar throughout every corner of the kingdom.

*

Duly, at the noon hour the next day, all thronged the square. The merchants had announced they would cease to trade, the blacksmith let his forge go cool, and the potter and carpenter laid their tools down upon their benches. From every part of the kingdom, the people gathered. Many, as soon as they were told the news, left their homes and walked to Treflan through the night. A few womenfolk had insisted they be there, but most had remained behind to take care of babes and children. This fair gathering, in the way of women, had made themselves as comfortable as they could by the entrance to the castle.

The mood of the crowd was one of expectation mingled with not a little anxiety, for the news that war was approaching had now reached all ears. Exhilaration had given way to prudence, voices were subdued, and an air of unreality stole over all. All changed when Brynan rode out of the castle gates. The king was flanked by Derwen and Caled, the latter a knight who might have been Derwen's twin. Their dark looks and even darker horses contrasted dramatically with the king, set proudly upon the back of Teryngar.

Upon his brow was the thin gold crown that a monarch will wear when he rides into battle. His silver breastplate had upon it a golden sun, its rays splaying out such as the waves do upon the shore. Some would swear afterwards this sun had pulsated with a divine energy. Brynan's leather jerkin was edged with the tone of blue that only royalty may wear, and from his belt hung a sword, the hilt of which was emblazoned with emeralds and rubies. As they took in this magnificent sight, the crowd gasped and all stared in wonder. The trio drew up before the crowd, and the two knights flanking the king drew their swords and raised them on high.

"Behold, Huan Brynan, the High King of Irlas!"

This heralding, cried out in unison by Derwen and Caled, was the spark that ignited the crowd. They began to call out for Brynan, and some even called out words from the oath of loyalty – phrases that they remembered from his crowning. Still more beseeched the blessing of Nen to be upon the king. It seemed that with the departure of Wythen and the rallying of the knights, any animosity that might have lingered towards Brynan had vanished. Such is the way of the crowd – a fickle creature at best!

At the moment Brynan turned and looked upon his people, the sun appeared. It seemed the play was being directed by a divine hand. A white gold disc in the heavens, startling in its intensity, filled the entire square with brilliant light. The towers of the castle seemed to grow immense and stand proudly over the crowd, a mighty symbol of the king's power and protection. Below, their hearts overflowed with hope and pride, and Brynan could have chosen no better moment than this to address his subjects.

"As long as my heart beats within me... my love for you O people of Irlas, can never be taken from me. But this heart of mine is now heavy because of what has come to pass in the Land of the West. Irlas is a land of peace and abundance, of joy and fruitfulness. We are a contented people, yet it is not so in all our world. Kingdoms that border with our own envy our lands and wish to deprive us of them... Prince Anfad has formed an unholy alliance with King Barud and King Galar. They would bring evil upon Irlas."

183

Shouts of alarm and bitter cries greeted the king's words, but Brynan held up his hand for silence.

"Fear not, my people. Your king, Huan Brynan, shall defend you against all who would wish to do you harm. Any who seek to oppress a single man, woman or child of Irlas must know they stand against the king and must first defeat *him*. I swore as much when the crown was put upon my brow at the Seat of Mawrinol and, know ye, I will always abide by that royal oath."

A lone voice was heard from the crowd, almost singing.

"None can forget that day... a golden light was about the king... heaven blessed him... even the birds did sing..."

This prompted a great cheer and, as if on cue, many doves flew out from under the eaves of the Great Hall.

"It is said that the best method of defence is attack!" Brynan shouted. "We shall go out to fight these wolves, and we shall destroy them. Together we shall vanquish our foes!"

A great roar went up.

"I come to tell you that our army must assemble, weapons be gathered and we must go to war."

A sound even louder than before came from the crowd.

"Be of brave heart, my people. It is the duty of your king and his knights... the duty to those we love and to the ancestors that we must go to war. We must fight, as the men of Irlas always have done, to defend our kingdom. We fight not just for ourselves, this is a struggle twixt liberty and tyranny... right and wrong... good and evil. With those men who follow me I shall lead Irlas to victory. Now will you who are men-at-arms march out with me on the morrow?"

The noise the crowd made was deafening. All arms were raised, and a great sea of clenched fists was to be seen. By the castle walls the women held their peace. It was not for them to cheer and be glad. All women see into the hearts of men. One old crone was muttering to herself in a melancholy whisper.

"There are neither good men nor bad – just men. And come the morrow, many will not return to their wives and children. And that loss will be the burden of women as always."

Other voices joined in with her.

"Perhaps it will change."

"Let us hope so. Let us pray for that day."

Nearby a man in a green and yellow cloak was pointing at the sky, where far off an eagle could be seen. He cried out to those around him.

"There... look you... the eagle of victory!"

The old crone could only see the ravens that had also gathered about the sky, making ready to garner the souls of the dead.

XV

When Rhaldon came into the courtyard of Melynas castle, a gaggle of servants were gathered about the door. He came down from his horse and strode up to them. At first, they quailed at such a stern presence. Their fears became mere puzzlement when they heard the words he spoke to them.

"Peace! I mean you no harm. I am a farmer, not a warrior. Where abides King Tulrech and the Princess Tegwyn?"

One of their number, less timorous than his fellows, answered.

"I am Waymeld, the Chief Steward. The princess attends the king in his chamber. Those cowardly rogues struck my master down, curse them."

"More than a few of them have also been struck down, if that gives you any pleasure, Master Waymeld. Now, lead me to the kin, if you will."

The steward hesitated for a moment, so dazed he was by the events of the last few hours, but he roused himself and duly led the way into the castle. Rhaldon followed him up a short flight of stone steps to a chamber where the Royal apartments lay. The steward knocked upon the door. There was no response at first, but finally a woman's voice, clear and commanding, was heard.

"Who is there? Speak."

"My lady, Prince Rhaldon would speak with you. He wishes to enquire of the king's health."

The reply was less than encouraging.

"Prince Rhaldon? I know him not. Who is he?"

Rhaldon spoke up.

"I am the brother of King Brynan."

Silence followed this announcement. Rhaldon could imagine the deliberations of the princess within. Finally she spoke again.

"Tell the prince he may enter, steward."

The door into the chamber was slowly opened by a handmaiden who, it seemed, was helping to nurse the king. His majesty lay upon a couch, his head bandaged, though he appeared to be taking in all around him. Immediately he addressed Rhaldon, in none too friendly a tone.

"So, you are the brother of he who is called Brynan. I suppose the kingdom must be grateful to you for seeing off that villain, Barud. But know this – Melynas is still no longer the ally of Irlas. The insults we have borne from your king cannot be forgiven."

Rhaldon saw the fierce glance that Tulrech gave his daughter, while also seeing that she did not quail beneath his gaze.

"I know nothing of the offences that you mention. I spoke with my brother Brynan but a few days ago. I had no doubt then that he intended to act honourably towards the kingdom of Melynas, and I see no reason to change that impression. It was he who requested me to defend your kingdom against any invader. In its history, the kingdom of Irlas has never had quarrel with Melynas, neither have we now with its present king ..."

Here Rhaldon bowed in the direction of the princess.

"...or his fair daughter."

Tegwyn blushed fleetingly at the compliment. She had been studying the prince. Despite the obvious resemblance to her former lover, which gave her a slight resentment, she knew her feelings towards Rhaldon were cordial. She spoke accordingly.

"Come, father, we should only offer our thanks to the prince for vanquishing a king who revealed himself as, not an ally of Melynas, but its foe. Our kingdom recognises a true ally in you, Prince Rhaldon. Please accept our thanks for all you and your men have done."

Rhaldon bowed once more.

"Willingly do I accept your thanks. And I am also most glad to see that no serious ill has befallen you."

King Tulrech appeared slightly gratified. He then proceeded to groan once or twice, in an exaggerated manner. His desire was to regain the attentions of his daughter. He perceived, quite correctly, that they had strayed too much in the direction of the prince. Rhaldon, for his part, thought the princess most fair, but also realised that certain matters were at this moment more pressing.

"King Tulrech, you have an army?"

The king replied with a certain comical dignity.

"Melynas has always maintained a fighting force."

"Indeed, and by all accounts a brave one. It would seem, for the sake of our two kingdoms, that you might have them assembled and given to march into Irlas to fight in this coming war."

This was too bold. The king almost roared out a reply.

"My men... fight for Irlas? What jest is this? What do I care for your kingdom? I was never fond of your father, a most difficult man, and Melynas cannot be involved in some domestic dispute. I refuse to entertain such an idea."

A silence ensued, broken only by the laboured breathing of the king. Rhaldon glanced at Tegwyn and their eyes met, not as yet in great affection, but a common purpose. Their determination was fuelled by the Divine Will, a force which brooks no opposition. It was this that made Tegwyn be resolute.

"Father, if you will not agree to do so, then I will lead our army."

Tulrech sat upright, to the great concern of the maiden attending him.

"Daughter, are you mad? What are you saying?"

"Did not my dream warn us of coming dangers, father? Now it is my heart that tells me Melynas must fight in this war that is bound to come... nay already with us. It is only right that Melynas, having been delivered by Prince Rhaldon, should in its turn go to the aid of Irlas. We must set aside old quarrels, be they ancient or more recent... this is not the time. If we do not act now, then it will be too late, and the Land of the West will suffer, perhaps in a way that can never be healed. I vow that I shall go with Prince Rhaldon as soon as my horse can be made ready."

King Tulrech stared in disbelief, then finally found his voice.

"Tegwyn, I forbid you to do this. Oh, how your mother would have rued this day that her daughter could even think of such a foolish thing."

Tegwyn answered her father coolly.

"I am certain my mother would have been proud of me, and I feel her spirit urging me onward. You, father, must do that which you feel to be right. I go to fight for Melynas... *as a warrior woman and as a mother* !"

The features of the king reflected horror and confusion in equal measure. After a while they assumed a certain resignation. Prince and princess stood together waiting for Tulrech to speak. When he did so, his voice had now assumed a tone of humility.

"Tegwyn, I ask you to forgive me..."

"There is really nothing to forgive, father..."

The king raised a gentle hand.

"Let me continue, I beg of you. Indeed you are right... your dear mother *is* with us at this moment... she watches over the kingdom and, indeed the world in all its travails, as she always did. I have acted foolishly, as old men sometimes do, and I am ashamed. Truly, I have no quarrel with Irlas or this brave prince who stands before us. I ask his pardon and yours also."

Tegwyn then went to her father, knelt before him and clasped his hand to her lips. He in his turn stroked her head with deep affection.

"One thing I have decided, however. You shall not go to war..."

Tegwyn looked up, questioningly.

"...without your father! I feel a new strength within me at this moment. Let us ride out and rid our lands of these evildoers! When again I set eyes on that Barud, I shall box his ears. Call the steward, gather our men, we shall set out at dawn on the morrow."

King Tulrech, fired with noble resolve anew, threw back the coverlet that had been over him and marched out of the chamber, followed by the anxious maid. Rhaldon took the opportunity to discreetly draw the princess aside.

"I think it wise that you are not to go to war. You serve Loenel better by being a mother to your child, as she is a mother to us all."

The princess lowered her eyes.

"It is true. You see more than other men it seems, Prince Rhaldon. I believe your perceptions to be as keen as your courage. I trust you as I do the rising of the sun."

The prince clasped her hand gently but tellingly, and thrilling to his touch, Tegwyn did not draw away. Neither did the princess question his wise words.

*

Hog had risen with the dawn. All was being made ready for the coming day of battle. Derwen had a reputation for being unforgiving of those who made any mistakes. Thus Hog, though he had gone over every part of the knight's equipment a dozen times, was busy making sure that nothing had been forgotten. To his great relief, when

Derwen strode into the chamber the knight found no fault with all the preparations that had been made. Gathering all together, Hog followed Derwen into the square to join the others assembling there. What a grand sight it was! Hog felt proud to be part of such a day though, deep in the pit of his stomach, a knot of anxiety had formed, one that would never quite go away.

At the sound of the herald's horn, the army of Irlas marched out of Treflan. The king was at their head, some three score of knights following behind him, and after that the captains, marshalling many score of foot soldiers. It was an impressive sight. Irlas was greatly proud of its nobility, its stock being of the fiercest warriors of the Old Era. The blood of heroes ran within the ranks of the men at arms, too, which was as well, for much would depend upon them also. A man on horseback has the advantage over the foot soldier, but it is the foot soldier who must engage with the enemy hand to hand.

All were in good spirits as they marched along, occasionally the ranks even burst into the old songs – ones that told of valorous deeds long ago. Over the years, little of the history of Irlas had ever been set down in writing, but much lore had been preserved in lyric. These tales of valiant men and their exploits had been passed down from generation to generation. As the family gathered about the fireside in the depths of Rhagel, grandfathers would delight their grandchildren with the exploits of Gwaed and Cledd, the warrior brothers, while the girls clamoured for stories of Degbryd, the Fairy King.

The lusty singing stopped abruptly when Brynan called the knights to a halt. The horses were left to graze, while men took their ease upon the ground.

The king knew that the Plain of Lanerch would be the scene of battle, and the army had been mustered on what little high ground there was there. The banners of Irlas were unfurled. Brynan, remembering the Temple of

Rhimlais, had insisted that the old standard of Irlas, depicting two golden serpents entwined together, was prominently displayed.

As always at the season of Hafwan, the sun was low even at noon. The king looked out over the plain. On the way, they had ridden past fields where the corn had recently been harvested. The earth, as always, was oblivious to the doings of men, simply waiting patiently to begin another cycle of growth. Unlucky Brynan! Before him stretched a land that would soon yield a more bitter harvest, one of strife and sorrow.

On top of the chain mail he had about his shoulders, Derwen wore armour plates, each fashioned to resemble a ram's head. He stood now beside the king, his dark features more grim than ever, as if he himself had become Marak, the God of War. The presence of that deity was felt by many in the ranks that forenoon. Above the field of battle, the god might have been seen honing a cruel blade, his taut limbs showing the intensity of his task as he readied himself for the impending storm. Marak had always been known to pour scorn upon those who were not bold. To the craven-hearted, the only reward he gave was one of fear and terror.

"My liege! The army of Blauwyg approaches from the south. They are but five furlongs distant. King Galar is with them."

Both king and knight stared at the approaching scout whose cries they heard afar off.

"Is Galar riding at their head?" Brynan asked.

"Nay, my liege," the scout said. "Some at the front of his army hold a banner, but the king is at the rear."

Derwen was suddenly alert.

"That means he has no hunger for battle!" the knight exclaimed. "Why else would he hang back like a lame dog? It is said that in the whole of Galar's kingdom, only a handful of hotheads desired to join with Anfad in this campaign, the rest of his people wished it not."

"Then we have the advantage in this first encounter," Brynan observed.

Derwen put a hand to his helm.

"Only if we strike this moment, as they are still marching... before they can group their knights... that is if they have any worthy of that name..."

The scout told that he had seen accompanying Galar's men-at-arms, less than a score of men on horseback. Brynan summoned his captains and made known his orders.

"Wait until all of them come into view... then let us swiftly make our move..."

Derwen nodded silently in agreement and stroked his sword haft.

"...tell the knights they are to form into three groups. Derwen will lead on the left, Caled the right, I will take the centre. Make all wheel around to a point twixt north and east, that will make our charge shorter and we will also strike them at the weakest place in their company. Let none move until my command is given. Go! Quickly now! "

The captains rode away to pass on the king's instructions. The knights had already mounted, the men held their weapons ready for the coming fray. Brynan continued to look towards the south.

"They must take the way that runs from the north across the plain. We shall see them before they see us, as soon as we do we shall ride out."

The king could feel the tension in the air. He was reminded of those days when he went a-hunting with his father, when the two of them waited for the game to spring a snare. This was far greater sport, he knew that, and the prize one he must win – that of freedom. All was still. Not a man in his entire army moved the smallest step. The horses' hooves seemed fixed to the earth. Brynan could hear the sound of his own heartbeat. Over the rise came King Galar's army. They had hardly time to see the banner the men of Irlas had raised before Brynan's voice rang out, loud enough for every man in both armies to hear.

"Men of Irlas! This is the hour! Stand together! All as brothers!"

Huan Brynan drew his sword and held it aloft. All saw the glistering brilliance of the blade, and felt within them the strength of the hand that held it. At once all their hearts were made bold, their sinews stiff with resolve. This was their leader, their King and, to some it may be said, their god. They would fight for him until the last. They would die for him if need be, though no man at that moment believed he would ever feel the icy breath of Angaz, the God of Death, upon him. As they go into battle, all warriors believe themselves to be invincible. The men of Irlas looked upon their king as immortal, and thus they became immortal with him.

"Now! Onward, knights of Irlas! Onward for the Kingdom!"

The king's words were still echoing across the plain as they began to charge, the foot soldiers following in their wake. The gap between the two armies closed far too quickly for Galar's troops to put themselves in any order. Moments before, their horsemen had been riding alongside the soldiery, exchanging banter with them and being far from alert. When they realised all that was happening, it was too late. As Galar's horsemen turned, they upset their own men to right and left. The curses of the soldiers added to the mayhem. Galar shouted orders and cursed the most, but the damage was irretrievably done.

The knights of Irlas fell upon the undefended ranks of foot soldiers and hewed great gaps in their ranks. None could withstand so savage an attack and, when the knights had ridden through their lines, they turned about and rode back through them again, hacking down all they could see before them. As the army of Galar started to flail this way and that – doing anything to avoid the stinging blades of the horsemen – the foot soldiers of Irlas were then upon them. With axe and sword did they cut at their enemy and showed them no mercy. Galar's knights retaliated as well as they might but, outnumbered by Brynan's own, and shaken to the core by the slaughter all around them, many quickly fell.

Derwen fought with incredible ferocity, in the first assault felling two knights with a single blow. Brynan slew another and he could see, either side of him, many of Galar's knights tumbling from their horses. Sword clashed against shield, and the rustle of chain mail was as the sound of the waves atop some bloody tide.

In the midst of all, rode Galar, parrying blow after blow that was aimed at him. Soon his army was so sore pressed that, realizing nothing could be gained from prolonging the battle, the king called to those knights that remained. Together they rode from the field. Most of his men now lay dead or dying and those that were still standing fled frantically in Galar's wake. Some of Brynan's army, drunk with the taste of blood, began to pursue them, but the king called out to leave this helpless quarry be. The day had been more than a defeat, it had quickly become a rout. Brynan could afford to be generous, and considered there had been quite enough killing for one day.

Some way from the field, Galar, being satisfied that they were not being pursued, slowed his horse.

"What fools were Barud and Anfad to say an easy victory was before us! Angaz curse the pair of them, if he has not thrown them into some dark pit already! What foolishness persuaded me to be part of this?"

Galar set his horse for Blauwyg, but he never did return there, for he was murdered by one of his own knights. He who killed the king had lost his brother in the battle, and blamed Galar for the young man's death. Thus, by the hand of one of his own, died the king of Blauwyg, leaving no heir to his kingdom. Such a dark deed was an omen of what was to follow in this, the most bitter of wars.

Only three of the knights of Irlas had fallen. One of the horses had been so badly wounded it had to be despatched. Less than a score of Brynan's infantry had perished. A few were bloodied, but they made light of their wounds. The mood of Brynan's men was one of triumph and celebration while their king was inclined to be more sober concerning the outcome of the day. He wished to share his thoughts with Derwen and finding him wiping clean his sword upon the grass, the king took him aside.

"I do not believe there will be another battle this day, but the morrow will be very different. Anfad will most certainly come at us then, and we will also have Barud to contend with, whatever has come to pass with him in Melynas. I trust that my brother will come to our aid at some hour, hopefully before it is too late. We shall be hard pressed against two armies, and Anfad's men have only a short march from Durasglyn. It will be a dawn battle."

Derwen sheathed his sword and faced the king.

"What would you have us do?"

"We must make camp tonight, ready for the morrow. I am moved to have our army proceed to Gornest."

"Gornest! That is a fair march for men who have just fought."

"I know that, Derwen, yet if any place will give us an advantage it is there. Consider, we will have our backs to the forest, and I do not believe either of our enemies would try to advance through those trees. Putting ourselves at the head of the Valley of Gornest will also give us the advantage. We may see from a long way off those who try to advance upon us from any direction."

Derwen had to agree with this strategy, and straightway took it upon himself to inform the other knights of the king's plans. While he did this, Brynan asked one of the captains to gather the soldiery together, that their king might address them. After a short time they began to assemble. Some walked proudly, some wearily shuffled into place, some even lay exhausted on the ground, but all gladly came together to hear the words of their king.

"Men of Irlas, you have fought like the heroes of old! Victory has been yours! The kingdom and your king is proud of you!"

A ragged cheer went up from the massed ranks before him. Brynan sensibly made do with a brief speech. A soldier likes to be praised for his prowess; he does not take so well to a lecture upon military tactics, or a sermon debating the morality of war.

Later, the king instructed his captains to see that there would be pasties and ale enough to give out after the march to Gornest. Then he surveyed the fallen and ordered that a modest pyre be made of the bodies. How tall a pyre would there be, he wondered, after the morrow?

Then Huan Brynan turned away from the field of battle. The King of Irlas wished to be alone. He walked for some time, till he could see in the distance the edge of the plane. The sun, behind a bank of slate grey cloud was of a deep rose edged with flaming gold. He tried to impress every detail of this sight upon his mind. He prayed that such a vision of beauty should be passed on, in some manner, to gladden the hearts of those who might come after him.

XVI

Paldarch knew his destiny demanded he make a pilgrimage into sacred lands. Battles for supremacy might be fought by others upon the earthly plane, but his path lay along the ways of magic. He would act, with due reverence to the divine powers, as he felt was right. That was all he could do, for he was still mortal man. Even if the struggle he anticipated was within himself then so be it – that was where the drama must be played out.

To gain a sight of this secret kingdom, he must pass through the northern edge of the Forest of Galtrin, and to the Marshes of Morfan beyond. These wetlands were shunned by all in Irlas, save for a few hunters of waterfowl. In their very centre was Ranweld, the place where magic continued to dwell and always would. Here Paldarch must enter the Otherworld, perhaps never to return. A wizard does not dwell upon his fate he accepts all, from beginning to end. If creation now saw fit to put Paldarch in a place where he would be poised between life and death, then so be it.

Confident that Irlas would survive the war, Paldarch had entrusted his horse to a steward in the castle at Treflan and, after swearing him to secrecy, confided that Brynan would ride Teryngar into battle. To this end, the wizard had spoken long with his loyal steed, for a man of magic has no difficulty in conversing with any living creature. Teryngar had listened intently, and then nestled his majestic head against the wizard's shoulder. Thus an understanding was reached, though Paldarch could not bear to meet Teryngar's questing eye when he left the stables.

Well before dawn Paldarch had silently left the castle in Treflan. After crossing the square he passed the dwellings in the centre of the town, the more humble huts on the outskirts, and entered the woods. Grasping his staff as he walked, Paldarch thought how fine was the air, and the ever-changing pattern of light that came through the trees gave him endless joy.

By noon he was looking out over the flatlands towards Ranweld. Here he had journeyed many times whilst he was learning of the secret arts. At Ranweld, under the watchful eye of his master, he had performed his first rituals. Now, as he walked, he took joy in every twist and turn of the way, playing a game with himself, pretending he had never seen these things before. In a sense this was true, for today, he was seeing all through new eyes. Paldarch took in the verdant grasslands and the immensity of the sky. The clouds were so low they seemed almost to kneel upon the earth.

Crows massed above him, whirling scrawls of dark ink on blue parchment. Trees, bent by the wind, stood crookedly by pools that resembled the shards of a broken mirror. Swans gathered among the endless reeds and suddenly the way became boggy. Paldarch was careful to keep to the paths that he knew of old. Surrounded by a cluster of twisted elder trees lay a mound that formed a miniature island in the marshes, while upon it stood a heron, graceful and erect.

This was indeed Ranweld, a place he had not visited for many a year, and Paldarch knew his quest must soon reach its end. He recalled the stone slab that was here and began to search for it. Unsuccessful at first, he persisted and soon, beneath a layer of matted grass, he discovered the stony seat. He laid his cloak upon it, fixed his staff into the soft earth, and sat upon his improvised throne. Closing his eyes and entering a world of deep meditation, Paldarch waited for whatever would befall him there.

It did not take long for an image to form in his mind. It was of the ring of stones that stood atop the Tower of Gafryd in Durasglyn. Standing in the very centre of these,

199

Paldarch recognised the figure of Gwirel. She was clothed in a blue and silver robe, and held a staff of gold entwined with lace that was as the black of night. She was as Paldarch remembered her, when they had known each other in their youth.

"Open your eyes, O wizard, and look upon me!"

The voice was all around Paldarch, within him and without. It would have made little difference if his eyes had been open or closed, for now only the realm of magic existed in that sacred place. Any who ventured into Ranweld would have seen no trace of all this. Even the cloak and staff that Paldarch had discarded had now passed into the Otherworld.

"I look upon you now, Gwirel, once my priestess, always the keeper of the secret way!"

Gwirel smiled, and the sun and moon met in the heavens. Her voice was as the song of the universe, the celestial music that causes the stars to shine and infinity to reign.

"Let fire from above, and water from below, now be in union together and create the timeless firmament. There we shall dwell together."

Now they stood upon the void, and together walked upon pure air. Their voices lifted in harmony, the resonance of which was more moving than any celestial choir. The words they spoke were beyond meaning, too sacred to ever be uttered by those who were not of the magical faith. Gwirel put away her staff and, at the same time, her robe parted to reveal she was bedecked in a lilac gown that splayed out around her. She looked as if her being was created entirely from the colours of the dawn.

A chalice, laced with crystal, appeared in her hands and she raised it high, an offering to god and goddess. Paldarch knew he was in that place where to walk upon the seas, to stand among shifting tides – and never once fall – was a commonplace. He and his companion were absorbed by the rhythm of ocean and mountain and at one with all creation. Truly, Paldarch now knew all there was to know. Great was the power of the Priestess! Now from out of this realm of pure silence, he heard the voice of Gwirel. The pure tone echoed the Goddess, that sound which, with eternal light, had first brought life to the galaxies.

"Let love flow down and around us, let it descend from the skies and give wisdom to the earth beneath."

Paldarch could feel once more the stone beneath him. He had returned to this world. A profound sadness overtook him, but only for an instant, for there before him stood Gwirel! Her feet were bare upon the grass, her arms were held aloft, and her eyes shone with radiance.

To the wizard, she was a temple maiden once more, and he a youthful magus in a velvet coat. Then, her hair had been as a raven's wing, glistening rose and carnelian her eyes, and the stars played within and all around them. Her lips were as coral upon the seas. She came to him, and he felt her hand upon his. He had known the touch of no other woman in all his days. Their union had been as constant as the rocks at the tide's edge, timeless and unending.

"Yes, Paldarch, I loved you," Gwirel whispered. "Long were the hours we spent in each other's arms. Many were the sweet words we exchanged. Those times were precious. Were they not so for you?"

Paldarch looked upon Gwirel, the love he felt for her having no bounds.

"I cannot deny it, ever were they most blissful, and I would wish that our love could now bring peace to a world at war."

"Alas, our own powers upon this earth wane. A New Age begins... it is for the Goddess to decide these things."

Paldarch sighed and Gwirel could see that he was troubled, even as he spoke.

"Are there no good men at all in the world? None who are noble and true? Never a hero that walked upon the divine path and did not stray from it?"

Gwirel put her head upon his breast, while speaking softly.

"You are a man, Paldarch, but you are not like other men."

Paldarch sighed once more, ever deeper.

"I am a man of magic, it is that which separates me from my fellows."

"But you have been touched by the Goddess. Any man who has such fortune is never as before. You are aware of the ways of me – your priestess – that is why she loves and respects you."

"Aye, perhaps it is only a magician who can truly know a priestess; it seems a king cannot ever hope to."

"You mean Wythen, our daughter?"

"Indeed," Paldarch replied. "But perhaps Brynan has now more to occupy him in this world than finding, and losing, the love of a handmaiden of the Goddess."

"He has not lost her love... he will find it again in the next world."

"That I know, and it consoles me a little. But there is a darker side to the coin. Now Brynan must wrestle with your son..."

"Anfad..." Gwirel whispered, and sat up, looking out into the land of Ranweld. Here was no time or indeed any situation. That was the nature of magic; it existed away from the world. But on occasion worlds collide and when that happens, all is changed. It was here in Ranweld that Gwirel, as a young virgin, had encountered Cythras, the Dark One. Alone and defenceless, he had taken her, not entirely against her will, and the fruit of that union had been Anfad.

"He is my shadow, Paldarch, as Wythen is the light. It is the strangeness of fate, that while we two have devoted our

202

lives to bringing light into the world, Anfad now brings death and suffering to that same world."

Paldarch, with some reluctance, freed himself from Gwirel's embrace.

"I cannot allow that prince to bring about such things," he said. "To destroy the Kingdom of Irlas would be to end all nobility. That which shone in the Old Era, I believe, should be preserved for others who will come. That is my belief, and it cannot be altered. "

Gwirel looked on as Paldarch grasped his staff and stood as tall as the very skies. She heard his voice, as of old, determined and forceful.

"I have known chaos and night all too well. I have struggled with the darkness much of my days; another battle will make little or no difference to me."

Out of the stuff of the air an image began to appear, as the sudden appearance of a figure in a mist will surprise a traveller. Paldarch could now see, suspended in the space above him, the Sword of Pengyron. He stared at the vision as if in a trance, his hands outstretched to grasp what he could so clearly see. Gwirel called out to him; there was a pleading in her voice.

"Paldarch, my love, return to me. That path is no longer for you! Your will has ebbed to nothing, as the stream that has run dry in its season. Come back!"

But Paldarch hurried on. To him, it seemed that the Sword was but a little way off, but, as he drew up to it and tried to clutch the haft, it seemed to retreat from him. The wizard took another step forward, and again the Sword moved away. In desperation, Paldarch began to run towards his prize and, to his horror, the vision of the Sword began to fade. Then it came again!

The wizard, try as he might, could not make his tired limbs move any faster. He tried to run but stumbled and fell heavily. He used his staff to raise himself and, having succeeded, he watched helplessly as the sword disappeared to nothing. At the same time, he could hear a voice close to him, though when he turned in the direction from where it came, no one was there.

"The Sword of Pengyron is no longer in your keeping Paldarch. The Goddess has decreed that another must own it...."

"Gwirel! This is your doing. Do you not realise that it is only the Sword that may keep the darkness from conquering all?"

The answer came, but the words were as if caught upon the wind.

"The Sword may be used for many purposes, and not only in the way that you think. How we believe the world should be is not always the way it must be."

"I beg of you Gwirel, listen to me. Your talk is all riddles within riddles. "

"Uncertainty is all we have, Paldarch. You cannot read creation as if it were a merchant's docket."

The wizard's appeal to her was desperate.

"I have tried to keep man from fighting man all my days. Will he never be given a chance to right his wrongs? Who can say that we might not again know an age of kings that is golden with peace and concord? The struggle we have is against the darkness within us. The enemy is ourselves – only when we conquer that, can we win."

Gwirel's answer – when it came – was as the judgment of Angaz, changeless and final.

"The time of discord and conflict is near its end. The Goddess is now ready to return. She awaits only the end of the last battle between the kings. Their Age – of which you still to speak -- is forever gone. No longer will be heard the sound of sword against sword, shield against shield. Discord will end and harmony rule. The Waters of the West are building and soon will rush into the world with the mighty Goddess at the head of the tide."

Paldarch struggled to keep his balance upon the earth, he was falling once more. He knew he would never rise again.

"No, no," he heard himself saying. "All grows dim. Am I to drown in this tide?"

"All must be dark before the light returns."

Paldarch, though he blinked and rubbed his eyes, could no longer see any forms. All had become a colourless haze. He closed his eyes, and in his inner mind saw a vision. A hawk filled the sky, its talons gripping the crest of the mountains, its wings blotting out the sun. There was a rush of mighty winds and the air was filled with the feathers that covered the bird's eternal form.

The wizard knew that his life was now held only by the thinnest of threads, and soon even this would break. He did not cry out for mercy, for he knew that none would be offered. Soon no part of him would remain – even to witness that which he saw. His life upon this plane was about to end. Paldarch would soon be a spirit, and that only. Of this he had no choice.

He opened his eyes for one last time in this world and looked into the heavens. The sky suddenly seemed to fall upon him – as if an enormous weight was forcing him down into the very earth. He fell to his knees, then upon his back. He lay on the thick grass of the moor, his cloak spread about him, his magic staff useless and abandoned by his side. Then, all that was about him began to disappear. Trees, distant hills, the horizon, all were whirled away, until he was aware of nothing that remained.

Now he found it difficult to breathe, his lungs, desperate for air, pained his chest and he made strange gasping sounds. None would ever hear them. The wizard could feel the sweat gathering on his brow and his heart pounding within him. To faint was inevitable, and as he did so, his hands made one last gesture of appeal before they lay limp upon the damp of the moor. The earth, that element often so scorned, would have the final judgment.

Paldarch left the material world and felt himself falling further and further into what seemed an endless void. The darkness was like none he had ever encountered before, a clinging blackness that gave no sense of here, there, or indeed, above or below. Incapable of thought, his mind was numb with such endless motion. Only a single feeling remained to him, some instinct at the very core of his being – a speck of understanding, given to him by an ancient hand, some god beyond time, one who had bestowed this seed of the infinite into the deeps of his soul. He knew with a certainty, beyond all mortal wisdom, that it was not Angaz who would meet him at the end of this final journey. This was not Death.

And so he continued into the abyss – without fear, without hope, but no longer with any anxiety. An acceptance of the divine order, a total surrender to fate, he had. The destiny of Paldarch had been decided by the heavens before he had been born into the world. A mere interlude before he continued upon his chosen path – the blink of an eye in the face of Time. Paldarch realised that he was giving up of his entire self to the whim of whatever forces mastered him. That same power now guided him to the gate he must pass through. In a rush of light, his magical personality was taken from him, but what he was to gain would be even greater.

XVII

Brynan woke to the sound of doves murmuring in the trees beyond the camp. It seemed a strange music to herald a day of battle, but he knew only too well that the goddess Cyngerl had never concerned herself with the ways of men. Brynan threw aside the rough blanket that covered him, realising he was stiff from the chill of the night. The dew upon the ground was also cold but he was grateful to feel its touch upon his face.

Behind him, the wind thrummed in the trees. The topmost branches shook sending showers of twigs below. The king looked out over the valley, where a sliver of gold was rising over the hills – a false dawn. Rain had fallen in the night, and the clouds were already descending upon the distant hills to make an array of differing shades of blue. As long as the storm kept back until noon... all might be over by then.

But it would prove not be so.

Before he had lain down to sleep the previous night, the king had prayed to Nen. He had asked to be kept from fear and pain. In the morning light, he reflected on what an empty plea that was. What else does war offer but pain and fear? It was likely that most of his army had prayed to one god or another or fingered amulets and charms. He doubted that any had confronted Angaz. All men in war simply hope for death to pass them by, or if not, for that end to be swift.

He had dreamed, too, of Anfad and Wythen, walking upon the battlefield hand in hand. The image had so troubled him that he woke in a cold sweat. He had prayed once more then, this time to the Goddess asking for rest. His prayers were answered: he slept until the dawn. Now he could hear the camp coming to life, and the captains ensuring that all were able to break their fast. Supplies had been brought in from the surrounding countryside, so that at least none would go out to battle on an empty stomach. He saw Derwen approaching carrying a platter in each hand.

"Have you any appetite this morn, my liege?"

Brynan surveyed the bacon and bread offered him and his stomach gave its approval.

"It seems I do have a good appetite, Derwen."

"This may be our last meal in this world, my liege. So let us enjoy it."

Each drew their dagger and set to. No sooner had they finished their meal than a scout rode up to the king.

"What news?"

"Anfad approaches from the east, Barud from the south. Both will be upon us before the noon hour."

The scout hesitated as if not wishing to impart any more tidings.

"Is that all?"

"There is word that many Northmen are gathering beyond the forest. If they make haste, they will be here by the forenoon also."

Derwen cursed loudly.

"The Northmen! They never leave their stinking dens unless there is something to plunder. Anfad has promised them much treasure, no doubt. Three armies against us, my liege! A pity your wizard is not here to work his sorcery now!"

Brynan felt strangely calm. He had, on the other side of the valley, noticed the last wisps of the moon. This gentle vision of the Goddess was fast disappearing as the sun came once more to rule the sky, but it had been an omen. The king was lost in silence and Derwen wondered if he had heard all the scout had said. The knight was about to question him to this end when Brynan suddenly gave orders to one of his captains, in tones that spoke of his resolve.

"Let the men finish breakfasting in peace. Tell the captains to let them gather their arms and I will speak with them soon enough."

Derwen appeared grim.

"Take care not to tell them that they are outnumbered three to one or they may flee back to their huts."

Brynan was in no mood for such talk.

"Never have I shirked from telling my people the truth, Derwen, and I do not intend to do so now. The warriors of Irlas long ago would have thought it only greater sport to face such odds. Nen will be with us... and I believe, also Loenel."

Derwen went off to make ready his horse and perhaps chide Hog a little. He wondered briefly at the words of the king, but did not seek to question them. Neither did the army of Irlas who, as Brynan had predicted, merely cheered their king the louder when he told them of the battle ahead.

"Let it be that when our children's children come to talk of us here in years to come, they will say that we stood fast against our enemies and never once did we think of surrender."

As the forenoon wore on, both knights and men-at-arms stood by, waiting for the first assault. It would not be long in coming, but what would occur, not even the wisest seer could have predicted.

*

Surrounded by the remnants of his army, King Barud lounged indolently in the saddle. His mood was not of the best, particularly as he had just received word that Galar and his men had abandoned the cause and departed for Blauwyg. As yet, there was no sign of Anfad, and so he had been forced to make a decision as to how to play his hand. His inclination was to put his army out of sight and wait for Anfad's men to arrive. Having ordered his scouts to spy out the land, he had, on their findings, decided to lie low with his men in a nearby valley.

The Carrug valley had been so named as to mean 'strife' in the old tongue. Some fell deed among men, now long forgotten, had happened there. The minstrels often sang of the place and spun tales of a time when giants ruled and, at their peril, warriors fought with them. It was said that to defeat a giant might only make one a very temporary hero, for the victor often ran the risk, at a later date, of being torn to pieces by the giant's comrades. But the day of the giants was now long gone, or so the people believed.

Barud led his men between two rock pillars that made a narrow entrance into the valley. From there they descended to the valley floor and huddled in that sunless place, many grumbling loudly. Barud perhaps complained the most, for he had no notion of how long they must wait for Anfad's men to appear. The king was in no mood to face Brynan's army alone. Having been soundly beaten by Rhaldon's army he was not anxious to risk another defeat at the hands of his brother. So they waited, getting colder and more miserable by the moment, while the scouts kept watch as best they could for any sighting of Prince Anfad.

Barud suddenly shivered, not a common occurrence for one so amply bestowed with flesh. He was certain, too, that the air had suddenly become damp, though there appeared to be no sign of rain in the skies. A mist began to rise from the floor of the valley, an eerie white vapour that eddied about the ankles of his troops.

There was little that Barud could do to allay their anxieties, and he was not willing to quit the valley, either. Uncomfortable it might have been there, but at least they were out of danger, or so he thought. The king had to admit that all was becoming more dank by the moment.

The jerkins of the men were now dripping with water. The mist, too, was becoming thicker and was rising higher. Now it was difficult for any of them to actually see each other, and many of his army were in a state of panic.

Barud decided that he, at least, would not be enveloped by this milky cloud. Abandoning his men, he clambered up the path towards the valley entrance where he could be free from those clinging wraiths. Below him all was hidden, nothing but a vast pale blanket could be seen. Barud looked around him and was astonished to see a figure standing between the rock pillars dressed in a silver shift with a blue circlet about her brow. The maiden might have appeared to be slight, but even Barud could feel she owned an aura of tremendous power. He called out to her in a voice dulled by the mist.

"Who are you?"

"I am Wythen, handmaiden of the Goddess. Take one final look at the world, O king, for you and your company will not live to see the setting of the sun."

Barud could not believe his ears and shouted coarsely back at her.

"What! You threaten me, you impudent wench. Wait until I come there! I believe you need to be taught some manners."

Barud started up the steep way towards the rock pillars, his features twisted with murderous rage. Suddenly Wythen's voice rang out, clear as a crystal spring.

"Behold my powers! I am Wythen, the spirit of the waters."

With unseeing eyes, Wythen looked down upon King Barud, all the while slowly raising her arms high above her head. The mists began to turn to a fountain, a waterfall, then to become a rushing, rolling tide. The roaring of the torrent began just below where Barud was standing, and he stared in amazement and then horror as great waves jostled against each other down the length of the valley, whirling and twisting as they went. With a frozen stare, he saw in an instant his entire army swept away, their cries of terror whirled into oblivion by the sound of the rushing waters. Not one moment longer did Barud watch, his heart was fixed now only upon revenge.

"Vile sorceress! Now you shall die also!"

He was but a few paces from Wythen who stood, still as ever, her eyes closed, intent on weaving her spell. Barud was nearly on her, his claw like hands ready to clasp her throat. Then, as if a jester had stepped upon the stage to enliven the scene, came a knight – but no ordinary member of that calling. Sir Bulwas raised a rusty sword with a shaking hand and his voice had an equal tremor.

"I am the servant and protector of the Goddess. Thou shalt not harm her handmaiden."

Barud's reason had almost deserted him, but if nothing else, he was determined to first strike down this caricature of a knight he saw before him. He went to draw his own sword but the scabbard was damp and he could not free his weapon. In trying to free it, Barud slipped upon the wet ground and fell. He clutched at Sir Bulwas who, in overbalancing, tumbled against the king. The old knight recovered his footing but Barud was not so fortunate and began to slip and roll down the steep incline.

Although he clutched desperately at the rocks and tumps of rough grass, Barud could not slow his descent. Eventually he fell into the waters that still roared and rushed down the valley. A scream, and Barud was gone. Thus perished the last king of Techlyn, drowned with all his army in the valley of Carrug where strife had never entirely been absent.

Sir Bulwas picked himself up and sought out Wythen, who smiled upon him in a strange, ethereal way. The muddied yet unbowed knight began to splutter out his thoughts.

"The Goddess sent to me a vision of you, O Spirit of the Lake. I once brought king Brynan to the sacred Temple of Rhimlais... and I hastened here to the valley of Carrug to ensure you came to no harm."

The knight looked upon the figure of Wythen which, before his astonished eyes, began to fade until there was no trace of her. Sir Bulwas realised that in evoking the Waters of Justice, Wythen had ensured that she would become, for all eternity, part of them. Her spirit was now as the mists and damps that still hung over the valley. Wythen had sacrificed her own being for the Kingdom of Irlas. A selfless gesture, one that showed her love for the kingdom, and for the king. As she knew only too well, they were as one and the same.

In a kind of trance, Sir Bulwas returned to his horse, and saw Anfad's coming across the plain. It was as if the scene was frozen in time, beneath the grey skies of a forenoon in Hafwan. Brynan and his army were as still as if they were part of the landscape. Like a rock was every figure, and every face, proud with no fear of man or death, true warriors all. Brynan felt a surge of pride to be their king. As for Sir Bulwas, perhaps he too was destined to return to the aether from whence he had come, but they heavens had decided he had one more appearance to make.

*

Brynan's men watched, in puzzlement and some alarm, as the enemy's knights, when they were some way off, broke into two groups and moved wide intent on attacking both their flanks. Brynan was in a dilemma, if he ordered his knights to wheel around and engage those of Anfad, he exposed his own infantry, and they were already outnumbered. He quickly realised he had no choice but to move forward with his knights, and engage Anfad's foot soldiers, who were already advancing at a run towards them.

The king hoped his knights would quickly subdue them, then return to support his own troops against the enemy. It was a risky course but one almost forced upon him. Anfad had quickly shown that, as a tactician, he was not to be underestimated. It would remain to be seen if he was equally skilled as leader.

Brynan then raised his sword on high and all of his knights echoed the gesture. In perfect order, they urged their horses forward. They fell upon Anfad's troops like wolves upon a flock of sheep, though their quarry was not as defenceless. Many of the enemy perished in that first assault, but at the same time, many of Brynan's troops were also lost. Anfad's knights had pressed them hard, and realising this, the king ordered his knights to draw away and engage Anfad's knights on the right. This, he hoped, would draw the rest of the Prince's horsemen to support their comrades.

Brynan's ploy was only partly successful as their foes, reading the king's intentions, drew together behind his own lines and made ready to repel his attack. Any surprise that Irlas might have gained was lost. Little was achieved during the mounted combat either. Several knights on both sides fell from their mounts, as the result of ill-luck rather than the skill of any opponent.

Meanwhile the two companies of foot soldiers continued to fight for supremacy. They were evenly matched, and the advantage went first one way and then the other. This stalemate prompted Brynan to establish a defensive position on the rise that his troops still occupied, and from that point venture out to attack the enemy. At the very moment the king made this decision, another player stepped upon the stage of war.

*

Hog had played no part in the battle so far. Like the rest of the group of squires, he was relegated to a position behind the battle lines. From there he had experienced his first taste of war, at first with trepidation, then excitement, and finally a state bordering on indifference. But as he watched, he saw the standard fall and without a second's thought he left his post and rushed into the fray. Such was his pace that he knocked to the ground one of Anfad's soldiers who was about to pick up the banner. Those about him simply stared as Hog retrieved the standard of Irlas and made as if to lead his countrymen into battle. At the same moment Brynan left his knights, intent on personally engaging Anfad's men-at arms.

The king and Derwen, stepping out of the heaving throng ready to lead an assault on foot, were astonished to see Hog. Derwen was all for sending him back, but Brynan was loath to do so. Somehow he knew that the sight of the young Hog, proud and erect, even though he was unarmed, would make stronger the resolve of his men. With him holding high the banner of Irlas, with its twin eagles, the trio advanced at the head of the army and became much more than mortal men.

Hog stood in the centre protected by the two fiercest fighters in all the land. The king was transformed into a lion with a tawny mane streaming past his shoulders; the strokes of his stinging sword his deadly claws. The silver breastplate upon his scarlet tunic now gleamed so brightly, that it blinded those who looked upon it. On Hog's right Derwen, grim and ruthless, in his black armour became as living darkness. Anfad's men suddenly believed they had encountered a three headed beast out of some fabulous legend.

The battle continued to rage, and ravens began to gather in the trees above the battlefield, a sure sign that death held sway. The air was rent with the cries of the wounded and the dying. Blood, spilled so wantonly as it is in war, stained the grass and its stench filled the nostrils. Still did swords pierce flesh, and axes shatter bones. Suffering and violent death were all around, enacted with a vicious intensity.

Once, Brynan looked up from his gory task and saw, at the edge of the plain, the sight he had prayed for – Rhaldon at the head of an army, and in his wake, King Tulrech leading another company. They immediately entered the fray, to the great dismay of Anfad, for his men were now greatly outnumbered. Brynan would have rejoiced but for Rhaldon's shouted words as he came near.

"We have seen the Northmen gathering !"

Brynan called back over the din of battle.

"Let them come! We shall stand together and fight! Brothers that we are!"

Rhaldon acknowledged his words by raising his sword and, as one, Prince and King of the Royal House of Irlas plunged into the fray.

XVIII

Brynan's conviction that no enemy would come from the direction of the forest had been proved wrong. From behind the trees began to appear grotesque, misshapen creatures many resembling trolls and gnomes. These were the Northmen, squat and hairy, all with a curious light in their eyes, as if they had imbibed some awful potion to make them immune to their wounds. Once they had left the shelter of the trees, these twisted versions of men leered and cavorted before Brynan's ranks.

Many were naked, apart from a thin covering of tattered skins and rags wrapped about them. Some looked like slavering beasts; others were like crippled birds hopping from one foot to another. They began to swing their axes and wave short swords, while hollering and chanting in some coarse tongue. Then, with cries like the screech of wolves in the mountains, they threw themselves upon the men of Irlas.

"Hold! Do not let them pass! For the Kingdom, and the Ancestors!"

At the sound of Brynan's voice, the tremor of fear that had passed through the ranks at the sight of the monstrous Northmen disappeared, and a new courage replaced it. To Derwen, gripping his sword hilt anew, they were merely vermin to be slaughtered. He summarily struck down an ugly beast with one eye that stood before him. The knight then stood fast, and soon bodies began to tumble all around him. No Northman within a sword's length of Derwen remained on his feet longer than a few moments. One bigger than the rest, who approached Derwen with yells and curses, had his head taken from his shoulders in mid-curse. His comrades behind were splashed with his blood and immediately fell back, squealing in terror.

217

A pair of stunted axe men scuttled towards Brynan. He kept them both in his sight, knowing that at any moment they would rush upon him as one. As the king had anticipated, one went to feign an attack, while the other fixed Brynan with a vicious stare. Brynan did not move, merely waiting until they both came at him. When they did, he felled the first with a cross-bladed stroke, then turned the grip on his sword and smote the other as hard, who tumbled to the ground emitting a gurgling sound.

All this time, many more of the Northmen plunged into the heart of the battle, while countless more emerged from the forest. A miracle would be needed to save the day for Irlas. That supernatural event would be shaped by the youth next to the king, still bravely holding high the banner of the kingdom, whose life, it seemed, might be charmed no longer. Already the attack of the Northmen had driven the men of Irlas back and given Anfad's men the added will to press them even further. Both the king and Derwen, as they fought, had a look of desperation about them. The knight cried out in anguish.

"There are too many of them…"

It was at that moment that Hog could hear the voice of Paldarch calling to him. The words were there in his inner being, and Hog listened intently so as to make out their meaning.

"Take and hold the Sword of Pengyron; it is bequeathed to Brynan, he who wears the Ring of Anwen. Beware those who would give this to a prince when it is intended for a king, and beware also another king, one of the underworld, who would wish to take it for himself."

The last words were almost too faint for Hog to hear, but it made little difference to their portent. In the air before them was suddenly the Sword of Pengyron, the Bounty of Haelmaw. It glowed with a fierce light, the blade pointing to the heavens. The bejewelled haft awaited the grasp of the one to whom its power had been bestowed. At the moment the sword appeared, Hog could also see the shadow of a wraith standing beside the king. He too was a king, but one long dead and only returned to this world for a fell purpose. Existing in a kind of half-life – made more terrible as it was sustained by the blood of the fallen – his only desire was to hold the world in a state of stagnant darkness.

Hog watched in amazement as the wraith reached for the Sword of Pengyron, while Brynan seemed incapable of moving. Indeed, the whole scene seemed to slow – as if frozen in eternal time. He watched in horror as the skeletal fingers closed over the sword haft. At the same moment, Prince Anfad strode from out of the ranks of his soldiers, his features a mask of triumph.

The wraith, now holding the sword aloft, began to utter words that chilled Hog to the marrow. His voice was as dust and things long gone.

"The Sword of Pengyron is mine at last! The Old Kings will rise once more and rule the Kingdoms of the West!"

Then Anfad's voice rang out.

"Hear this! It is I, Anfad of Durasglyn, who will possess the Sword, for *I* am destined to be ruler of all the Six Kingdoms."

The prince then made to take the sacred weapon for himself, but could not understand what unseen force prevented him. He could not see the shadow, let alone wrestle with it, for he was no man of magic like Hog, who stood beside him.

Hog heard the voice of his mentor Paldarch once more, faint but insistent:

"It is he who bears the Ring of Anwen that must be given the Sword."

With the power of the wizard bestowed upon him, Hog leapt into the air. He flew over the heads of both king and prince and seized the Sword of Pengyron. The vision that Paldarch had seen in the Mirror of Insight, of the youth with the gift of flight, was made manifest. Alighting upon the earth, he presented Brynan with the glowing blade, now blinding in the intensity of its light. The king flung away his own weapon and gripped the haft of the Sword. It responded by glowing the more, as if it knew full well the hand that grasped its haft was its true owner. Brynan turned to Hog with a battle-weary smile and mouthed but a few words.

"I thank thee, Magical Master Hog."

In the middle of that desperate *melee*, Hog smiled – proud of his master and of himself. He had fulfilled the promise of his wizardry he had shown when he was Paldarch's pupil, neither had he forgotten that he had been plucked from obscurity by the hand of the Goddess.

Brynan wasted no time in employing his new found weapon. When he raised the Sword, he seemed to grow in height and even when he cut the air about him, those before immediately fell back and would not engage in combat with him.

Anfad, who had been ashen with rage when he realised he had lost the Sword, was now nowhere to be seen. The wraith king had also vanished, but back to whence he came beneath the Earth. Even the underworld could not sustain his unearthly presence now that he had failed to claim the Sword.

Brynan, with Derwen at his side, went about the task of demolishing the enemy ranks with new vigour. None could resist the Sword, and those foolish enough to attempt to fight with the king were swiftly dispatched with a single, telling blow. The Northmen, who had threatened to turn the battle, were now a tide that speedily ebbed.

If a hero may be said to be naught else but a lucky fool, then the bold attack upon which Brynan had ventured was enough for fortune to smile upon him. From being a fearful threat, the enemy had now become a floundering mob. The Northmen were broken and beaten back, almost to the forest from whence they had come. Nothing was left for them but to return to their own lands. They left their dead, and many of their wounded, and lurched away. Many were cursing Anfad, as Galar had done.

"He told us there were easy pickings and the men of Irlas could not fight."

It seemed this was far from being so.

*

Now Prince Anfad, and those still loyal to him, attempted to surround what remained of the armies of Rhaldon and Tulrech. The knights of Irlas still held fast, but many had fallen and there were but a score left. Now the Northmen had withdrawn, Brynan and Derwen now turned their attention to engaging with the prince. They advanced upon the enemy's outer ranks and caused great alarm. If anything, the Sword of Pengyron had gained a greater potency, and Brynan's prowess with his magical weapon had become scarcely believable.

Anfad, realising what was happening, set himself to force his way through the melee, intent on confronting Brynan and reclaiming the Sword. Anfad slowly worked his way into a position where the king's back was to him and in his craven way, made to attack him. Brynan was engaged in fending off a trio of the enemy who had braved the stinging arc of the Sword. Unaware of Anfad creeping upon him, the king was knocked to the ground by a blow across his shoulders. Immediately, his three attackers aimed blows at his prostrated form, while others, seeing the king had fallen, ran to join them, also intent on killing him where he lay. Derwen, seeing Brynan's plight, let a cry like thunder ring out to the heavens.

"You may be brave enough when there is a score of you attacking a man who is down. Let us see how you fare now! Let Marak give me strength and Angaz be at one with my blows."

The knight then ran at them, slashing to right and left. Two of the king's attackers immediately went down before his blows. The others fell back and Derwen stood over his monarch, who was still unable to rise, intent on defending him to the last. They were on the knight again before long, and Derwen skewered the first through his chain mail, but his blade caught, and in the moment he took to free it, they were on him once more. A sword cut into his shoulder and blood began to flow freely, staining his tabard. But the wounded beast is not so easily cowed, and Derwen, though breathing heavily, stood his ground.

One thought went through his mind; he would die defending his king, as any true knight should. It seemed as if every combat he had known before was merely a prelude to this, the last moments of his life that he would know. Soon he would thrill to the horn blast of Marak, the sound that greeted all warriors when they entered his Hall of Victory. Derwen could not know, and he would have thought but little of it, that minstrels would forever sing of his mighty deeds. Such is the way of a truly noble man, that courage fills his heart as naturally as the blood flows through his veins.

Though still stunned, Brynan now struggled to his feet. His first thought was to recover the Sword that had been knocked out of his grasp. At the moment he took the haft, Anfad was upon him.

"Ah, the boy king! You cannot hide behind your wizard's skirts now. This is no game of foolery that I play! See, here is my sword, one that yearns for your blood."

Brynan did not reply, saving his energy for this final encounter. King and prince closed in combat. Brynan was no master of swordplay, but his thrust had always been true, and with the Sword in his hand, he would have been a formidable enemy for even the most practised warrior.

Thus the two were evenly matched, Anfad all earthly cunning, Brynan guided by the hand of heaven. Blows were offered and parried; relentless attack was met with stout defence.

Brynan was aware that all about him men were twisting and writhing, some engaged in dealing out death, others attempting to avoid its icy breath. Pale figures came into view, weaving their way through the scene, then drifting away. A glimpse of Sir Bulwas gave a dream-like air to the grim proceedings. All these things began to swirl about the king and as his weariness began to conquer him, all that was real began to slip away.

It was at that moment the sword pierced Brynan, but he almost did not feel the blade enter his body, so swift was that blow. Now all disappeared save for an image of the sun setting, and as the last bands of gold dropped past the horizon, Huan Brynan, the last king of Irlas, fell dying upon the Field of Gornest. The Sword of Pengyron was loosed from his hand. Even before it struck the earth, Anfad reached for it – the last move the prince ever made in this life. Derwen's sword twisted in the air, almost of its own volition, and came down, cutting through Anfad's helm and skull. Thus ended a line whose blood was mingled with Cythras, the Dark One, and it was fated that no king would ever rule that kingdom again.

Then, many of Durasglyn were upon Derwen to avenge the death of their leader, and the knight, helpless before so many, died from a welter of savage thrusts. He looked to the skies before he also fell forever, to pass into the Halls of Victory where Marak holds court, and be welcomed with godly acclaim. Above Derwen the Sword of Pengyron had risen once more into the skies and disappeared, never again to be glimpsed in this world.

The killing of Brynan – the king and his own brother – poured liquid fire into Rhaldon's soul. With a fierce energy, the prince gathered all those knights who remained – a dozen in number – and ordered a charge into the ranks of the foe. Rhaldon led the attack with the fury of a demon freed from its chains, and within a short time Irlas had gained the field. Weakened in spirit by the loss of Anfad, what remained of his army quickly crumbled into defeat. The men of Irlas and Melynas gathered about Rhaldon, a bloody but victorious band.

"The day is ours!" he cried, exhausted but triumphant.

Those knights who had endured the day raised their swords, wearily, as high as they were able.

*

The pyre burned high in the dusk and could be seen from the furthest reaches of the plain. Standing together, Tegwyn and Rhaldon wept over Brynan's body, while the knights mourned with them. Their fallen comrades they also remembered. As they left the field the rains came, and with the dawn a pile of smoking ash was all that remained of warriors both noble and common.

By the next Gwan no trace would remain of this funereal occasion, and in time the memories of the place would also fade. It was marked that, in the coming years, travellers who crossed the Plain of Lanerch avoided the paths that passed by Gornest. It was said that in Rhagel nights, the tumult of battle could be heard and the Sword of Pengyron would hover in the sombre skies above the battlefield.

*

Brynan's last impression of this world was of how the clouds resembled hills and the skies, the sea. All the elements had become one and he had, like Paldarch, entered the spirit world. In the place he had come to, no sound came. His life was seeping from his body, and as soon as his soul parted from its shell, a figure appeared before him, filling all his vision. She wore the mantle of black and crimson that signified she was the consort of Angaz. She was Tandurol, Queen of Uffern – the Underworld, where the souls of all must pass. The faint smile upon her pale lips contrasted with the darkling jet of her hair. Beautiful and terrible, she held out a slim hand to Brynan.

"Come, O blessed one. Nothing ails thee now."

The voice held no terrors; rather it was of that soothing sweetness Brynan had known before, at Mefynon, the Spring of Wisdom, and in the Temple at Rhimlais. His own words, when he spoke, sounded far away to his ears, as if they were echoing into nothingness.

"Must I go with thee?"

The eyes that looked down upon him were instantly filled with a soft light, and the smile grew a little more.

"You must."

"Why so?"

"Because only in the place where I take you shall be found the peace you seek."

"I feel peace now."

"That is because you have laid down your life for your world. As a true king, you made the ultimate sacrifice, as a god does also. You have shed tears, not for yourself, but for others."

"Are you the Goddess?"

"I am one of many faces of the Goddess. Only true men of magic can see the Goddess as she is. I will take you to one such."

She moved slowly towards him, and Brynan clasped her offered hand. The king followed Tandurol into the mist, to wherever she would take him. Brynan was led to Golarwein Cefnor, which means 'the Hill of Kings in Sight of the Great Sea,' a name known to him from the song of minstrels. Here was to be found Paldarch, who had once told the king, 'The Goddess will wait for us in the West'. And it was so. Brynan and Paldarch smiled upon one another, and the deep bond of understanding that had always been between them was now beyond the exchange of mere words.

The place of Gwynfar – the world beyond – awaited them. Thus did Paldarch the Wizard and Huan Brynan, the Last of the Old Kings, pass between the two great pillars of Colofewin, and into Gwynfar in the West. As they did so, the setting sun made an aura about them in orange and gold. And when they had passed further into that unknown land, they could no longer be seen, as they had become as the very light itself that fills that sacred place.

The voice of the Goddess now came to the spirit of Brynan.

"Do you wish to be united with Wythen once more? For she is here in Gwynfar."

"I would wish it more than anything, but she told me I could not know love until I truly knew the Goddess."

The Goddess laughed – a blissful sound.

"My handmaidens are far too modest! You, Brynan, who have loved Wythen, have known the Goddess already. Wythen and I are one and the same."

Then the spirits of wizard and king passed into the House of Fire, and at the same time their souls were taken to the realm of Loenel. And Paldarch marvelled for Gwirel was also there; she had willed that she would pass into Gwynfar also. All held the hands of each other in the triumph of celestial joy. Brynan looked into Wythen's pale blue eyes, and they became again as one. The Raven and the Dove walked together in all eternity. The skies were all alight in Gwynfar where the mirth of creation lies beyond the form of the universe. Gwirel looked upon every one of them in turn and each soul sang to her words.

"We are made eternal through the divine light of the Goddess."

XIX

With Rhaldon and Tulrech at their head, the three armies marched slowly but triumphantly along the way that led to Treflan. All would sleep in the Great Hall that night, and those who belonged to Melynas return to their kingdom in the morn. The wounded would be tended, and all the soldiery given a full repast, not just mutton pasties and ale, but all delicacies and spirits that could be found for them. As they entered the town, they were cheered by the townsfolk. Their rejoicings were at first muted when they learned the fate of Brynan, but still they found much to celebrate.

The knights departed to their quarters, while Rhaldon and Tulrech approached the castle. The stewards, like the townsfolk, saw that Brynan was not leading the army, and feared for the fate of their king. Nevertheless, they welcomed Rhaldon and Tulrech warmly, and bade them occupy the late king's chambers. However welcome such an invitation, it was a melancholy air that pervaded the place. A heavy silence descended upon the two of them as they sat where once Brynan had held court. Often did King Tulrech glance anxiously at Rhaldon, for the victor always maintains an aura of power long after the battle. At last, the king of Melynas spoke.

"Now that peace has been restored to the Six Kingdoms, what must be done to maintain it?"

Rhaldon reflected for some time; he was weary, but knew that certain decisions would have to be made before long.

"We must consider carefully, King Tulrech. I am now the ruler of Irlas, but there is no successor to the throne of Techlyn or that of Blauwyg. Durasglyn has no ruler either, and Tarth has never seen kingship."

Tulrech was anxious to voice his thoughts.

"Then the Six Kingdoms should be united once more... under a strong ruler..."

The king looked upon Rhaldon, who steadily returned his gaze.

"I have no desire to rule as a king, neither over Irlas, nor any land."

"But you are warrior who has defeated all his enemies," Tulrech protested.

"I disagree. I am not a warrior, and they were not my enemies."

Tulrech looked baffled at this.

"But those we fought would have destroyed us all..."

"They were simply men. I do not see them in any other way. I cannot. To me, many men are a mystery... they fight and they kill – why, I do not know. I live in the forest with my sheep and cattle. I have no wish to deal in death. Farmers do not kill, only when the wolf preys upon their flocks. That is perhaps how I saw the Northmen, as wolves."

Cydlon the Chief Steward entered, announcing that Tegwyn was to join their company. The princess had remained in Irlas during the days of the fighting. Although sure that Melynas would not be threatened a second time, she had preferred to ride to Irlas and seek shelter there. Tegwyn had sought out the priests in Treflan and been most welcomed in the temple, where they provided her with lodging.

Her father and the prince greeted her warmly, she was eager to tell of that which she had experienced while in her holy retreat. When Tegwyn spoke of a vision of Loenel, it was as if her words echoed from the heavens above:

"The Goddess has promised to bring harmony to the world, and in some way I am destined to help her fulfill that promise, this I know. And I have sworn a sacred oath that I shall endeavour to bring joy into the hearts of those I love."

Tulrech failed to understand his daughter's words, but as she spoke she looked intently at Rhaldon. The deeper she gazed into his eyes the more astonished he was at the strength of his own feelings.

When Tegwyn had gone from their presence, Rhaldon reflected deeply upon the words she had uttered.

*

The next day, all gathered in the square at Treflan. Word had quickly gone abroad that Rhaldon would speak to the people of Irlas. Some even said that he would be crowned king that very forenoon. An equal mix of loyalty and curiosity brought many from all around. A crowd, perhaps even greater in number than that which had assembled for Brynan, filled the square. Now the voice of Rhaldon rang out in the crisp air of Hafwan.

"People of Irlas, know you that I am Rhaldon, brother of your beloved king, whose soul is now in the West. Much do I mourn Brynan, and I know it is the same with you all. May his soul enjoy great peace! That will ever be his reward for serving the kingdom. Brynan laid down his life for us, and deserves all our praise."

Here, the prince called for a moment of silence in honour of Huan Brynan, before he continued.

"But, there is an ancient saying, older than any may remember, 'the king is dead, long live the king'."

Rhaldon paused, and from the crowd came a cry, soon taken up by other voices.

"Rhaldon will be our king!"

Rhaldon did not answer immediately, but all watched in awed silence as the Princess Tegwyn walked out to be by the prince's side. Then Rhaldon spoke the words that would change the Kingdoms of the West forever.

"People of Irlas, will you now give your love and loyalty to your queen?"

The words echoed about the square and the crowd saw that Tegwyn carried a child in her arms, and they marvelled. A silence that seemed endless filled the square, so that not one sound was heard. Then, as if the Goddess had ordained that very moment, a murmur became a great cheer. It was the sign that woman, the Great Mother and the Well of Creation, had been acknowledged in this moment, and forever.

It was the first time that the voices of women had been heard in such number and with such freedom in that place. The feminine spirit – crying, singing, laughing – all the many tones of the Goddess flowed unrestrained. And from the heights of heaven, Loenel saw the compassion and love that had come to the world was manifest in this great ocean of joy. This was her victory, not one gained with arms, but with love and celebration. It took only a few moments before the voices of men were also raised in unison with their womenfolk.

Soon the whole of the crowd was calling out the name 'Queen Tegwyn'. In their hearts they had already crowned the figure who stood before them. In that moment she possessed Divine Favour. Wythen had proclaimed that Tegwyn was a handmaiden of The Goddess and was thus most favoured in The Heavens. Was it not by the will of the Divine that a beautiful woman, and a mother, would come to rule this world? Queen Tegwyn of the Six Kingdoms of the West she would be, and all those who ruled would follow her from that day on. The Goddess had chosen wisely.

Tegwyn stood before the people, holding her daughter Siricyn for all to see and soon they almost worshipped her. Many in the square called out their praises to her beauty and goodness and some continued to openly weep. For many, the sight of Tegwyn before them brought a rush of

231

gladness to fill all their hearts. At last they could put aside the torment of war and the suffering and pain that it brought.

Tireless and majestic, the queen smiled upon all. She was as the goddess Cyngerl, and the power of the earth and the waters flowed about her and through her soul. The dawn was in her eyes, and from her lips flowed songs of joy. Blooms sprang from between her graceful fingers and, through the spirit of Tegwyn, the land would swell with abundance. At her touch, the very trees would seem to burst from the ground where they were confined, to glory in the light. Tegwyn was nature herself, the queen that has the power to unfurl the leaf, colour the petal, and sweeten the very air.

Rhaldon looked upon the princess and realised that he loved her. At that same moment, Tegwyn turned to him and the joy in her eyes told of how she regarded the prince. Such was the power of these silent exchanges that the crowd began to cheer, and chant the names of prince and princess together.

"Rhaldon... Tegwyn... King and Queen ..."

At this, the couple smiled the more upon all that were there before them.

*

The ocean lapped upon the western border of the kingdom of Irlas. There, a coast of high cliffs, worn away by constant pounding from the waves, greeted travellers. Unless they intended to take ship to unknown lands, there the journey must end. Perhaps they would pause momentarily to regard the wild tides that sent the creamy surf to roll upon a narrow stretch of sand. That morning, Rhag had hinted that soon it would be the death of the

232

year. The trees had lost their leaves, and stood as skeletal shapes, frost made the tufts of grass as white and hard as marble – all this reflected the season's cold and stillness.

Rhaldon and Tegwyn had ridden to the coast of Irlas, the prince knowing that they must commune with the powers there. He knew not what they might be, but a strange urgency drove him to persuade the princess to accompany him on this journey. A day's ride it had taken from Treflan, and had been tiring.

They tethered the horses as best they could to a tree that stood upon the cliff top, one bent and battered by the wind. A path led to the beach below, and this they followed. The frozen pools that met their gaze on the beach mirrored the grey sky. The light was such that the edge of each rock was etched against the next, and their grey and ochre hue spilled into one watery tone.

Prince and Princess looked out on mist so near to the water that it was impossible to tell where sky ended and sea began. Rhaldon took the Princess by the hand, and they stepped over pebbles and rocks until they found a cove, where they sat.

About them they heard the sound of sea birds – lapwing and wimbrel, mixed with the plaintive call of the curlew. A raven flew above them, its ebony plumage made even darker seen against the frost-covered cliff. Rhaldon was certain he could see figures in the mist, appearing to walk upon the water. Tegwyn, noticing his intense gaze, spoke.

"What do you see, my beloved?"

"Only imaginings from when I was a child, returning for an instant. The storytellers at court would speak of Awren the Hero, the Sword of Justice in one hand, the Spear of Destiny in the other. I thought that I beheld him."

"And the Ring of Power, my darling, was he wearing that upon his finger?"

Rhaldon looked at the princess, surprise upon his features.

"You know the tale, Tegwyn?"

"Of course, it was probably the same storyteller who came to my father's castle when I was a child."

"I once dreamed I would venture across the Great Sea too, but..."

"You may one day, my darling one."

Rhaldon took her hand in both of his.

"No, I have every reason now, not to venture forth."

Tegwyn looked upon him with a great love, so much so that she wept silently. Rhaldon took her head in his hands, and kissed away the tears from her eyes.

"Tegwyn, promise me you will never be sad."

The princess looked out to sea, not able to look upon the face of Rhaldon. Her lips began to tremble, and she could hardly speak the words she wished to say.

"Your brother Brynan is the father of my child."

Rhaldon also looked out to the waves, and saw there only eternity, and the great blessing that was creation.

"I know."

"Now he is gone."

"Yes. Like the greatest of kings, he gave his life for his people. He loved them so."

"I loved him, too," Tegwyn said.

"And for that, he was the most fortunate of men."

"Perhaps. It is all so sad."

"Yes, but it need be no more. I can never be my brother, and indeed I would never wish to be, but I love you dearly. And if you will allow me, I will care for you and Siricyn as if she were my own."

Tegwyn began to weep.

"I do not deserve this. I am not worthy of a man as noble as you."

Tegwyn would not show her face to Rhaldon. The strange sense of shame she felt would have marred the love in her breast if the Goddess had not chosen this moment to come to Tegwyn's aid. The princess looked again at the endless waves, and it was as if the waters suddenly washed away forever any regret that might have lain upon her soul.

Her heart became light once more. Rhaldon, sensing that her pain had passed, spoke softly.

"You know when you and I and Brynan played together as children, I always wanted to be the one that kissed you in our games."

Tegwyn's eyes were wide.

"Is that true? I did not know."

"I loved you first in those times, and when you were promised to Brynan, I could not bear the thought that I had lost you. That was the reason I hid myself in the forest with the animals, though I came to be part of that life and cherished it."

"Oh my darling, you did that because of me?"

"Yes, but now I have found you once more."

Stars played within Tegwyn's eyes and she smiled. She took Rhaldon's hand and looked deep into his eyes.

"Pray with me."

"Of course I will."

"It is to Loenel that we should pray from now on, for although she is the consort of Nen, she is about to become more powerful than him for a time. She does not seek to dominate him, just to make the world a place where men and women are as equals. That is her purpose. That is the reason of her coming at this time."

"I know. It is why I wished that you should become the Queen of the Six Kingdoms."

Tegwyn trembled with the power of the Goddess that she felt, and it was always at heart the power of love. The prince put his arms about her and, for them, time disappeared from the world. The sun danced briefly in the skies, and from the rocks behind them, they could hear the soft patter of the ice melting. The sun's setting was not long in coming. The two lovers waited until flecks of purple grey stood against the turquoise sky, and pink and orange lit the horizon. Then they rode through the night, returning to Treflan.

*

Soon after Nadoman, Siricyn, a child as fair as the sun, began to take her first few faltering steps. From that moment on, Rhaldon doted upon the child and would spend as much of the day in her company as he was able. He marvelled at the great miracle of life that the heavens had bestowed upon mortal men. Truly was there no more joyous a time for the royal couple and all in the kingdom. The feasting went on for many days, to celebrate Siricyn's first birthday, and to hail a new era in the world.

At the time of Gwan in the next year, Tegwyn was crowned Queen of the Six Kingdoms and Rhaldon was named her consort. The feasting and celebration continued, and the time was forever known as the Years of Joy.

XX

A year had passed since the Battle of Gornest. The lone figure of Sir Bulwas walked once more upon the field of war. Although restored to his former self, to be seen now with rubicund features covered in smiles, he had been restless. For a time he had accepted the hospitality of the court at Treflan, and the welcome of the company of knights, but he had always known his destiny lay elsewhere. He would return to the Temple at Rhimlais, and remain there as its guardian until such times as he also would be summoned to Gwynfar in the West.

This faithful servant of the Goddess had served her well, and his reward would be to end his days in peace and contentment. He had, through no sin of his own, once ventured into the darkness of doubt and despair that comes to many. Through faith alone he had eventually gained the light. His destiny resolved, the old knight strode for a time upon the Plain of Lanerch, then mounted his steed once more, and took the way that led to Tarth.

The Goddess had another faithful servant in Hog or *Hawdren*, as his new found role demanded him to be addressed. He was known as the Voice of the Goddess, and Tegwyn and Rhaldon oft sought his wisdom. His fame since the battle had spread, and many regarded him as the natural successor to Paldarch. Hog tended to shrug off such accolades as was only fitting for such a modest personality. With great joy he had been reunited with his father, Helryn.

Hog was quite content to spend the time, when he was not wanted at court, in the woods. This, too, suited his partner Rhi who had sought him out desiring a permanent union with him. Within a year, child was born. Now that the ways of the Goddess pervaded everyday life all the more, the times were more sympathetic to women who

237

practised magic. Hog founded a school of magic for children of both sexes who showed promise in the arts, and he and Rhi taught them together.

Another year passed, and little Siricyn, eternally doted upon by mother and father, celebrated the second year of her life. Life was fair and good in the Six Kingdoms, and Tegwyn ruled in a manner that gave no cause for dissension or unease. The spirits of Gwirel and Wythen were always in her dreams and at her side in her waking hours, to guide her. Truly the vision that Paldarch had seen in the Mirror of Insight had come to pass.

The icy days of Rhagel began to retreat and another Gwan came to the world. The sun did not, as yet, have rule. Upon the first day of the season, the sky was as whitened lead and the wind from the east swept the plains like a vengeful blade. Newborn lambs ran bleating to their mothers when a hawk wheeled and dived overhead. But not only harshness was reflected in the season, for snowdrops sheltering in the forest glistened whitely and promised warmth and new life.

As if unconcerned by all that She could claim to have created, the feet of Loenel - the Goddess – glided over the stiff grass. Finally, the world was hers. She had waited long, and now none could question her right of ownership. It was also the decree of Nen that this be so. The Goddess had not come to make her claim as a swordsmith – though she had mastery of that cunning craft – she had brought healing and words of love. These were the gifts she would give to all, and this was the moment to bestow them. Though it was only the noon hour, there was aura of silver and midnight blue about the Goddess, and at each step she left behind her moon trails upon the sacred ground. She had brought – as the seers had foretold – the Dawn of the Goddess.

~oO0o~

Other Books by Gordon Strong
Available from Mutus Liber:

King Arthur: The Waste Land & the New Age

This is one of the most strongly individual and imaginative reinterpretations of the Arthurian legend that I have ever encountered. It proves again how the story can be made fresh and new for any age.

~ Professor Ronald Hutton

A very different approach to the matter of King Arthur and his legends... Gordon Strong has gone for a much wider canvas, drawing on tradition but also looking at Tibetan mantras, Apocryphal texts, magical writers and mages and sages... He shows that inner themes of search and loss and captivity are universal and that the main characters are to be found echoed in many ancient sources of wisdom... a myriad of fascinating clues.

~ Marian Green, co-author of *The Grail Seeker's Companion*

The stories about King Arthur, and the Waste Land that must be crossed in order to attain the Grail, continue to fascinate, inspiring writers from Geoffrey of Monmouth in the twelfth century to T. S. Eliot in the twentieth.

This new study of the Arthurian legends combines exciting insights into the nature of the Holy Grail, our modern yearning for spirituality and romance, and the relevance of Arthurian myth in the technological age.

Arthur and Guinevere, Merlin, Morgan le Fay, the Lady of the Lake and the Knights of the Round Table... all are brought to enchanted life on the mystical stage in the heart of sacred Albion: Glastonbury and the landscape of Somerset.

ISBN: 978 09555230 14

Tarot Unveiled

Tarot Unveiled speaks with a friendly yet informed voice. The author's familiarity and enthusiasm provides a well grounded introduction to the subject including practical advice for readers and guidance for the spiritually adventurous. Right from the start Gordon Strong sets the right tone by reminding his audience that Tarot is part of a magical philosophy, not just a method of divination. Unveiling the Tarot is a lifetime's journey, and this book offers a good starting place.

~ Naomi Ozaniec

The Tarot is a philosophical document, a wisdom tradition and a gateway to the unseen. It has the power to reveal the ebb and flow of existence - the divine rhythm.

An invaluable guide for the beginner and the professional reader alike, Gordon Strong perceptively explains all the cards of the Major and the Minor Arcana. A brief history of the Tarot, an intimate guide to Divination, Tarot Correspondences, numerology and Tarot meditation exercises are also included.

ISBN: 978 09555230 21

Bride's Mound: Gateway to Avalon

With Jane Marshall
Illustrated by Jen Delyth

Bride's Mound: Gateway to Avalon celebrates one of Glastonbury's most important, but least known, mystical sites.

The destination of sea-borne travelers from the West, Bride's Mound is also the portal into the Other World, that of Avalon, the Arthurian paradise. Like Isis, Bride is the Goddess of the Moon - to the Romans she was Minerva, to the Christians, St. Bridget. She is the swordsmith, the healer and the poet, and excels in each calling.

Associated with Mary Magdalene, the Black Madonna and the Celtic festival of Imbolc, Bride is also the sister of the archangel Michael. Her colour is white like the lamb, and the snowdrop that symbolize her. Bride protects the young mother and the old sinner alike - she owns compassion and devotion. Today, she may have exchanged the mantle of Pisces for that of Aquarius, and become the independent, radical female.

Jane Marshall is the secretary of the Friends of Bride's Mound.

Jen Delyth is a Celtic artist based in San Francisco.

ISBN: 978 09555230 45

Sun God and Moon Maiden:
The Secret World of the Holy Grail

The medieval troubadour saw the Holy Grail as a vision of heaven. In the twenty-first century, the quantum physicist locates heaven in parallel universes. The shaman, spanning prehistory and the modern world, travels in other dimensions to experience the limits of existence.

In *Sun God and Moon Maiden*, Gordon Strong argues that the metaphor of the Grail questions not only space and time but perception itself. The philosophy of Plato, the psychology of Jung and the nobility of mythic kings lie in the Grail's domain; an interior landscape where we discover gateways into Inner Space, the nature of the universe, and ourselves.

From legends of Atlantis to Arthur's Camelot, the path to Avalon awaits. In this fascinating book, drawing together mythology, magic and modern physics, Gordon Strong explains how the ancient wisdom of Qabalah, Tarot and Stone Circles open the way for new discoveries in expanded consciousness.

An approach to the sanctity and mystery of the Grail which combines tradition, insight and invention in equal and exciting measure.
– Alan Richardson, author of *Priestess: The Life and Magic of Dion Fortune*

This revealing and original study sheds important new light on the paradoxes of the Grail which we find, ultimately, are paradoxes of the Self. Joining Gordon Strong's mythic quest to unlock the secrets of its divine truth will reward the reader handsomely.
– Geoff Ward, *Mysterious Planet*

ISBN: 978 1 908097 019